## ONE DEATH TOO FAR

"An intense and addictive thriller. You'll be hooked."

— BOOKWORMROOM.COM

Dennis Koller's One Death Too Far delivers a compelling blend of political thriller, military action, and emotional depth that keeps readers on edge from its explosive opening to its high-stakes conclusion. With a gripping narrative that spans continents, government agencies, and criminal underworlds, the novel deftly weaves personal tragedy with national intrigue.

— AMMAR HABIB, EDITOR-IN-CHIEF,
THRILLER MAGAZINE

# ALSO BY DENNIS KOLLER

**THE OATH**

"Dennis Koller's mystery-thriller debut is a strong one. The novel has it all; intrigue, politics, murder and romance. Combined with characters and dialogue that are ultimately believable, The Oath is a real page-turner."

– The Irish Herald Book Review

**THE CUSTER CONSPIRACY**

"A first-rate thriller! Koller ratchets up the suspense in this fast-paced tale of history gone awry. Crisp writing and intricate plotting will keep you turning the pages."

– The Martinez Gazette

**THE RHYTHM OF EVIL**

"A fast-paced, can't put the book down, suspense thriller. If you liked the Harry Bosch series by Michael Connelly, you'll love this book. The Rhythm of Evil is a top-notch thriller! The suspense escalates in Koller's fast paced tale of a simple murder that turns out to be anything but simple. Tight writing and believable characters will keep the pages turning."

– Vivian Roubal. Columnist, Martinez NewsGazette

# ONE DEATH TOO FAR

## A THRILLER

## A RED SQUADRON NOVEL

## DENNIS KOLLER

Publish Authority

Editor: Janie Mills
Cover design lead: Raeghan Rebstock
Interior Design: Teresa Evans

ISBN 978-1-967213-01-6 (Paperback)
ISBN 978-1-967213-02-3 (eBook)

Published 2025 by Publish Authority,
300 Colonial Center Parkway, Suite 100
Roswell, GA, USA
PublishAuthority.com

Printed in the United States of America

*To Sarah:*
*Whose inspiration and nuanced critique never allowed me to*
*abandon the dream.*

# PROLOGUE

*It's a good day to die.*

Thirty-one years ago, Walt McArthur greeted every sunrise with that very thought as both he and his men geared up for battle in the streets of Mogadishu.

Thirty-one years ago, the grim reaper gave Walt a pass.

Today, the reaper wasn't going to be so generous.

# CHAPTER 1



Walt McArthur awakened early that Monday morning, flicked on his bedside lamp, grabbed his cell phone, and scheduled an Uber to take him to San Francisco International Airport in time for his flight to El Paso. He padded down the hallway into the bathroom. As he entered, he quickly sneaked a glimpse of himself in the full-length mirror. Staring back at him was a DEA Special Agent with a sagging face, a full head of wavy hair now almost completely white, and a stomach that hadn't felt a sit-up in years.

The mirror also reflected the two lumpy scars running across the top of his chest, armpit to armpit, courtesy of the '91 firefight in Mogadishu where he found himself lying on a concrete floor while a Delta Force medic frantically worked to cauterize both bullet wounds before he bled out. Thankfully, that image morphed into one where his eleven-year-old son,

Kenny, frolicked on the bed with him while he plucked at the bullet-wound scars as if they were guitar strings.

Those images quickly disappeared, however, under an avalanche of unwanted memories—starting with his wife, Betty, who divorced him when their son turned seventeen and had the audacity to move with him to San Diego.

Walt dried himself and made sure he had all his papers with him when the Uber pulled up in front of his house. Arriving at SFO, he boarded United Flight 560 to El Paso. At precisely 10:00 a.m., the big plane rolled down the runway and glided gracefully into a sky heavy with clouds. Banking left, the plane headed over the West Bay hills as the pilot's calm voice announced they were passing through 10,000 feet on their way to a cruising altitude of 36,000. *As soon as I get back from this trip,* Walt murmured to himself, *I'm going to call Kenny and tell him I'm retiring from the DEA … effective immediately.*

He leaned back in his seat and smiled, knowing it wouldn't be long before his son, his only son, would be coming back home … and this time to stay.

DEA Special Agent in Charge, Bill Gilardi drummed his fingers on the desk while glancing at the clock hanging on the opposite wall. 10:10 a.m. "Come on, come on, you SOB," he shouted. "Answer your damn phone."

"Federal Aviation Administration. Phil Cruz speaking. Can I put you on hold?"

"NO, YOU CANNOT PUT ME ON HOLD," Gilardi said with all the venom he could muster. "This is DEA Special

Agent William Gilardi online in San Francisco. The Deputy Director in DC gave me your name and phone number." Gilardi went silent for a few beats, then said, "United Airlines' Flight 560 took off not more than twelve minutes ago from San Francisco International. You've got to get that plane to return to SFO ... IMMEDIATELY!"

"I'm sorry, sir, I can't authorize anything like that unless—"

"Please don't interrupt me, Mr. Cruz. There's no time for *I can't authorize it!* You've got to get that plane back on the ground. Immediately!" There was a slight pause, then ... "there's a bomb on board that aircraft."

Gilardi heard Cruz suck in a deep breath and knew he was pulling up Flight 560 on his computer screen. "The plane had wheels up at ten-ten," Cruz told Gilardi ... "and has just now cleared the coastline over Pacifica. I've already alerted the pilot to return to SFO immediately." Gilardi could hear a few faint clicks from Cruz's keyboard in the background. "Thank God he got the message," Cruz said. "The plane has already started to turn." He paused, "How much time do we have?"

Gilardi peeked at his watch and shook his head. "I wish I knew."

AFTER PARKING their nondescript car in one of the many regional parks dotting the coastal hills from San Francisco to Santa Cruz, two men crested a ridge to their liking at 9:25 a.m. Both wore black parkas to ward off the cold, drippy mist rolling in off the Pacific Ocean, plus blue baseball caps emblazoned with the logo of San Jose's professional soccer team. The smaller of the two pulled out a stopwatch as they both watched the 737 begin the wide turn that would bring it back over the coastline.

"Are you ready?" the larger one asked in a thick Mexican accent.

"Sí," his partner replied, keying a string of numbers into the phone he was holding. Looking at the plane that had just started its rollback, the smaller of the two men tapped the phone's "call" button. Lifting his eyes skyward, he smiled as he saw the big plane shudder violently as it erupted in a giant orange and crimson ball of flame, scattering pieces of Walt McArthur and 208 other poor souls over three square miles of the blue Pacific below.

When Gilardi heard Cruz whisper, "Holy Mother of God," he knew their time had run out.

FORTY MINUTES after Flight 560 went down, a white van bearing the name *Expert House Cleaning Services* pulled into Walt McArthur's driveway. Witnesses later reported there were two men in that van, both of whom went into McArthur's house. There was general agreement that both of the men wore blue overalls and carried what looked to be three large laundry bags. It was in those three large laundry bags that the two men carried out the contents of Walt's safe —including the flash disc containing his Snowplow file, the computer's hard drive, and the contents of the top drawer of his filing cabinet.

# CHAPTER 2



Alex Navarro arose later than usual that Monday morning and was rinsing the toothpaste from his mouth when he heard a loud explosion out over the ocean, half a mile to the west of where he and his wife lived. Patting his mouth dry, he put on his glasses and walked toward his front room window when his wife, Kathleen, caught up with him. "What the heck was that noise I heard?" she asked, a slight tremor in her voice. "It shook the house like crazy."

"I'm not quite sure myself," Navarro replied. "The only thing I can think of is it had to be an airplane that blew up. Somewhere close, but still out over the water. And it was explosive enough to cause that damn painting in the living room to jiggle off its hook." He put his arm around her.

"Yeah," she said. "It wasn't something I expected."

"Me neither," he said. "If that airplane had come in just a bit lower, it might have hit us."

"I'll take your word for it," she said. "Had to be some kind of miracle ... no doubt about it."

"And while I'm in the mood, let me grab a cup of coffee while I dial up Inspector Murray on the phone."

Murray greeted Navarro with silence, then said, "I'm sorry, sir, but I've been instructed not to use my cell phone to speak with someone pretending to be a police officer." After another short silence, Murray said, "Hey, wait a minute! Come to think of it, I once knew an officer named Navarro ... an Alex Navarro, if I'm not mistaken. He was not only my partner, but a good friend, too. Then one day last week, he up and told me he was taking a sick leave. It was the last I ever heard from him." Murray chuckled, then said, "Hey Nav ... I knew you were just kidding with me, but I do have to tell you ... when you took that sick leave at the beginning of the week, you had me worried." He paused, then asked, "You doing okay?"

"Yeah!" Navarro responded. "I was down for a while, but I'm making a comeback." He chuckled, then said, "Is tomorrow quick enough for a comeback?"

"Well, heck yeah," Murray said. "I'm looking forward to getting your butt back here."

"Tomorrow for sure."

"Good!" Murray paused for a minute, then said, "But before I let you go ... wasn't that a United jet that went down close to where you live? Did you actually see the plane go down?"

"You're right about the plane's location. I not only heard the explosion, but I'm close enough to it that the shockwave hit my house like a sledgehammer." Navarro paused, then said, "It was a United flight, huh? That's bad news! From my house, I could actually see parts of that airplane falling into the ocean."

"That's a picture I'm not looking forward to seeing," Murray replied. He paused, then said "Hey ... I'm really sorry, but I do gotta run. It's really chaos around here. So much so that our main switchboard has already gone bonkers. I only answered my phone because I knew it was you calling ... and, as you can imagine, we've already got a gazillion people calling us to ask if we could check to see if their great-great-grand uncle twice removed just happened to be on that airplane. I'm sure you remember how that goes."

"I do, indeed, my friend," Nav said with a chuckle. "But if you don't mind, I've got a quick question to ask. Does anybody on the Force have any idea about what actually caused that plane to go down?"

"Lots of talk," Murray said. "But it's way too early. You know how that works. No matter what any of us say over the next few hours, the chances are that most of the chatter will be dismissed as nothing more than rumor. But, if I hear anything definitive, I'll for sure give you a quick shout-out. Otherwise, I hope to see you all well by tomorrow."

# CHAPTER 3



Having decided to go to Mollie's, but not pig out, Nav and Kathleen were almost out their front door when his cell rang. Recognizing Murray's number, he shrugged and mouthed to Kathleen that he'd be just a minute.

"Hey, man, what's up?"

"Sorry to bother you, Nav. Just thought you'd want to hear the latest on the airplane investigation. Right this moment the speculation is it was a bomb."

"A bomb? Are you kidding me?"

"You know I wouldn't kid you on something as important as that, Nav," Murray said. "And to make matters worse, there's a group of people here starting to play around with the idea that this could possibly be a terrorist hit. And as you know, once a notion like that starts to make the rounds, our department will unceremoniously be dumped in favor of the big boys from Homeland Security."

"What prompted the 'bomb-on-board' thinking?" Nav asked. "How'd they come up with that?"

"Oh, come on, Nav … you're aware that every guy who does this kind of work instinctively thinks that onboard bombs bring down every damn plane—mechanical problems or not. That's just how they view the world. Factually, however, it's still way too early for anybody to come up with a definitive answer. I'm hearing, however, that by mid-afternoon, they'll have possibilities about what the heck happened to take that aircraft down." He paused, then said, "Okay, my friend, I gotta get to work. You stay well, okay? If anything happens around here, I'll be back to you."

It was midafternoon when Murray called back. "Just wanted to give you a heads-up, Nav. The scuttlebutt around here now is that Homeland Security is taking over the United Airlines explosion … lock, stock, and barrel."

"I'm really sorry to hear that," Nav replied. "So you're telling me the Department might be left out altogether?"

"Maybe not at this exact moment, but no doubt within the next hour or so. With them finding convincing evidence that it was a bomb that took the plane down, you know our involvement will end very soon. From now on the investigation will be solely in the hands of Homeland Security. This bomb business is way over our heads anyway, Nav, so I'm cool with letting them handle it." Murray paused, then in a more somber tone said, "But all that is minor league stuff compared to what I'm about to tell you." He paused, then said, "the FAA sent us one of their *For Eyes Only* passenger list. You know the drill—

to see if we had any active investigations going on with any of the passengers."

"And?"

"We didn't." Murray went silent again, then in a soft voice, said, "There's a friend of yours, however, whose name is on that passenger list, Nav. In fact, he is ... or at least was, a friend of all of ours." He paused, then said, "Walt McArthur."

"Walt McArthur? Oh my God ... no!" Navarro breathed into the phone, his throat constricting as his pulse quickened. "Tell me you're kidding."

Kathleen, on her way to the kitchen, heard the anxiety in her husband's voice and returned to sit with him. She held his hand as he took a deep breath. "You're sure it was Walt, huh?"

"Positive ID, Nav." He paused again, then said, "I knew how tight you guys were, so I knew you'd want to know."

After a momentary silence, Navarro whispered, "It's a tough one to swallow. But, yeah, Walt's an old friend of mine. I appreciate your heads-up."

Navarro and Murray spoke for a few more minutes, then disconnected. By this time, tears were running down Kathleen's cheeks. "I'm so sorry," she murmured into his shoulder. "He was a good man."

"A good man and a good friend," Nav responded, letting out a long sigh. To erase some of the tension lingering in the air, he turned to Kathleen and said with a half laugh, "Guess we won't be going to Mollie's for lunch today, huh?"

Through a forced smile, she dried her eyes and put her arms around him. "Guess not. What can I do for you?"

"Just being here with me is all I could ask. And I've got a tough phone call still to make."

"To McArthur?"

"Yeah ... McArthur."

She leaned over and kissed his forehead. "I'll be here next to you for as long as you need me."

NAVARRO HAD Kenneth McArthur's cell phone number from the time he had met him in San Francisco a number of years back. His cell phone rang several times before going to voicemail. In no way was Navarro going to leave the news of Walt's death on his kid's personal voicemail, so he searched for McArthur's office number in Virginia. A woman answered, telling him Kenneth McArthur was on an overseas assignment and that she was not authorized to say where. However, she did say he called in every day at 7 a.m. Eastern.

"Won't work," Navarro told her. "I have to talk with him immediately. It's an emergency ... and it's personal."

"I'm sorry, sir, I'm just a temp. The woman whose place I took became ill this morning and went home. She left me numbers of a group of people to contact in case of an emergency. Would that work for you?"

"Absolutely it would work! Shoot."

Four phone calls and half an hour later, Admiral Doug Moore, Deputy Director of Joint Special Operations Command, answered his phone.

"I don't know you," Moore said. "You've got exactly ten seconds to tell me who you are and why you're calling on my secure line."

"I received your number from Kenneth McArthur's

secretary," Navarro said forcefully, not in the mood to be pushed around. "A commercial airplane went down over San Francisco this morning. Homeland Security is all but certain there was a bomb on board. McArthur's father, Walter, was on that airplane. I was a good friend of their family. I thought you should be aware of what happened to Walt."

"Walter McArthur?" There was a silence, then another pause, "And your name is Alex Navarro?"

"Yes, sir, it is."

"Thank you for being persistent, Mr. Navarro. I'm sorry, but I can be a hard person to corral. I promise you I'll get word to Kenneth McArthur ASAP."

# CHAPTER 4



The last smoldering embers of our small fire winked out behind the high peaks of the Hindu Kush. In those peaks, I sat with my other three retired SEAL brethren to help monitor the images being transmitted by our *Bird* to the iPad cradled in Stinger's lap. The *Bird*, an RQ-20A Puma, showed the thermal signatures of two sentries a klick east of our current position. After recording their presence, I told Stinger to send the *Bird* back to scan the rest of the compound.

"Doesn't look like those two dudes are gonna give us much of a problem, Mac," Stinger whispered through his frost-covered mustache that curled down past his upper lip. "They're sitting on the path that leads into the compound. Sittin' there just shootin' the bull and smokin'... just waitin' to die."

"And being the good people we are, we're gonna do the right thing by them," I whispered, as Stinger passed me the iPad. The freezing air condensed my breath into a small cloud of tiny droplets that pasted themselves on my triple-layered balaclava. "But before we get too obliging, let's just slow down a minute or two to make sure we know what else is waiting for us over this here mountain pass. Our Bird is taking thermals of their compound as we speak."

As if on cue, images began appearing on the iPad. "Looks like we got ourselves a problem, Mac," Stinger whispered after watching the iPad's images.

"Gather round, people," I said, as the squad clustered around me in a tight circle to stare at the Bird's screen. I brought up a picture of a bearded man in traditional Muslim garb. "This, as you might expect, is a fellow named Advik Varujan," I said. "He's the guy the spooks in DC targeted as a *quote*—high value target—*unquote*. They want us to bring this dude back to them."

"Weren't those DC spooks also the ones who assured us that Varujan had already taken up residence in this small village and all we had to do was snatch him and bring him back to Jalalabad ... preferably alive?"

"Yeah, but it now looks like our pal Varujan has made friends ... seven to be exact ... who are all heavily armed shooters who've taken up residency in both Cabin One and Cabin Two."

Wolfman spit on the frozen ground and whispered angrily, "We just got flat out lied to, Mac. Our own people told us that the two small shacks on the flatland were only going to be used for Varujan and two friends. But now we find out he has seven friends, and that they've split the bunking arrangement in half." He shook his head in disgust. "There's truth in that old mantra ... you're kept in the dark and fed only horse manure."

"So true, Wolfman," I said. "So true. But this isn't anybody's fault. Remember that the Bird's imaging only captured a few signs of life in the smaller cabins nestled in the mountains to the north. Looks to me like those people who've already taken up residence on the mountain slopes shouldn't be a problem." Waiting a beat, I added, "And just so we've all counted correctly here, there are only four dudes in Cabin One and four in Cabin Two. Cabin Three is vacant, so it's not in play."

"But now that we're here discussing the alternatives," FT said, "I'm looking at numbers that still could put us right on the edge. What's your best guess, Mac?"

"We're going to do our job so thoroughly and quickly that the only thing these fighters will hear will be our shell casings hitting the floor right before they die. Once that's finished, we'll be getting our butts back to civilization."

"Okay, that's all I needed to hear," FT responded with a nod of his head. "You still want me on the ledge above the village watching for any movement coming in our back door, Mac? Or would you rather have me on the assault team?"

"Better to have the back door, FT," I said. "You'll probably have some bad guys up there that you'll have to keep honest by firing a few rounds into their hooches. And hey, I'm conceding that the number of bandits in shack one and shack two actually might offer us a challenge, but nothing we can't handle."

"As long as you're confident about it, Mac, we're all good to go," Stinger said. "Let's just get on with it so we can get back home."

"Ditto that," Wolfman said.

"Thanks, guys," I responded. "Having FT watching our backside while the rest of us take care of the business in those two shacks reminds me of a walk in the park." I laughed, then said, "But if any of us, including you, FT, have to go hot, we all know the drill, right?"

"Keep shooting, keep moving, and always protect each other's back," Stinger said without hesitation. "And remember, at the end of the day, the only thing that matters is we're all still alive ... and on our way home."

"Amen to that," I said. "Any questions?" Only silence. "Good! What say we go kick some butt so we can return to civilization at a reasonable hour."

Twenty minutes later, we crested the hill and found ourselves on the path where the Bird showed the two sentries were stationed. Stinger raised his fist for us to halt as he quietly disappeared down the path.

As I watched him go, my other senses kicked into overdrive. For me, there was no drug on earth that compared to the rush of adrenaline immediately before combat.

Five minutes later, I heard two suppressed shots from Stinger's MP7. Three minutes after that, he was back. Raising two fingers on his left hand, he curled them into a fist, then emphatically jerked his thumb downward.

"Showtime," I whispered with a smile.

FT went to position himself on the village overlook, while Stinger, Wolfman, and I quietly moved to Cabin One. The Bird showed there were four heat signatures inside. I could only hope it had the count right. Stinger walked silently forward and tried the door handle. Good fortune number one

... the door was unlocked. Good fortune number two ... the door opened inward, right-to-left, with nary a squeak. My night vision goggles quickly surveyed the darkened room. It was approximately twenty feet by ten feet with four hostiles racked out on cots scattered haphazardly around the room. All were asleep, but all had weapons next to them in their bunks. After determining the CIA's high value target was not in this cabin, I nodded for Stinger and Wolfman to go hot. Eight rounds later, we were outside and walking quickly toward Cabin Two, about a hundred yards away.

When we got to the cabin, we were surprised to find there were five fighters there, not four as we were expecting. And, to make matters worse, just as we entered the room, FT unexpectedly went hot above us. Even though suppressed, the bark from his MP7 echoed down the valley, awakening everyone in the cabin.

"Full auto," I barked into my mouthpiece as I kicked open the door. "Try to save the HVT," I yelled, "but everybody else dies." The fighters were now fully awake, and all were fumbling for their weapons. The one directly in front of me, a kid with black, squinting eyes who couldn't have been more than fifteen, glared back at me with a hatred that penetrated me to my very core. I put a short burst into him just as Wolfman and Stinger shot the other two dudes to our front.

It was then that I caught a glimpse of the last two fighters who were trying to escape by climbing out the back window. Both had strapped a rocket-propelled grenade launcher to their backs.

Both may or may not have been a high value target, but by this time, I couldn't have cared less. I did what I was trained to do ... I shot the guy. As he collapsed halfway through the window, the RPG launcher attached to his back got stuck in the window frame. One of my rounds had, unfortunately for him, punctured his launcher, causing the rocket's fuel to ignite. Flames of red and orange shot out the back of the tube, roasting this particular rocket man. I actually felt sorry for him.

But not so with the second person carrying the other rocket on his back. He had climbed to another window and, seeing what had happened to his partner, pulled out what looked like a Glock from his waistband, stuck it in his mouth, and with a wide grin, blew out the back of his head.

"The desk jockeys in DC are going to have a hissy fit," Stinger said as we walked through the carnage into the outer room.

"The first HVT dude to blow his head off was, in fact, an enemy combatant," Wolfman replied, "as was his partner. In both cases, we had little choice. Them or us. We chose us."

"Amen to that," I said. "And while I'm at it, take a look-see at this." Pointing to the guy hanging out the back window with the RPG strapped to his back, I said, "Doesn't rocket man look familiar?" I took the CIA's photograph of the HVT out of my pocket. "Not sure this is gonna be good news to our friends in DC," I said, "but I'm pretty sure that the rocket man is the dude they wanted us to bring back alive."

"Hey, Mac, want me to take his picture?" Stinger asked with a smirk. "I'm thinking *just hanging out* would be an appropriate tagline."

I nodded and laughed. "Go for it. I'm sure they'll love it."

"What say we get these bodies checked for intel, retrieve FT from the mountain back there, and get our butts outta here?" Wolfman intoned.

"Agreed," I said, keying my mic. "All clear here, FT. Time to come home. I'm dying to know what made you go hot."

"Sorry, Mac. But I gotta tell you the CIA's intel was way off target. There were at least six bandits in two of the cabins up here. When the shooting started at your end, I engaged them so they couldn't come down to join in the fight. I nailed all six of them—four in a cabin and two trying to sneak past me to get down to where you are."

"Good going, FT. We're starting to rig all the cabins with explosives. Care to join us?"

"What better way to have fun?" he said. "I'm on my way."

I told Stinger and Wolfman to set the charges with twelve-minute delays. Stinger spoke into his mic a few minutes later, saying, "We're finished here, Mac. Everything's wired."

"Then let's giddy-up and get home. We're running out of time."

We were halfway up the goat trail when a giant fireball illuminated the mountainside around us.

# CHAPTER 5



The helo picked us up at 0320. Thirty minutes into the trip, the crew chief handed me a headset. "For you."

"This is Ensign Michael Dowling on the line, sir. Major Cavanaugh is here and wants a word with you." Cavanaugh was the commander of the Special Forces Forward Base at J-bad.

*These guys are something else,* I thought, as I waited for Cavanaugh to get on the line. *They can't even wait 'til we return to base before reaming our butts out because we lost that HVT dude.*

Turned out Cavanaugh's phone call had nothing to do with losing the HVT.

"Mr. McArthur? Major Cavanaugh here. A short while ago, I received a message from Admiral Douglas Moore at Joint Special Operations Command. He requested I set up a secure line for you and your men the minute you land. He wants you to be aware he's bringing Red Squadron home immediately. I'll fill you in with as much as I know when you land."

Minutes after getting the Bird on the ground, my team and I were sitting in Cavanaugh's office waiting for the Deputy Director in DC to dial us up on a secure line.

"If this has to do with that HVT dude we didn't bring back alive," said Wolfman, "I'm gonna go crazy."

"Let's send them the picture of that dude after he made himself a human sparkler," snapped FT. "At least it'll show these desk jockeys we weren't messin' around."

"Perhaps we should wait a minute or two before we all get hot and bothered," I responded. "Let's see what the Admiral wants. Could be something completely different."

"Yeah, right," Wolfman replied through a generous dose of sarcasm.

The team was issued headsets, allowing them to listen to the conversation I was about to have with Admiral Moore. A drained coffee pot later, the phone in Cavanaugh's office lit up. "Headsets on, gentlemen," Cavanaugh said.

"Mac? Admiral Doug Moore here." He paused a few beats, then said, "I'm sorry it's been such a long time since we've talked. I want you to be aware that I hear nothing but good things about you and your tcam. Congratulations!"

"It's been a while, Sir, that's for sure. It's great to hear your voice again."

I'd known Admiral Doug Moore for over seventeen years. He was a legend in the Teams. A former member of SEAL Team 6 and commander of SEAL Team 3, Moore had been decorated multiple times, including the Navy Cross for gallantry in the Battle of Mogadishu in '93, where he took four bullets saving a Delta Force unit trapped in an apartment complex. My father was a member of that unit and was so badly wounded, he barely made it home. If nothing else, Admiral Moore was instrumental in getting me accepted into the SEAL Team 6 training program.

"How'd your mission go last night?"

I gave him a short debrief, including the part about not getting the CIA's HVT out alive.

"Well, don't worry about the CIA, Mac. You did what was necessary to protect your squad. Your mission didn't fail. Just think of that HVT as someone who deserved to die."

"Agreed, Sir," I said with a chuckle. "He left us no selection."

There was silence between us for a few moments before I heard Moore take a deep breath and say, "Mac, I didn't contact you to discuss the so-called high value target your squad was after. I have some bad news and don't know any other way to tell you than straight out. Are you there with your team?"

"I am, Sir," I responded, not at all feeling comfortable with the tone in Moore's voice. "We're all wired, Sir."

"Good. I want your entire team to hear this," He clicked off for a moment, then came back on. "I received a call this morning from a retired San Francisco Police Officer who introduced himself as Alex Navarro. Do you know him?"

I thought for a moment, then said, "As a matter of fact, I do, Sir. Though not all that well. He's a good friend of my father. And, yes, he's a police officer. Or was. Recently retired, I think."

"You're right about him being a good friend of your

father," Moore replied. "Alex Navarro called me twice this morning trying to get in touch with you. He didn't have your number, so he called around until someone from my office gave him my number and told him to call me. Which he did." I heard Moore take a deep breath before saying, "I'm sorry to have to tell you this, Mac, but I don't see any way to sugarcoat it. Alex Navarro told me your father died in an airplane explosion over San Francisco. He wanted you to know."

It took a moment for me to fully comprehend what the Admiral had just said. Talk about an explosion going off inside your head. While my father and I had many issues over the years, especially as it related to his treatment of my mother after their divorce, he was still my father and I still loved him. I glanced around the room, not knowing how to respond. My shoulders slumped. The next ten seconds felt like an hour. The best I could do was sink back in my seat and mouth a quiet *give me the strength, Lord.* I closed my eyes and pushed back a few feet from the table. The team, after hearing Moore's message, all bowed their heads and sat quietly in silence for a few moments before Stinger walked over and placed his hand on my shoulder.

"I know how you must feel," the Admiral continued, "but I'm afraid it gets worse. Approximately seventeen minutes and forty-two seconds after takeoff, the plane exploded. As you no doubt know, that's a very rare occurrence in modern aviation. There was, and is, some early speculation that the plane was brought down by a surface-to-air missile ... or possibly a bomb placed on board.

"Nothing has been confirmed yet, Mac, and we won't know for certain one way or the other until sometime tomorrow afternoon at the earliest. Whatever happened up there, your father was one of 209 people that perished." Moore paused, then said, "I want to thank all your teammates for being with you during this time." There were nods and pats on the back as the squad gathered around me. "And forgive me for having to skip right to business, but there's been a lot of activity here that you all should be aware of." He paused, then said, "Less than fifteen minutes ago, I was in a meeting with the President of the United States." He went quiet for a minute before asking me, "Mac, did your father ever speak to you about a plan of his he code-named *Snowplow*?"

Closing my eyes, I leaned forward, concentrating as best I could on Moore's question. I shook my head and said, "As you probably know, Sir, my father and I have been semi-estranged for some time now. Actually, for the better part of twenty years, though truth be told, we quietly reconciled as best we could a number of months ago. But, yes, I do remember him mentioning a Drug Enforcement Agency operation he was involved in that was code-named *Snowplow*. He told me it was a plan that many people in the DEA hoped would be a game-changer as to how we wage war on the drug cartels. That was it. Nothing more. No details."

"Interesting," Moore replied. "Were you aware that your father was on his way to El Paso to finalize, one way or the other, the Agency's interest in putting this *Snowplow* plan of his into operation?"

"I did not, Sir."

"The DEA confirmed to us," Moore continued, "that they were flirting with taking *Snowplow* operational even though some in the Agency were having second thoughts about not only its efficacy, but also its lawfulness."

"My father never mentioned any of that to me, Sir, so I don't know what to tell you."

"Given what happened to your father, we're all curious about what the President will do next. He's still being squirrely, even after being debriefed by that fellow named Gilardi, the DEA Director in Charge of West Coast Operations. It's Gilardi's group that will take charge of *Snowplow* if all parties involved give it a thumbs-up." He paused, then asked me if I knew Gilardi.

"Mostly by reputation, Sir. Over the years, it was a rare occasion when my dad spoke to me either about his job or about the people he worked with. But in the case of this Gilardi fellow, my father didn't hide the fact that he wasn't one of his all-time favorite people."

Admiral Moore went silent for a few seconds, then said, "Okay. That, in and of itself, is good info. But enough about *Snowplow* and Director Gilardi. I mentioned, did I not, that the President and I had a conversation about Red Squadron?"

"You did, Sir." Furtive glances swept the room. "Anything we should know?"

"I told the President that, in my opinion, Red Squadron could be a real asset to us in the drug war. I'm saying this because both the President and I think the drugs coming into the country through the cartels could easily be considered an act of war. And, without any concrete knowledge as of yet, I sincerely believe the cartels had something to do with bringing down the airplane your father was on."

"Do you have any evidence of that, Sir?" I asked, sitting up a little straighter, and leaning into the phone's receiver.

"Only speculation, Mac. That's why I'd like to invite you and your crew to meet with me at 0900 this coming Thursday at JSOC Headquarters in Coronado. By then, we should have a lot more info on whether there's a connection with the cartels and your father's death. Can you do that?"

I looked over at the team. All nodded in the affirmative. "We'll all be there, Sir."

"That's good news, Mac. Given what happened to your father, I had hoped you'd be part of our team." Following a brief silence, he asked, "Is there anything else I can do for you or anything you want to talk about?"

I glanced around the room, seeing only a shake of heads from my team. "Nothing here, Sir."

"Good. We'll talk about this again when I see you next Thursday. In the meantime, I've requested that Major Cavanaugh arrange transportation to get your team back to the States." He took a deep breath, then said, "Again, Mac, I'm very, very sorry about your father. I knew him well. He was an exceptional man. I promise we'll help you to get the SOB's who murdered him." He went silent for a few beats, then said, "Godspeed, gentlemen."

After Moore disconnected, the room went quiet ... a silence I completely embraced. No trivialized conversation could overcome the emotions coursing through me at that very moment. I put my head down, my chin firmly tucked into my chest. I began picking imaginary dirt off the legs of my fatigues.

Wolfman spoke first. "Mac, you know we'll do anything for you." Stinger and FT nodded in agreement. "Looks like we're all being asked to be in San Diego at 0900 on Thursday. Why not fly with us from here to Coronado and spend a few days clearing your mind before we meet with Moore?"

There was silence in the room as they all gazed at me. "I appreciate your concern, guys. It means a lot to me that you've got my back at a time like this. But while you're lounging around in San Diego before our meeting on Thursday, I'll be going over paperwork associated with my father's estate."

"Are you the executor?" FT asked.

"I have no idea. But whether I am or not, it'll still take me a few days to decide what to do with the house and all his belongings. No matter what, though, I'll be with you guys at JSOC HQ on Thursday." I peered down at my watch. "It's now 4:15 a.m. Let's sleep 'til noon and then get our butts on an airplane and go home."

"You're on, Mac," Stinger said, as the others nodded their approval.

"And just so you all understand where I'm coming from ..." I paused, looking into each of their eyes. "No matter how many people died on that airplane ... my father's death was one death too far."

# CHAPTER 6



Making sure we were going to be with him in San Diego on Thursday, Moore arranged for us to ride a military airplane from J-Bad to Qatar's Hamad International airport. As a personal gift honoring my father, Moore purchased four first-class tickets on Qatar Airlines for the non-stop, eleven-hour-plus flight to San Francisco International. All four of us had to admit that when you fly on Uncle Sam's dime, it's a whole different experience. Not only did Qatar Airlines offer real beds to sleep in, they also served gourmet international foods accompanied by the finest of French wines. None of us, however, were sophisticated enough to tell the difference between an expensive bottle of French wine and a twenty-dollar bottle of an Alexander Valley Cabernet. No one was surprised when Alexander Valley won out. And, to make the trip even more special, by traveling east to west over the

International Dateline, we got part of Tuesday back. Is this a great country or what?

I AWOKE from a much needed eight-hour sleep, took a shower on the plane, had a gourmet breakfast, and changed my watch to California time. Since the airline gave us access to a satellite phone, and we weren't scheduled to land in San Francisco for another six hours, I took the opportunity to call and reintroduce myself to my dad's friend, Alex Navarro. It was he who alerted the Admiral that my father had been murdered by the Mexican cartels. If Navarro hadn't done that, I wouldn't be sitting on this airplane getting ready to sort through my father's life. When I told him I was flying into SFO, he offered to drive me home.

After hanging up, I sat back and tried to imagine what my father had been doing the day he died. Admiral Moore told me he was headed to El Paso to put the final touches on what he had named *Operation Snowplow*. Knowing my dad's attention to detail, he was probably still piecing together the final touches when his plane exploded.

At 2:15 p.m., we began our descent into San Francisco International. The flight path took us over the Bay Bridge, sparking childhood memories of the 1989 Loma Prieta Earthquake. That particular night, I was sitting with my dad and mom in the bleachers of Candlestick Park anxiously awaiting the third game of the World Series. Since the San Francisco Giants and the Oakland Athletics were both in the Series that year, the games promised to be a neighborhood brawl. As fate would have it, the "brawl" that particular evening would be trying to *crawl* your way out of a Candlestick Park that had been pounded by a 6.9 magnitude earthquake. Since I was all of eight years old, little did I realize there was only nine years remaining in what I viewed to be an idyllic life.

It just so happened that in the middle of my junior year in high school, my parents divorced. Upon receiving the final decree, mom moved us to San Diego. That decision, and the strain it placed on my relationship with my father, was the catalyst for me traveling east for college, and then joining the Navy after graduation. Three years after enlisting, I was awarded my Trident and became a Navy SEAL. My father never made it to the ceremonies. That, coupled with my continued deployments over the years, made it hard for me to reestablish my relationship with him. My mom's passing seven years ago also didn't help bring my father and I closer together.

Looking down at the city, I was reminded of all I had missed by not being a better son to my father. I just now realized, for the first time in many, many years, how much he meant to me. The irony of it all was, of course, overwhelming. At that very moment, I found myself on an airplane returning home to spend some quality time with my father. But now? But now, I was on an airplane returning home not to reconcile with my father, nor to care for him in his old age, but rather to bury him after the cartels murdered him.

AFTER DEPLANING, I walked the concourse with my three brothers-in-arms while they checked the screens to find their flight to San Diego. When they saw their flight was scheduled to take off from the next terminal over, they gathered around me.

"See you mutts later," I said, giving Stinger a hug and pat on the back.

"I'll be looking forward to seeing your ugly mug come Thursday afternoon." Stinger responded with a smile.

Wolfman shook my hand and pulled me close. "Take care of yourself, bro," he whispered in my ear. "Sorry about your father. I'll be thinking of you."

"Thanks, mucho, my man." I paused, then said, "Got to tell you guys, it's going to be weird bunking down in my old house."

"I'll bet," Wolfman responded. "How long has it been since you were home to see your father?"

"Long time, my man. Went to San Diego to live with my mom when I was seventeen. A year later, I traveled back East to go to college. Four years after that, I met you guys in the Navy."

"And we all thought you were such an old dude," FT chuckled, stepping forward and giving me a hug. "Take care now, ya hear?" he said.

Not being sure what else to say, I simply smiled and said, "Have a safe flight."

# CHAPTER 7



Ten minutes later, I found myself in baggage claim giving Alex Navarro a bear hug. "It's been a long time, old friend," I said. "Let me apologize for not communicating with you sooner about that job opening we talked about. My life these past few months has been particularly complicated."

Navarro put his arm around me and returned the hug. "Hey, no problem about the job opening, Mac," he exclaimed. "I want to tell you how sorry I am that your dad was on that airplane that went down over the coast yesterday."

"Thanks, Uncle Alex. What bothers me the most, though, was he and I weren't fully reconciled when he died. I had so much I wanted to say to him."

"Your father told me just two weeks ago that he had decided to retire and reconcile with you once this plan of his ... he named it *Snowplow* ... was either accepted by the DEA or buried by it. He told me either would have worked because all he really wanted was to get straight with you."

"Funny how that works, isn't it? I had those very same thoughts. It's the reason I'm here with you and not flying to meet the Admiral in San Diego." I hesitated, then said, "I'm going to stay in the area until I find out what caused his plane to go down."

"It's still under investigation, Mac. I've been retired from the SFPD now for over a month, but fortunately still have close ties with most of the guys who still work there. I called this morning to see if they had any further info that they could pass off to me that I could pass on to you."

"And ...?"

"And I did get a friend of mine who's still on the Force to tell me that there's been heavy-duty speculation that a bomb had been placed on board."

"I was afraid of that," I murmured.

"Yeah. I'm sorry about your dad, Mac." He put his hand on my shoulder. "And, as a consequence of it being a bomb that was planted on board, the SFPD was unceremoniously dumped from the investigation in favor of Homeland Security." He paused, then said, "Sorry for the lousy circumstances, Mac. In my estimation, your father was a stand-up guy and one of my best friends. We called each other brothers-in-arms. And we meant it."

"Thanks, *Uncle* ..." I hesitated, thinking the name "uncle" probably wouldn't be appropriate anymore. I flashed him a grin, and said, "Tell me ... by what name should I call you? Uncle Alex? Al? Mr. Navarro? Or ... what?"

"Hey, you can dump the entire *uncle* business," he said.

"Nav works just fine. It's what most everyone calls me ... except my wife, of course." He paused, then said with a smile, "But that's another story." He smiled and patted my shoulder. "And while we're at it, how about you? Do you go by Ken? Or Kenny? Or Mac? Or maybe something more military, like Lieutenant?"

"Well, Admiral would be cool, but I'm just a wee bit too young for that title, and now that I'm a civilian, I can't be called Lieutenant anymore, either. Nor any other military title, for that matter."

"They disowned you, huh?" Navarro shook his head, then laughed. "Hey, at least they gave you a pat on the back, didn't they?

"That's exactly what they did. One lousy pat. So, since I'm no longer in the military, most people just call me Mac. But Ken, or Kenny, would work in a pinch."

"You have a favorite?"

"You know ... the name Mac has worked for me." I paused, then said, "Which reminds me. I have a duffle bag that needs to be rescued from Carousel 10. You want to come with me while I retrieve it?"

"You bet! Just lead the way."

My duffle appeared a few minutes after we arrived. I picked it up and carried it to the nearest bench. "Can you hold on for just a minute, Nav?" I asked, unzipping the duffle. I carefully went through it until I found my Sig and slipped it into my jacket pocket. "Sorry," I said. "I had to pack quickly out of Afghanistan and didn't have time to obtain a special carry permit. Showing my US Department of Defense credentials, however, got me a pass to stow the Sig in my luggage."

"What a world, huh?" Navarro said with a scowl. "But that's the way things are nowadays, unfortunately." I nodded just as he changed topics. "What's it been, Mac? Twelve or so years since I last saw you? It was right before your mom and dad divorced ... and you ended up in San Diego. And all I can say is that you haven't changed much at all."

"First your memory goes, then your eyesight," I said with a chuckle. "Anyway, yeah! It's been a while. Seems like forever, doesn't it?" I paused, then said, "So, catch me up. You got married again, right?"

"That I did. Best thing that ever happened to me. Her name is Kathleen. And by the way, if you aren't too tired, she asked me to invite you over for dinner tonight. She's an outstanding cook. If I were you, I'd take her up on it."

"Thanks, Nav. I appreciate the offer. But would you and the missus be offended if I took a rain check? I honestly wouldn't be very good company tonight. Been on airplanes for the better part of two days now, and, while we were treated well, there's still nothing like sleeping in your own bed. And in my case, the bed of my youth, for goodness' sake. It may sound silly, but I'm looking forward to climbing into that bed and falling into a deep, peaceful sleep."

"Hey, no problem. I've been in the same place many times, so I know how you feel." He guided me to the elevators and punched Level 3. When the door closed, he said, "Before I forget, let me give you these." He reached into his jacket pocket and passed me two keys on a small chain that had a flashlight attached. "This one is your front door key, and the other is the key to the desk in your dad's office. Walt gave them to me so I could watch over the place when he wasn't in town. I'm thinking you should probably have these now."

"Thanks, Nav," I said. "Before you so graciously offered to pick me up today, my only other course of action would have been to wake up old man Popovich—the guy who lives next door. Or at least used to."

"Hey ... he's still there."

"Small world. When I lived in the house, my father gave Popovich a key. For emergencies."

"He was a funny old guy, but he no longer has the keys. I do."

As we drove out of the lot, Navarro said, "You know, Mac, about a year ago, your dad dropped by my house and, out of the blue, asked if I would mind being the executor of his estate. It sounded so ghoulish to me, that I resisted at first. Besides, I just assumed your dad would outlive me by many years." He turned to me and said, "I was sadly wrong, Mac, and I want you to know, I would've given anything to have been right."

# CHAPTER 8

SAN FRANCISCO, TUESDAY EARLY EVENING

Forty minutes later, we arrived at what was now my house. "Come on in for a drink, Nav. It's been at least ten years since I was last here, and truth be told, I'd feel somewhat strange walking into my house by myself. Would you mind at least holding my hand while I reintroduce myself to the old place?"

"I don't think I'll hold your hand, but would giving you a pat on the back work?" he said with a smile.

I nodded. "Thanks. I have a ton of memories about growing up in this house. At this very moment, however, they're still tiptoeing around the back of my head." I unlocked the front door. "It feels so strange now, but you know what the most vivid memory I have of this house is?" I didn't give him a chance to respond. "It was where my dad kept his liquor." I paused, then said, "In the cabinet above the kitchen sink, right?"

"Well, hate to tell you this, but you're a wee-bit late to the party," Navarro said with a chuckle. "Your father, being the thoroughly modern fellow he was, kept the rotgut in the kitchen. The class stuff, for close friends like me, and now you of course, he kept locked up in the bottom drawer of his office desk." He gave me a pat on the back. "Many a night the two of us would sit in that office with a bucket of ice and a bottle of Jameson's and just shoot the bull for the next few hours. It was during those years that bottles of Jameson took up permanent residency in that particular desk drawer. Tell you what ... let me get two glasses and ice from the kitchen, and I'll meet you in the office. Sound good?"

"Absolutely. While you're getting the glasses and liquor, I'm going to take my duffle upstairs, unpack, and check out my old room. Can you wait a few minutes before you pour?"

"You bet. Go for it."

"Thanks. See you in a few minutes." I grabbed my duffle and sprinted up the stairs, making a sharp left at the top of the stairs, and entered my old bedroom. Placing the duffle on the bed, I removed the Sig from my pocket and placed it on the nightstand. Retrieving a towel from the bathroom, I laid the weapon on the towel, quickly took it apart, then oiled and reassembled it. Slamming home the magazine, I jacked a round into the chamber. Not that I was expecting trouble, but I learned early in my career that carrying a gun with nothing in the chamber was akin to being in a gunfight with an unloaded weapon—a tried and true method of getting yourself killed.

Finishing with the Sig, I gazed around the room, surprised

that not much had changed since I had left the house nearly two decades earlier. I still felt a kinship with my old dresser sitting in the far corner of the room where I'd left it many years ago. I smiled at the memory and promised myself I'd clean and polish the old girl first thing in the morning. The mirror that used to hang on the wall behind the dresser, the one that held pictures of friends—girls that I had fallen in love with and sports heroes I admired were no longer there. *One less thing Dad had to clean*, I mused.

Standing, I walked to the closet and opened the door. It was full of clothes, mostly old suits of my dad's. What did surprise me, however, was finding some of my mom's old outfits hanging there as well. It puzzled me as to why my father kept them. As a sign he still loved her? Missed her? That he expected her to come back? When no plausible explanation punctured my brain, I closed the closet door and walked back toward the bed.

It was Navarro's yell to get my butt downstairs immediately that interrupted my walk. Hearing the urgency in his voice, I grabbed the Sig off the bed and bounded down the stairs, two at a time.

Navarro stood outside my dad's office doorway holding a bucket of ice and two highball glasses—his body language a concert of uncertainty. Casting a glance at me, he motioned with his head toward the interior of the room. "Take a look-see in there, will you? You're not going to believe it."

# CHAPTER 9



As a young boy, my father's office was my favorite place to hang out. Staring at it now, more than eighteen years later, it looked exactly like I remembered. Of all the childhood memories assaulting me that very moment, the most vivid was the faint smell of Lemon Pledge. When I was growing up, my dad never went on a trip without first polishing his office furniture with Lemon Pledge, and I'm sure his Monday trip was no different. Only now, it smelled of Lemon Pledge ... and death.

In the years leading to my mom and dad's marital storm clouds, the three of us used to stand at the kitchen sink while doing the dishes together. In those early years, a favorite mantra of ours was *the family that did the dishes together, stayed together.* Unfortunately, the mantra didn't last beyond my sixteenth birthday. For no reason I could think of, I was sent off to my room to do homework right after dinner. My mom would do the dishes then go to the family room to watch television. My father retreated to his office ... and closed the door.

Over time, that office became his man cave. No one was allowed in the office without his express permission. The room was dominated by an expensive black walnut desk that always seemed to me to be newly polished. Even back then, if my dad knew he'd be out of town for a few days, he took a polish rag to that desk before he left.

A large computer screen now dominated the middle of the desk in front of a high-backed leather chair. The telephone sat next to his chair to the left of the screen. Behind the desk was a mahogany table on which was placed a copier and fax machine.

But what captured my full attention was the two oak filing cabinets in the corner, their security locks having been drilled out, leaving a dusting of wood shavings covering the floor like a fine mist. The top drawers of both filing cabinets were open and empty.

"Better that we don't disturb anything," Navarro said. "This is obviously a crime scene, so let's not compromise it or ourselves, okay?" I nodded in agreement. "And even though I'm no longer an official SFPD officer, let me call Robbery. I'll get some techs over here." After a few minutes of chatter, he hung up. "No one's in the office right now. The supervisor told me they'd be at your door no later than 9:30 tomorrow morning. I assured them the scene would not be touched until they arrived. You cool with that?"

"Absolutely."

"Good." He glanced over at me. "And you're sure you don't want to come and stay the night at my house?"

"Thanks, Nav, but I'll stay here. I may get lucky and have the dirtbags come back for round two"

"We can only hope," he said with a smile.

"What do you think they were after?"

"Normally, I'd say they were just gangbangers waiting for the newspapers to publish the names of victims ... like they did of everyone that was on your dad's plane. Then, while the next of kin were at the coroner's office filing a death certificate, or like you flying in from who knows where, these dudes come and burgle your home." His eyes slowly perused the room. "But, to me, this looks more like a direct hit. Going through the house just now, I couldn't find another room that was messed with. Whoever broke in here knew exactly what they were after, and exactly where to find it." He glanced over at me, then put out his hand like a stop sign. "But, before jumping to any conclusions, let's just wait to hear what the department's techs have to say tomorrow."

I stared at the mess. Shaking my head slowly, I said to him. "I want you to know I appreciate all you've done and are doing for me, but there's nothing more to do here tonight. Why not just head home to that pretty wife of yours and get some sleep? You'll be here tomorrow when the techs show up, right?"

"Absolutely, Mac. Nine-thirty. However long it takes them, I'll be here to watch. That'll give you some time to perhaps visit a few of your dad's DEA cohorts."

"That's on the top of my to-do list. Besides scheduling a meeting with them tomorrow, I'm going to call an old SEAL buddy of mine. Guy named Vince Delgado. The last time I checked, he lived over in the East Bay near Berkeley. Haven't seen him since he left the Teams three or so years ago. He was one tough hombre. Don't know what he's been up to these past couple of years, but I can tell you from what I'm seeing, I just might need someone with his kind of tenacity. You okay with that?"

"Absolutely," Nav nodded. "Go for it."

# CHAPTER 10



As the de facto CEO of the twenty-first largest company in the world based on revenue, Victor Serna was, if nothing else, a shrewd businessman. As with so many of life's unexplained coincidences, however, one person's *shrewd businessman* is another person's *sadistic butcher*. Serna fit most easily into the latter category.

Serna was a second-generation Tormenta, the first cartel leader not to have emerged from the Mexican army. To his friends, he was *Ángel*, the Spanish word for "Angel." To his enemies, Victor Serna was known as the *Ángel de la Muerta*, the "Angel of Death."

Serna had sealed his reputation years ago by boiling alive three of his closest rivals in fifty-five-gallon barrels of grease, and then leaving their overly cooked remains on the side of a major Mexican highway.

As befits one of the wealthiest men in the world, he was in the midst of hosting a lavish dinner party aboard his 164-foot Delta Marine yacht he named *M-40*. His guests that evening were Enrique Sanchez, the country's Minister of the Interior; Leon Cardenas, the chief of police in the Mexican state where Serna headquartered his Tormenta cartel; and Alejandro Morales, known to everyone as El Papa, the editor of Mexico City's *Gaceta Oficial* newspaper. They were seated in the 1600 square-foot salon on the yacht's enclosed second level, smoking expensive Cuban cigars and sipping Camus Cognac served to them by four scantily clad women.

Except for the women and the twenty heavily armed guards strategically stationed on various levels of the yacht, the attendees could have been at a high-level business meeting anywhere in the world.

"Sir," Enrique Sanchez stated, "it is not possible for the coca plant to be grown on Mexican soil."

"That used to be true, Minister," Serna replied politely. "But not anymore. Tell him, El Papa."

"Señor Serna is right, Minister," Alejandro Morales said. "The reason you are here smoking a Cohiba BHK 56 with the lovely young señorita on your lap is because I met someone recently who recently developed a similar hybrid coca plant. He assured me it would grow in Mexico and graciously allowed us to have it."

"Why have I not heard of such a breakthrough?" Sanchez asked dryly.

"Because you are not *El Papa*," replied Morales with a smile, blowing a stream of cigar smoke in the air.

"You need not know, Minister, who developed this plant,"

Serna sighed, while absentmindedly picking lint from the sleeve of his coat. "All I want from you is ownership of the first five kilometers of hill country bordering Guatemala ... and to be assured, of course, that no one from the government will harass me."

"How can I promise you such a thing, Señor Serna? I am but a lowly minister with little or no power."

"Minister Sanchez," Serna replied in a calm voice. "I realize you will find a way to do the right thing. I won't dishonor you by threatening your family. Please ... keep having fun with your playmate there. She is yours for the entire night ... if you can handle it," Serna said with a chuckle. "And when you leave, be sure to pick up the suitcase Jefe Cardenas has sitting next to him. It will handsomely finance the people you will need to assist in our project."

A bodyguard appeared and whispered in Serna's ear. He nodded, waving the man away. "You will have to excuse me, gentlemen. I must take a phone call. Ladies, show my friends a good time while I'm gone." Serna walked to his office, closed the door, and raised the phone to his ear. "Rinaldo ... to what do I honor this phone call?"

"My contacts alerted me that someone of interest is coming from Washington, DC to nose around in our business," Rinaldo Ruiz replied.

Ruiz was Serna's boyhood friend, confidant, and the second in command of the Tormenta cartel. Serna flashed a smile. "Tell me, my friend ... who is this someone of interest?"

"His name is Kenneth McArthur," Ruiz replied.

"Ah, isn't it always the same?" Serna whispered as he

massaged the back of his neck with his off-hand. "Family ... the bane of our existence, eh, my friend? Your contacts know us too well." He snickered.

"They knew we'd be interested, *Ángel*," Ruiz replied. "They are concerned about any potential problem accruing from them being the ones you chose to eliminate senior McArthur."

"And what do we know about *el niño* McArthur?" Serna asked.

"He's a former Navy SEAL, *Ángel*. So, he could be a problem. But he'd only be a problem if we let him live."

"Then let's not let him live," Serna replied.

"Exactly what I hoped you would say, but wanted to make sure. I will tell the gringos that we'll make the arrangements, but it's going to cost them mucho dinero."

Serna hung up and tapped the top of the desk with his fingertips. He shouldn't have been surprised the dead DEA agent had a family. It's just these kinds of situations where families come seeking revenge. It's the reason he, the *Ángel de la Muerta,* makes a point of killing the family of his enemies in the most gruesome of ways before they become a problem. It serves as a warning. *If you want your family to live, do not become my enemy.*

He remembered the DEA spy within his own cartel. The one they called Munoz. The man who told the Americans about the bomb they planted aboard the airplane. Not only did he execute Munoz, but his wife and two children as well. Their mutilated bodies were dumped in an open sewer in Piedras Negras, on the Texas border. He grinned, not thinking he was a bad man, nor even a butcher as some people called him. He was nothing more than a businessman discouraging competition.

Though Señor McArthur's military background posed a threat of a different order, Serna wasn't worried. Rinaldo would handle it. He always did.

# CHAPTER 11



Rinaldo Ruiz, known as *El Rhino* to his friends, was a practicing trial attorney in San Diego, California. He was Victor Serna's best friend ever since they attended kindergarten together forty-five years before at Our Lady of Guadalupe in Tecalitlan, a small town in the Pacific coastal state of Jalisco.

If anyone doubted that opposites attract, the relationship between Serna and Rinaldo Ruiz would have erased all doubts. Victor Serna had always been big for his age and was never shy about exerting physical superiority over everyone around him. On the other hand, Rinaldo Ruiz made up for his lack of physical strength with a mental acuity bordering on genius. He'd never beaten up anyone physically, but his intellect had, on many occasions, ground the most muscular physical specimens into dust.

It was Rinaldo Ruiz who saw the power in coupling his and Serna's unique skills to become a force in the emerging world of cartels. When they were twelve, they enlisted as mules in the La Familia cartel, delivering drugs throughout the states of Jalisco and Colima. Ruiz was the one who figured out ways to skim the drugs, and then resell what they had stolen without being caught. If a consumer made a fuss about not receiving the amount he paid for, Serna stopped the complaints by beating up the consumer's sister or mother. Their business made them piles of money. Ruiz watched over the business side by heavily discouraging Serna from spending money frivolously.

By the time they were sixteen, they'd risen to the rank of captains in the Jalisco cartel. They were now toting guns and making a reputation for themselves in the shooting wars that broke out between rival cartel gangs. One such gun battle changed their lives forever.

On a hot September night, a group of five armed men from a rival cartel arrived in Tecalitlan looking for Serna, Ruiz and their childhood friend, Diego Velasquez. The rival gang members found them in the central plaza during a Virgin of Guadalupe celebration. Opening fire, they missed all three, but killed eight innocent bystanders. Serna, Ruiz, and Velasquez managed to escape, but recognized, because of the gun battle, their time in Tecalitlan had come to an end. They took to the surrounding mountains and lived in them for four months while discussing a new course of action. Those discussions evolved into a plan by which the three managed to save more than $70,000 via various illegal schemes. Rinaldo Ruiz took his third and went to America, settling in Tucson with his aunt while he went to college. With certain modifications along the way, Ruiz ended up staying in the States. He earned his college degree in three years, then went to law school, specializing in immigration law. They all decided Ruiz should stay in America and handle their business enterprises from there.

It was the long-ago agreement between them that decided the path their individual lives would take, including that they would watch each other's back. Ruiz's first bit of business after receiving his law degree was obtaining Victor Serna's signature appointing him as chief attorney for the Tormenta cartel. This gave Ruiz immediate wealth plus unlimited trips to Mexico to "advise" his client.

During the time that Ruiz spent earning his law degree, Serna was making his bones in the Tormenta cartel. The fight he waged to secure his position as the head of the Tormentas allowed him to become one of the wealthiest men in the hemisphere. The downside, however, was that his name was on the DEA's most wanted list. That irritation didn't perturb Serna, however, as he was certain his enormous wealth would be his shield.

The path Diego Velasquez, the third member of the triumvirate, chose to take unfortunately landed him a fifteen-year jail sentence for insurance fraud. Having Rinaldo Ruiz as his attorney, however, resulted in a commuted sentence and a well-paying job as Serna's full-time bodyguard.

THE CALL from his contact in San Francisco came at a particularly inconvenient moment for Rinaldo. But then, any calls coming in after two in the morning would be considered inconvenient. That's because virtually every night Rinaldo Ruiz lived up to his nickname, El Rhino, with an enthusiasm that would have ordinary men swearing off Viagra by the fourth month.

Amber, one of his most desired women, was with him that night. Knowing he received many mysterious phone calls in the dead of night, his instruction to her was always the same: never cease what she was doing to him unless he told her explicitly to stop. Many nights, Ruiz found himself conducting business in what he would call a *deliciously compromised position*. But, unfortunately, not this night. This night, he recognized the incoming phone number and knew the message would be of critical importance. He told Amber to stop and bring him a Sapphire tonic from the bar. While she was gone, he listened to the short voicemail, then dialed a phone number he knew by heart.

"Lupe," he purred, "I need you to find me a competent shooter for a job I have in the San Francisco area. Can I trust you to find one?"

"Si, Patrón," she replied.

"Excellent. I'll wire the money to your bank account tomorrow, along with the name, address, and MO of the target; a fellow named McArthur. Kenneth McArthur. A dossier will be delivered the usual way. You want to be sure not to underestimate this gringo. Because of his background, he could very well prove to be a tougher kill than most. You're authorized to tell your shooter there's a $5,000 bonus if he kills the mark before the week is out. As soon as he finishes that job, I'll wire you the bonus."

# CHAPTER 12



I'd already completed a two-and-a-half hour, ten-mile run through San Francisco's Forest Hill neighborhood and was about to shower when Navarro and his robbery techs arrived at the house. They slowly filtered into the kitchen and started to set up shop.

"Looks like it's going to be a busy day, Nav. How long do you think this will take them?"

"I'm guessing 'til noon," Navarro answered. "And just so you're aware, these guys are gonna make a real mess here. But don't worry, they're professionals and will clean up before they leave."

"I'm sure they will," I said with a smile. "In any case, I'll leave you guys alone. I've got to get cleaned up myself, and then make a few phone calls."

After showering, I sat on my bed and called Vinnie

Delgado. I was looking forward to talking to him after all these years. He answered on the fourth ring. "Is this Vincent Delgado?" I asked, deciding to mess with him a little.

"It is," the voice answered tentatively.

"Yeah, well who the heck cares?" Not wanting him to hang, I waited just a beat, then said, "Wait! Turns out I *do* care!" I chuckled. "Vinnie Delgado—this is Ken McArthur. Better known to you as Mac."

There was a long pause, then ... "I can hardly believe what I'm hearing. This better not be some kind of joke."

"No joke, Vinnie. It's really me, Kenny Mac, in the flesh."

"Well, I'll be a son-of-a-bitch. What a great surprise. I've been out of the Teams now for what ... almost four years? I heard through the grapevine that you retired, too. How long ago?"

"A little over a year and a half, Vin. I'm now working for the Teams off and on as a contractor. I'm in the Bay Area because my father just died."

"Ahhh, man, I'm sorry to hear that."

Yeah ... thanks, Vin. I appreciate the thought." I hesitated for a few ticks, then said, "Anyway, while I was on the West Coast, I thought I'd look you up. As I told you, I still work on a contract basis for people you would recognize. That's why I'm calling. If you don't have anything critical staring you in the face this very minute, I could use you on a job I'm putting together. I'm thinking five to ten days ... maybe more. Just like old times, man. You game?"

"If you be the dude hiring, Mac ... well, heck ya, I'm game. You calling me from San Francisco?"

"I am."

"I'm living in the East Bay, Mac. A town named Martinez. Give me your address, and depending on traffic, I could be at your place faster than small town gossip."

"Hey ... you still got a way with words, Vinnie," I chuckled.

"How 'bout an hour and a half. Will that work for you?"

"Well, heck ya, it'll work. Looking forward to seeing you, my friend. Been way ass too long." After giving him my address, I hung up and called the DEA's San Francisco office, asking for Special Agent Gilardi.

I introduced myself, and after Gilardi's *I'm sorry about your dad* banter, I asked if it were possible for me to meet with him and his team. Gilardi sounded genuinely pleased that I had called, and promised to get back with a time that would allow him to round up his guys.

I hung up, walked downstairs, and sat with Nav in the living room. "Remember I told you about an old SEAL buddy of mine named Vinnie Delgado?" Nav nodded. "Well, he's on his way over as we speak. One of the good guys. Just the kind of professional you and I would want watching our backs. And while I'm at it, I also called the head of my dad's old DEA team ... run now by a guy named Bill Gilardi. I asked him if I could meet my dad's old teammates just to let them know how much he thought of them. Also, I'm hoping they could provide me a lead on the Mexican cartels. Care to come along?"

"I probably should stay here, Mac. The techs always do better when they have a fellow officer, even a fellow *former* officer like me, peeking over their shoulders." He bent down to wipe something off his shoe. "I don't blame you trying to put these cartels out of business, but, just so you know, you'll probably need to get the permission from the head dudes to carry out a mission like that."

I pursed my lips together. "And just so you are aware, Nav, whether I get permission from these guys or not, I'm still going to take care of that particular cartel ... personally." Just then, my phone rang.

"Ken? It's Bill Gilardi speaking." He paused, then said, "The entire team is looking forward to meeting you. Can you be at my office today by twelve thirty? We'll give you lunch."

I cast a glance at my watch, then asked if I could bring someone with me ... "a fellow who was in the Teams with me early on."

"No problem, Ken, as long as you and your sidekick bow down to kiss my butt," he answered with a laugh, then hung up.

I WAS STILL SITTING at the kitchen table with Navarro when Delgado arrived. "Vinnie, let me introduce Alex Navarro. He's a retired SFPD homicide inspector who was a good friend of my father." I paused. "I know he's an older dude, but since he was my dad's friend, I have to be nice to him. And, since he's already at retirement age and no one else would hire him, I felt sorry for him and agreed to take him under our wing."

Delgado chuckled and put out his hand to Navarro. "Nice to meet you, sir."

I threw Delgado a smile and asked him if I should give Nav the long version or the short one?"

"Short, for sure," Delgado said without hesitation.

I smiled. "Vinnie was a SEAL with me and three other of our Red Squadron guys you'll meet within a few days. He was the toughest SOB I ever met. Don't let his long hair, pockmarked face, and five-foot-two frame fool you."

"Five-six," Delgado corrected, sitting up a little straighter. "Tom Cruise size."

"Give or take a few inches," I chuckled. "Anyway ... he still owns the record for the most bare-handed kills in the entire SEAL community. Tell you what ... I never met anyone who wanted to mess with him." I paused, then said, "So, why is he a former SEAL, you ask? Well, that belongs to what version of the story he wants me to tell. He gets embarrassed easily."

"Hey, if it's embarrassing, I don't need to know," Navarro offered. "I've got enough embarrassing things in my closet to choke a horse. My motto is 'you stay out of my closet, and I'll stay out of yours.'"

"I knew I was gonna like this guy, bro," Delgado said to me while shaking Navarro's hand.

"But before we get all slobbery as a hog in slop," I said, "let me change the subject for a minute. Do either of you know a Mexican dude who drives an older model blue Mercedes?"

I glanced over at Nav, who shrugged. Turning back to Vinnie, I said, "Guess the answer is *no*."

"Well, while I was driving up the street here looking for a place to park, there was a Mercedes in front of me. It slowed down and drove past the front of your house at a snail's pace, peering up here the whole time. Then the driver drove down the street, did a U-turn at the bottom of the block, pulled over and parked. I swear to you, Mac ... it looked to me like he was casing your place."

"Don't have a clue as to why anyone would be interested in me or this house," I said. "Fact is, I just got in yesterday evening. Haven't had time to get people that angry at me ... at least yet." I put my arm around Vinnie, and said, "Tell you what, my man! Nav's gonna let me use his car to meet my father's DEA guys. If your antenna is up, why don't you follow a block or two behind me in your car."

"Sounds good to me, Mac. Let's roll."

# CHAPTER 13



Delgado pulled into the underground garage of the Federal Courts Building five minutes behind me.

"You gotta tail," he said, as we stepped into the elevator. "It's that same dude I saw early on in the blue Mercedes. I had this premonition he was casing our house, but if that were true, why would he be following you? And when you drove in here to park, he just kept right on going, never making an effort to follow you. The only thing I can think is he's probably casing your house so his pals can burgle it when nobody's home. Good thing you've got some of your people staying there."

"Yeah, I guess that's a good thing," I said. "But I'd love to be there when, and if, that idiot and his friends walk in on us. We'd be visiting him in the hospital for the next month or so." I smiled, paused, then asked, "Did you happen to get an eyeball on him?"

"Not as good as it'll get if he's still there when we get back," Vinnie said.

"Probably better if we coordinate that with Nav," I said. "He's got the law enforcement creds, not us. You get in a scrape with jerks like this and, all of a sudden, you find yourselves up to your eyeballs in lawyers."

Before Delgado could reply, the elevator door opened on the twentieth floor. Special Agent Gilardi stood waiting to greet us. He was immaculately tailored in a dark blue pinstriped suit, a crisp white shirt, and sporting a navy and red club tie. If nothing else, I thought, the guy knew how to dress.

He grasped my hand with a grip slightly too firm for the occasion. "It's such a treat to meet you," he said, a disarming smile dancing on his lips. "Your father bragged about you constantly. Let me tell you, it got really tiring." His grin and slight chuckle were quickly followed by a practiced look of sorrow. "I'm really sorry about your father. He was an exceptional man and a good friend."

Acknowledging his sentiment, I nodded and said, "Thanks again for seeing us on such short notice. My father always spoke highly of you and your team." I was stretching the truth a bit since my dad, at least in my presence, never once mentioned Gilardi, nor any member of his team. "Let me introduce Vincent Delgado to you. Back in the day, we served in the military together."

Gilardi shook Delgado's hand then promptly forgot him as he grasped my elbow and guided me down a long corridor lined with offices.

The corridor abruptly ended at a steel security door, complete with Iris Recognition Software. Gilardi gazed into the screen, allowing the software to do its job. The steel door clicked open, and he escorted Vinnie and me into a small conference room featuring a round table surrounded by six executive-style office chairs ... three of them already occupied.

"Gentlemen," Gilardi said, facing his people. "It's my pleasure to introduce Walt McArthur's son, Kenneth, though he answers better to just plain Mac. And this is his friend, Vincent Delgado." Vinnie and I nodded our heads.

"Now allow me to introduce your father's team," Gilardi said. "This is Agent Michael Gray."

Gray leaned forward and shook both of our hands. "We admired your father very much. We're sorry he's not with us."

"Thanks. Your words are appreciated," I replied. For some reason I took an immediate dislike to Gray by just the way he murmured "we admired" and "we're sorry" instead of "I admired" and "I'm sorry."

"Agent Pete Torres," Gilardi said, introducing the next man in line. Torres stood and leaned over the table. He shook my hand while at the same time giving Delgado a nod of his head. "Forgive me for not wearing khaki's," he drawled, glancing at his jeans while pulling down on the black Nike jacket he wore. "This was supposed to be my day off. I was fiddling around in my garage when Bill called."

Gilardi waited for Torres to sit, then said, "And last but not least, Agent Brian Jackson." Jackson was a thin Black man of medium height, a painfully short buzz-cut and dull dark eyes. *Ex-military*, I thought. *Probably JAG.* He stood, and we shook hands. That he didn't acknowledge Delgado's presence told me everything I needed to know about the guy. I smiled at the thought of what Vinnie would do to him if they ever got into a brawl.

Gilardi politely requested everyone to sit. "Before we start to reminisce about Walt," he said, "I want to acknowledge the contributions Walt made to *Operation Snowplow*. The factual truth is he gave his life, both literally and figuratively, to the operation. Without him, our being here and about to go operational would not have been possible. Let's all welcome Walt's son, and his friend, Vincent Delgado, here with us today. But more than anything, let's honor Walt's memory today with a moment of silence."

The men in the room stood and placed their hands over their hearts ... all except Mike Gray. He stood, but kept his hands at his side. His non-gesture didn't escape either Vinnie or me.

# CHAPTER 14



"Okay, now ... as to why we're all here," Gilardi began. "Ken is with us today to meet the team his father worked with so long and so well. We are also here to find out the latest on who placed the bomb aboard the plane that was taking Walt to El Paso." Looking at me, Gilardi asked, "A fair assessment?"

"It is." I paused, then said, "But could you do me a favor and call me Mac?" I smiled. "That's how I'm known in the real world. Most people who know me, know me as Mac."

"Fair enough ... Mac." Gilardi paused, then said, "Let me then start from the beginning, though any of you ...," he pointed his index finger at the three agents sitting at the far end of the table, "... who want to ... or who need to ... add something, please feel free to do so."

He drew in a long, deep breath, then, looking over at me,

said, "To bring you up to speed, Mac, *Snowplow* was a plan devised by your father to win this country's so-called War on Drugs once and for all. Most everyone who read the plan considered it brilliant. Unfortunately, the President remained, and still remains, resolutely opposed to some of its provisions ... the biggest being sending Special Op troops into Mexico to shut down, once and for all, the cartels who flood this country with narcotics. And nary a peep about those responsible for your father's death."

"And, if I may be so bold," interjected Agent Jackson, "once we learned about your father's death, we were sure the President would change his mind ... allowing us to bring the cartels to justice. But he didn't. A real shame. Your father was our leader and mentor ... and we for certain don't want his death to be in vain."

"Can I interject here and change the subject for a quick minute?" I asked. When Gilardi nodded, I continued. "There's something that's been on my mind from the very beginning of this tragedy. How did you know there was a bomb on board that plane before it exploded?"

There was silence in the room before Gilardi wiped his mouth with the back of his hand and said, "I'll take this one." He gazed at me and said, "We cultivated a person high up in the Tormenta cartel ... a fellow named Munoz. He found out the cartel was planning to place a bomb on board the plane upon which your father was a passenger and tried to alert us. In fact, he sent us a message about the plot four days ago. For some reason, and believe me we're still investigating what that *reason* was, his message didn't reach us until early Monday morning, just five or so minutes *after* his plane took off. The people in this room will tell you how I tried to get that plane back on the ground. It took me over eight minutes to contact the person in the FAA who could authorize the plane to turn back. The FAA guy was actually successful in contacting the pilot, and the plane was in the process of turning back when the bomb exploded. If I'd received Munoz's message ten minutes earlier, or if it hadn't taken me so long to connect with the FAA, we wouldn't be having this conversation.

"And to add to the tragedy, Munoz's role was somehow detected by the cartels. He, his wife, and two children suffered horrible deaths at the hands of Victor Serna, the worst of the cartel leaders."

"Can I ask a question?" Delgado said.

"Shoot," replied Gilardi.

"I've been listening to you talk about how you tried to get Walt's plane back on the ground after takeoff; how you knew there was a bomb on board; blah, blah, blah. For me, the most important question is the one that was never asked and therefore never answered: how in the world did the cartels know Walt McArthur was on board any airplane that day, let alone a United flight headed to El Paso for the explicit purpose of putting the cartels out of business? There had to be only a few people in the entire universe with that information. Most of them, I might add, are in this room." Delgado looked around the room, shrugged, then added, "Just sayin'."

A stunned silence gripped the room.

"I hope you're not accusing me, or any of my men, of leaking information to the cartels," Gilardi hissed, putting both hands on the table and half rising out of his seat.

"As my momma used to say," Delgado said, not breaking eye contact with Gilardi, "if the shoe fits ..."

"Hey, who do you think you are to come in here and screw with us like that?" Michael Gray exploded. Unlike Gilardi, he came all the way out of his chair—a direct, man-to-man challenge to Delgado.

Vinnie merely lifted his hooded eyes, cast a glance directly at Gray, shook his head slowly back and forth, and smirked.

Torres reached out and yanked Gray back into his seat. "Gentlemen, let's not squabble among ourselves, okay? Remember ... the four of us asked ourselves the same question. So, let's not get our panties in a twist when someone else also asks it. It's a legit question."

"We've struggled privately with the same question," Gilardi interjected, helping to solidify Torres's role as peacemaker. "We went through our entire department as to who had access to Walt's files. *What assistant may have inadvertently blurted out something during a coffee break? A 'loose lips sink ships' kind of thing. We did a thorough internal investigation. The only answer we came up with was the girl.*"

"The girl?" I asked quizzically. "That's a new one. And who might she be?"

"You want to take this one, Pete?" Gilardi asked. Torres pushed his chair back, and stood. "Hold on. I'll get her file."

When he returned, he placed a thin folder on the table. Opening it, he slid out a photograph and held it chest high. "This is a woman named Shira Lipkin." He put the photograph on the table and slid it over to me and Vinnie. "She's a thirty-something female Mossad agent your father met and then got permission from the Israelis to have her to work with him on various missions."

Vinnie and I found ourselves staring at an eight-by-ten publicity still of a very pretty woman with dark hair, striking blue eyes and an intoxicatingly innocent, girl-next-door smile that, on the one hand invited you to protect her from the big bad world, while at the same time begging you to participate with her in delights yet unfathomed.

"He recruited her from the Mossad?" I asked. "What timeframe are we talking about here?"

"Your father and the Mossad worked closely together over the past number of years, mostly as it related to illegal drugs flowing through the Mideast to America," Gilardi said. "Shira Lipkin was the agent the Mossad assigned to work with your father on various issues of mutual concern, and, because they had worked together before, the higher-ups agreed to have her work with us on a new and more dangerous version of fentanyl that's beginning to kill our young people in droves. She's been on our payroll for the past three years. We have the paperwork in the files if you'd like to read it."

I shook my head in the negative. Pushing the photograph back to Torres, I asked, "Since when have you folks been in cahoots with the Mossad? And what cartels are we talking about here?"

"There are two Mexican cartels in particular we want to crush," Gilardi said. "The Tormentas and the Nuevo Pueblos. They run a myriad of operations in this country, including more than fifty strip clubs nationwide. I mention this because that's how Walt wanted to approach the operation. He estimated the bottom line of each Tormenta-run club to be a staggering two million dollars per club—per year. Take the four clubs the cartels run in San Diego times two million each, and the bad guys are looking at a yearly gross income of close to eight million—just in the San Diego area alone."

"And this is what my father was going after?"

"For starters," Gilardi said. "Your father was a man of vision. Maybe you didn't know, but he went to Israel a little over three years ago to meet with various Mossad counterparts. They came up with a dual-purpose plan on how the two entities could work together. The Mossad's role was to free up Agent Lipkin to assist your father in thwarting the Mexican cartels' appetite to do joint ventures with the Egyptian Muslim Brotherhood. If those two entities ever came together, you'd see the largest worldwide distribution of fentanyl in history."

The room went silent. Torres looked over at me. "Before we break up today, Mac, I want you to know that as a group, the people in this room had some major reservations about this Lipkin woman. In our job, trusting anyone who's not one of us, no matter what he or she supposedly brought to the table, would be a major issue." He went quiet for a moment as he took a sip from his water glass. "Everyone in this room gave kudos to your father. The only thing any of us cared about was how Walt was using her. But you know how that goes ... even though we had no say in the operation, it was the center of conversation among ourselves. Brought on mostly by jealously," he said with a quiet chuckle. "And why not? I mean, look at this woman. Who wouldn't be jealous?" He smiled. "But seriously, when push came to shove, the only thing we cared about was how she was going to fit in."

I picked up her picture. "And did she?"

"Perfectly."

"Good to know. Can I keep this?"

Torres cast a glance at Gilardi, then nodded. "Boss says it's okay ... so I guess it's okay,"

As I HEADED BACK to the house, I dialed up Navarro. "How's it going with the techs?" I asked.

"Lots of prints to collect," he told me.

"Well, just wait until you hear about the Mossad agent Dad worked with."

# CHAPTER 15



The robbery techs had left by the time Vinnie and I got back to the house. The blue Mercedes, however, was still there.

"Whoever that guy out there is, he's got a single-digit IQ," Delgado said as we walked in the front door. "Thinking he can park in front of your house and not be made! Here's a guy I'm guessing doesn't have enough sense to spit downwind." He slowly shook his head, then asked me if he could go talk to the guy.

"We're gonna have to get Nav's okay first, Vin. He's in the kitchen."

We found Navarro with a rag in hand wiping down the kitchen sink. "My boys don't do a very good job of cleaning up, I'm afraid."

"No problem, Nav. Did they find anything?"

"Nothing of any real value, Mac. Tons of prints, of course. Just what you'd expect in a lived-in house. Most of them smudged because the same surfaces were touched over and over by the same hands. Even in the office where we know a computer and some files went missing, the only clear prints were Walt's and Lipkin's, the Mossad agent. In fact, her fingerprints were all over Walt's office. We got them to the lab quickly so we could identify them. And what did we find? That the Lipkin woman has been an agent in the Israeli Mossad for many years. Not that it really means anything, but it's certainly coincidental. Have either of you two ever met her?"

"No. We had never heard of her until today when she was simply a conversation piece at our meeting with the DEA. Like you probably already know, Ms. Lipkin is, or at least was, a field agent in the Mossad, and, it turns out, was not only a friend of my father's ... she actually worked with him on some of the high-profile cases the DEA and Mossad had, and maybe still have, in common."

"Hate to interrupt, people," Vinny interjected, "but can we switch to a different topic?"

"Absolutely. Ask away, Vin."

"Has anybody here figured out how perps got in Mac's house?"

"Good question," Nav said. "The tech guys spoke to the next-door neighbor—an old dude named Popovich. A guy in his mid-seventies. Said he saw two men drive up in a van that had the name of some house cleaning service on it. According to Popovich, two guys went up the front steps and into the house through the front door. Unfortunately," Nav said, "no useful prints were found anywhere in the house. These guys apparently had keys and knew what they were doing."

"Shouldn't we have at least seen the doorknob broken off?" I asked.

"You'd think so, Mac. The techs told us they were at least expecting the doorframe to be cracked. But the doorframe was, and still is, intact. So, they examined the lock for scratches that could point to a forced entry. Nothing! They then looked for evidence that the perps used tools to pick the lock. Still no scratches."

"So, the bottom line is ...?"

"The bottom line, Mac, is the tech guys think whoever got into your house ... had a key."

I threw a glance at Delgado. I could tell he was thinking the same thing I was: *Shira Lipkin*!

# CHAPTER 16



Delgado and I filled Navarro in on our meeting with Gilardi, but spent most of our time on the key Lipkin supposedly had to the house. "That's why Vinnie and I are heading down to San Diego tonight to have a chat with the Lipkin woman." I emphasized the word *chat*. "And then get the key to my house. Once we're through there, we'll spend the night at Naval Special Warfare Command, then meet Admiral Moore at 0900 Thursday."

"How're you going to tell if she's dirty?" Navarro asked.

"If she still has the key to this house, then she probably wasn't the one giving these guys free access. If I can establish that, then I'm willing to give her a pass. Sound right to you, Vinnie?"

"Yeah, but let's play it slow at first so we can find out for sure one way or the other." He walked over to the window. "In the meantime, we still have that dude and his blue Mercedes out there." Turning to me, he said, "I'm thinkin' it's about time we met the driver."

"What about you, Nav? That car's been on my tail nearly all day. The dude followed me all the way downtown. And then has the *cojones* to park right down the street again." I walked to the window. "Vinnie's been itching to get his hands on that guy, but I'm thinking the better part of valor is to wait for a real cop to make the collar." I paused, then said, "A real cop like you, Nav."

He smiled. "In the old days, that would have been me," Navarro said. "But not anymore. Let me see if there's a squad car in the neighborhood. Better to have the police here just in case our perp decides to make a gun battle out of it." He called dispatch, then turned to me and said, "They'll be here in five minutes. By the way ... are you carrying, Vinnie?"

"Never leave home without it," he replied with a smile, pulling his jacket aside, showing the holstered FN 509 on his waistband.

"Good, then I'll leave my rig home."

Vinnie, Navarro, and I walked down the front steps just as the SFPD cruiser pulled up behind the Mercedes. By the time the three of us got there, the two police officers had the driver spread-eagled on the trunk of his car.

Navarro walked over and thanked them. "This guy have a name?"

"Jorge Gallegos," the senior officer replied. "Gangbanger from San Jose."

"Why am I not surprised?" Nav answered with a smirk. He

turned toward the senior officer and asked, "Would you officers mind if my two friends here and I question this low-life punk for a few minutes? My two friends here are both retired Navy SEALs, so they know the drill. And we'd like to know why a tool like this jerk staked out Mac's house and then followed him downtown. We'd also like to know who, pray tell, hired him."

Both police officers conversed for a minute, then one of them said to Navarro, "He's all yours, Inspector. We'll be in our car. Be kind to the slimeball, okay? We don't want to be facing a civil suit because we, or you, were too rough on this poor SOB." Navarro smiled and walked back to where Vinnie and I stood. "They gave us their blessing."

"Geez, Nav," I said, "you got some serious juice here. I'm impressed."

"Hey, I've been a cop longer than both those guys have been alive, and they already know I'm a short timer. They're being nice because they know the sooner I'm off the active list, the better chance they'll have of being promoted."

We nodded and walked over to car's trunk where the perp was still spread-eagled. Navarro gave us a smile, leaned in close to the perp, and asked, "Name?"

"Get out of my face. You got no right to do this to me. I know my rights. I ain't broken no laws."

Navarro stood, looked back at Vinnie and me, then slowly bent back down and asked again, "Name?"

"You heard me the first time," the guy snapped back.

"Wrong answer, Jorge," Navarro replied.

"Mind if I take over for a few minutes?" Delgado asked, just loud enough for Gallegos to hear.

"Be my guest." Navarro said. Leaning in close to Gallegos, he whispered, "You just put yourself in a world of hurt."

Delgado walked up behind Gallegos, grabbed a handful of the perp's hair and yanked back violently. Gallegos' scream was loud enough that a few of the neighbors slammed their windows shut. Bending close to him, Vinnie kicked Gallegos's legs out from under him, causing him to drop to his knees and bang his chin on the trunk of the Mercedes, opening a two-inch gash that turned the trunk of the Mercedes from blue to red.

"Now listen carefully, you pile of manure," Delgado hissed again. "If I don't start getting the right answers, then you and I are going to have a serious *come to Jesus* talk. You understand what I'm tellin' you?"

Gallegos gave a short nod of his head.

"That's better," Vinnie said. "Let's try this again and see if we can finally get the right answer." He paused, then asked, "You got a name?"

"Gallegos. Jorge Gallegos," he spit through gritted teeth.

"See! Now that wasn't so hard, was it?"

Vinnie stood upright and walked back to me and Nav. "Got him talking, at least. Your turn, Mac. Don't want you to be missin' all the fun."

"Nah. Let's just get this over with."

"First, let me get him going," Navarro said. "I've seen a hundred guys like this ... most of them thinking of themselves as *somebody*. When confronted with the number of years they're gonna spend in prison, most end up blubbering like a baby. Let's see what this guy is made of, shall we?"

Pointing to the fingers on Gallegos's left hand which now

was splayed out on the car's trunk, Nav asked, "See those tattoos?"

Vinnie and I watched closely, as if whatever Navarro was about to reveal would secure Gallegos's place behind bars for the next forty years. "His index finger has the number 4 tattooed on it. See there?" Vinnie and I scrutinized the finger closely, trying to show Gallegos how interested we were in putting his butt in jail. "The middle finger has a 0, and the ring finger has an 8." Nav looked at us as if we were unmasking one of the seven secrets of the ancient world. "4-0-8, man! 4-0-8! That happens to be the area code for San Jose."

Vinnie and I pretended we cared, so again looked closely at the tattoo as if another wonder of the world had just been unveiled. "While we're here, take a peek at the tats on the fingers of his right hand," Nav said. "This boy is a *West Side Mongrel*, a supposed badass motorcycle gang." He leaned in closer to Gallegos. "Care to tell me why you were following my friends around?"

Gallegos remained silent.

"Maybe we should have another peek inside your vehicle. See what my officer friends here can charge you with."

"You have no right inside my car," he mumbled. "Illegal search. Go ahead, find something. My attorney will have me out within an hour."

"Don't count on it," Navarro whispered menacingly, putting on the pair of plastic gloves given him by one of the police officers. After a few minutes of rummaging through the car, Navarro backed out with a big smile on his face. "Well, gentlemen, look what I found! Mr. Gallegos here has a baggie full of what, upon closer inspection, will no doubt be cocaine.

A whole baggie, for goodness' sake. Think I'll just lay it down in the back seat and let the officers find it." He walked closer to Gallegos, bent down, and whispered, "It's going to be large enough to get you on at least one felony count. Minimum!"

"Planted," he mouthed through clenched teeth. "I'll just tell 'em you planted them drugs."

"You going to claim I planted this, too?" Navarro asked, holding up a gun. "A Glock 19. Nice piece. Gangbanger's favorite weapon." He walked to where Gallegos's hand was splayed on the car's trunk. Placing the weapon next to him, Navarro raised the prisoner's hand and quickly pressed all of his fingers on the gun. Gallegos struggled, but Nav held his fingers just long enough to transfer prints. "See what I mean? Your prints are all over it. And, bad news for you ... the Glock's fully loaded. Now we do have a felony. Probably more than one. Especially if you have a record, which I have no doubt you do." Gallegos remained silent.

Navarro walked over to the two officers. "He's all yours, gentlemen. From where I'm standing, I see one weapons charge and at least one drug charge in his future. Here's hoping they both stick."

As they stuffed Gallegos in the back of their black and white, Navarro leaned in and whispered, "Give my best to your attorney, dimwit."

As the officers drove Gallegos away, Vinnie turned to me and said, "Ya know ... the Lord must really love stupid people. I mean, just look at how many he's made."

# CHAPTER 17



Brian Jackson, Michael Gray, and Pete Torres were already waiting for Gilardi as he entered Foley's restaurant in downtown San Francisco at precisely 5 p.m. Being a known and respected public servant, the private dining room Gilardi requested was already waiting for them.

While dinner was being served, the conversation between the group was both varied and non-focused. But once the dinner was over and the waitstaff had removed the dishes and closed the door to their private room, the four were left alone to conduct business. And privacy this night was of critical importance.

"Let's start by standing and raising our glass to a fallen comrade," Gilardi said, pushing his chair back and standing. "While Walt wasn't officially one of us, he championed our cause and got it noticed." Everyone but Agent Mike Gray stood, raised their wineglasses, and took a sip.

"Now, let's get this show on the road, shall we?" Gilardi said. "As you know, we're here to discuss *Operation Snowplow*. Do we get it back on track or do we deep-six the entire operation?" He took a deep breath, then continued. "As you know, the President is now waffling on his commitment to send Special Op troops into Mexico to once and for all eliminate the cartels. Those jerks are destroying our country right in front of our very eyes, for goodness' sake ... and he's willing to do exactly zip about it."

"The President is a flat-out coward," Mike Gray sputtered, clenching and unclenching his fists.

"You can keep talking like that 'til you're blue in the face, Mike," Gilardi fired back, his annoyance made clear from the tone of his voice. "That's not going to get you or us anywhere. We've got to determine right now—tonight—*how*, and even *if*, we are going to propel *Snowplow* forward."

"Yeah? And how exactly are we supposed to do that, when our pissant of a President won't lift a finger," Gray continued angrily. "Even when it's one of his own trusted agents who gets himself blasted out of the sky."

Pounding on the table, Pete Torres stood and stared the room into silence. "Come on, people, let's grow up and lay off the President for a while, shall we? Let's cut him some slack! He doesn't have to deal with this drug stuff day-after-day like we do. But even as I say that, I happen to stand with Mike on this one. As each one of us knows, Walt McArthur wasn't really a friend of ours, but with so much about what happened to his flight being still unknown, I'll be darned if I'm gonna let him die in vain."

"Okay, since we all know what's at stake here, let's regroup." Gilardi said. "We still agree, do we not, that *Snowplow* is the best chance this country has of winning the drug war." Every head nodded in the affirmative. "So, we've got to get *Snowplow* off dead center and become operational. The question for us is *how and when.*"

"Let's start with the President," Torres replied. "*Snowplow* still depends on him saying yes. Am I right about that?"

"That you are, Pete," Gray replied. "We were so sure that McArthur's death was going to shove DC's paper-shuffling *sons-of-you know what* into action. But no, it's starting to look like McArthur might indeed have died in vain. Even though I never liked the righteous jerk, that he died by being blown out of the sky is still a tragedy."

"Hey ... we all know there's not going to be any weeping or gnashing of teeth in this room for McArthur," Gilardi interrupted. "So, let's deep-six any feelings we had for the guy, either good or bad, and move on to more important issues, okay?"

But Gray didn't let go. "It's really hard to move forward when it looks like we bought into a load of rubbish," he said, pushing the mop of black hair off his forehead. Facing Gilardi, he drew a long breath and asked, "Did anyone ever tell you what the President's objections actually were?"

"As a matter of fact ... yes, they did. The President told me straight out that everyone in the room favored the deployment of Spec Op troops into Mexico, except the Secretary of State."

"How come that doesn't surprise me?" Jackson snorted. "What a jerk! And her objection *this* time was ...?"

"Same as always," Gilardi responded. "She's concerned about the legality of the operation. Plus, something ..." he shook his head in exasperation ... "something about sending US troops into a foreign country uninvited."

"Where does she come up with that *invited* or *uninvited* crap?" Gray complained. "Hasn't anyone explained to her that Pakistan didn't exactly roll out the red carpet when we went in after bin Laden? Or, for that matter, when we went into Iraq?" Gray pursed his lips, then said, "As I remember it, the Iraqi people weren't overly thrilled about us being there. Same with the Taliban, who, as we all know, kicked our raggedy butts out of their country. And let's not forget that while they were at it, they commandeered every military weapon we left behind, including over two hundred fighter jets. Come on, let's stop kidding ourselves. That witch and the President are only concerned about the political fallout. You know like ... *gosh, what if we get caught in Mexico with our pants down around our ankles? Oh my,* he snorted. *What would we do?*"

"He's right, Bill," Jackson said. "I say it's time to raise the ante. It's our only chance. I, for one, am in favor of initiating phase two of *Operation Snowplow* this very minute. For me, *Snowplow* has always been our best bet. At the very least, it'll help keep drugs away from our young people." He hesitated, staring down everybody in the room. "So, we send troops into Mexico. What's that going to do to eliminate drugs in *this country*? Zip, if you ask me. And besides, it's the only thing we have left. If *Snowplow* doesn't work, I'd be in favor of shutting the whole freaking operation down."

"Hey ... that's not up to you, Brian," Gilardi shot back, angrily slamming his fist on the table. "You're just one voice here."

The room went silent, the challenge clearly laying on the table. The two measured each other for a few seconds before Jackson raised his hands in surrender. "Sorry, Bill. I was out of line. It's just I'm so darned frustrated with all this, I could barf."

There was a brief silence in the room before Gilardi relaxed his lips from their tight grimace. "Apology accepted," he said, taking a sip of water. "And let's never forget that we're a team here, and we must always maintain our sense of comradery and integrity." He took another sip of water and returned the glass to the table. Looking around the room, he said, "Just so you know, for the record, I'm more than a *little* concerned about McArthur's kid coming back for his father's funeral. I can see him as a potential loose cannon, capable of screwing up our plans big time. There's just too much at risk here."

"Granted," Gray sighed. "I didn't even know Walt had a son. He never spoke a word about the kid—at least in my presence. I'm now in favor of us pushing back on his kid if he becomes a major league pest. And from where I'm sitting, he's already got himself right on the edge." A short silence ensued before all the heads in the room nodded their agreement.

Gilardi smiled. "Okay, done! Now let's get back to more important issues, like phase two of *Operation Snowplow*." Gilardi took a breath, then said, "As things stand now, we have to be extraordinarily careful in how we roll it out. Without McArthur, I'm not sure we have the capabilities to make it work."

"McArthur's gone," Gray said. "And I, for one, am glad he's finally out of our hair. We all heard his story about that collateral damage crap. He actually started talking openly about closing down *Snowplow* altogether. Something we certainly didn't need."

"I'm with Gray a hundred percent," Jackson remarked. "What a two-faced jerk McArthur turned out to be. It was his baby from the get-go, and what … he starts having pangs of conscience? Give me a break! Casualties? Well, absolutely there are going to be casualties. After all, we're in a war, for goodness' sake. Walt just happened to be one of them. Couldn't be helped."

"I hear you both," replied Gilardi. "But my other concern is whether or not we have the capabilities to carry out the plan to its conclusion." He went silent, then, impatiently tapping his fingers on the table, asked, "Well, do we?"

All heads nodded in unison. Gilardi beamed, raising his fist in the air. "Okay, then! Let's get *Snowplow* into action." A cheer bounced off the walls, causing one of the waiters to peek into the room. "Do we still have the product ready to go, Pete?" Gilardi asked, once the waiter had closed the door. "What's our timeframe now for becoming operational?"

"We can get into the local distribution channels almost immediately," Torres replied. "Tomorrow's Thursday. If we start tomorrow, we can seed incrementally by region, and then by state. First reports of illness could possibly be Friday, but, for sure, no later than Saturday. Then it will quickly grow region by region, state by state."

"Then let's get at it, gentlemen," Gilardi said excitedly,

pounding on the table. "I guess I won't be expecting any of you at the office tomorrow."

There were a few chuckles before Gray said, "One last thing, Bill. What about Serna?"

"What do you mean, *what about Serna*?"

"How are we going to deal with him?"

"Don't worry about Serna, Mike. He's just another distraction in this stage play. It's why the United States of America has a military arm. Once the President gets the *cojones* we're going to provide him, Serna will be dead within a week."

"Amen to that," beamed Jackson. "Tell you what, Bill. If you can arrange it, I wouldn't mind being in on the Serna kill personally. He's such a complete jerk." All at the table nodded.

They sat in silence for a few moments before Gilardi stood and raised his glass, "Let's at least raise our glass one more time for Walt. No matter what you thought of him, he got us to where we are today. We owe him at least a sip."

AT FIVE MINUTES past eight that evening, Rinaldo Ruiz received a call from Lupe.

"I have failed you, Patrón. My gunman didn't kill the younger McArthur. In fact, he got himself arrested in the attempt."

"Is your gunman in jail?"

Si, Patrón. Santa Rita."

"Kite him, Lupe," he ordered, referring to a method gangs had of carrying out targeted killings inside prison walls. "We have to send the message that there are consequences when someone fails the Tormentas."

"Si, Patrón. And I'm sorry."

"Not to worry, Lupe. These things happen ... but only once." There was silence, then "Comprende?"

"Si, Patrón."

"Bueno." He waited a beat, then, with a note of relief, said, "Just so you know, we're also planning a nighttime finale for the younger McArthur."

# CHAPTER 18



Vinnie and I landed in San Diego at 9:35 p.m., picked up a rental car at the airport, and drove up Highway 101 to the Magic Kitty.

"I'm gonna love runnin' with you, Mac," Delgado blurted out, staring at the garish purple neon sign dominating the entrance to the Magic Kitty Adult Theater.

"Don't get too comfortable, my friend." I warned, nodding my head towards two Hispanic-dudes watching us from the doorway of the *"Open 'til 3" Taco Plus* restaurant located on the floor directly below the Magic Kitty. "What do you make of them two hombres?"

"Well, for one, they work the right hours," Delgado chuckled. "Let's see ... nude theater closes at two, taqueria closes at three. Think they're serving eggs rancheros to the club's patrons before they go home to *mama*?"

"I'm thinkin' you got 'em spot-on, Vin," I said with a chuckle.

"Seriously, Mac, do those two guys look like chefs to you?" Delgado powered down the window and waved. "Hey, how you guys doin' tonight?" he yelled. "Business been good to ya?" They stared back at him through dead eyes.

"Cute, Vin ... but let's cool it, okay? We're not here looking for trouble."

"Sorry, Mac. I'll be on my best behavior ... promise. It's just those kinda guys ..." He shrugged, letting the thought die. "I'll tell you what, though. Them dudes ain't chefs."

"Shrewd deduction," I answered with a smile as I parked the car in the club's lot. "Maybe their sole function is to keep riffraff like you and me away from this fancy club." We started the climb up the wooden staircase leading to the second floor. "Speaking of riffraff, Vinnie ... were you ever a customer of this place? I mean back in the day?"

"Nah. Made it a practice never to frequent strip joints located on the second floor of old, broken-down strip malls. Especially those advertising 'live' nude girls. You know ... like maybe some people would come wanting to see the alternative?" He chuckled at his joke. "And tell me, Mac. You're a smart guy. What kind of genius puts their sex club on the second floor, for goodness' sake?"

"Perhaps someone who wants plenty of lead time to clean up anything messy or inconvenient before the cops arrive. Could it be what our two *friends* downstairs are? Cleaners?"

"Yeah, could be," Delgado said before he went off in a different direction. "Can you imagine what kind of poor lounge lizards frequent a place like this? I'm guessing forty-five or older? What about you?"

"Forty-five still sounds a bit young to me, Vin. I'm thinking fifty-five or older."

"And fat," Delgado responded with a chuckle. "Having to climb all those steps to stare at naked girls gotta be a killer if you're overweight. Maybe those two gents downstairs are doctors or ambulance-chasing lawyers. But way smarter cuz they're right at the source." He shook his head through a quiet laugh. "And I'll bet the chicks in this place are a real piece of work, too. Nothing against the lady we're looking for, but I wouldn't let any of them get too close to me. Would you? I mean, what if one of you had an open sore or something. Know what I mean? Never know what you might pick up."

"Geez, who wound you up all of a sudden?" I asked with a smile. "But to tell you the truth, I don't plan on getting close to anyone."

I ponied up two twenty-dollar bills to pay both of our twelve-dollar entrance fees. When I insisted on the change, they acted like I was stealing their money. "Just so you know, Vinnie. I'm here to find the Lipkin lady, and then collect my dad's house key ... period! Then we're out of here."

"You're no fun at all, Mac."

IT TOOK a few seconds for our eyes to adjust to the club's dark interior. There were two stages, one at either end of the oblong room. On the far wall, curtains hid a small booth area where the private dancing took place.

"I count thirty-two customers. Twenty-eight single guys and two couples. You?"

Delgado slowly gazed around the room. "Same."

"Anyone here look like trouble to you?"

Delgado's eyes again trailed slowly over the room. "Nah. Even the two bouncers remind me of, forgive the pun, pussies."

We made our way to a table on the outer fringe of the room, the ones used by guys who want nothing more than to stare. Only trouble with doing that is we became a mark for the girls roving around looking for lap dance suckers. We'd been seated for all of about two minutes before a young, raven-haired girl wearing a paisley G-string, matching pasties, and sporting a large nose ring put her arm around me. "What're you drinking, sweetheart?"

"Not sure yet. What's the cover?"

"Two drinks per hour. Minimum darlin'" nose ring answered distractedly. "Since the girls dance nude, we can't serve alcohol. Only soft drinks, coffee, and water."

"How much for the coffee?" asked Delgado.

"Twelve dollars."

"And a Coke?"

"The same."

"Each?"

"Each!"

"And we have to order two?" Delgado asked, now having fun with her.

"Per hour." She stopped, then said, "Come on, guys, don't give me a hard time, okay? Y'all know the drill. I don't set the prices. I just work here. If you want to know, I don't like the high prices either. They cut into my tips, which are, for the most part, the only way I get paid. Means I have to work my tush off to make anything." She smiled as she wiggled her money-making derrière, then eyeballed the both of us seductively. "You guys want company?"

"What's your name, sweetheart?" Delgado asked as he put his arm around her waist and pulled her to him. She didn't resist.

"Tiffany," she answered with a big smile.

"Well, Tiffany, I think we'll order Cokes for now. You're cute and all, but my partner here is springing for this, and he's notoriously cheap."

She cracked a smile. "That's what all you big spenders say … at first! Hey, I'll be back in an hour, and you'll be begging me to sit with you. Or better yet, a private dance, just for you." She gave Delgado a bump with her hip then a big hug, squishing her fake boobs into his face.

"Geez, Vin. Never knew you were such a smooth-talking Mexicano."

"Lots you don't know about me," he laughed, pulling Tiffany closer.

"Nice to meet you, honey child. Got a quick question for you."

She snuggled into Vinnie's lap then looked over at me. "I'm looking for a female named Shira Lipkin," I said. "Do you know her?" I gave her a twenty.

"Shira? Yeah! She's new. Believe me, though, she's not all that sexy."

"I'm not looking for this Lipkin woman because she's sexy. I'm looking because I've got a note from a friend of hers concerning a guy named Walt McArthur."

"We hear that same spiel from a lot of guys like you. Sounds to me like you're trying to come up with an excuse for the girl to wiggle on you for a few minutes."

I shook my head in amusement as the MC introduced Dawn as the next dancer. Dawn stood no more than five-foot-two inches and was more than pleasantly plump. I felt sorry for her, but I'll be darned if that extra weight didn't dissuade any of the male losers from scattering dollar bills all over the stage.

While Dawn was doing her thing, I leaned over to Vinnie and said, "I want you to check out if there's a back door to this place, okay? Maybe find another way down to the taco place. I'll buy the Cokes. And, hey, I'll even save one for you."

"You mean I'm gonna miss squeezing Tiffany? Oh, well," he pouted. "It's either Dawn or Tiffany. Me? I'll take Tiffany. If she comes by, tell her I'll be back."

"I'm sure she'll be breathless."

# CHAPTER 19



I was about to take a sip from my second Coke when I felt a tap on my shoulder. Turning to my right, I came face-to-face with the bare midriff of a girl who obviously knew her way around the gym.

"You asked for me?" came a soft voice with just a hint of an accent that I couldn't quite place. She laid her hand on my shoulder. "Do I know you?"

I looked up, immediately getting lost in the deep blue of her eyes. "Don't think so."

"Then how did you know my name? I only give my name to very special people. And the last time I checked, you weren't on that list."

"My name is Ken McArthur. Mac to most people who know me. Walt McArthur was my father."

That heartbreak smile hadn't as yet picked up on my use of

the past tense. "Oh my gosh," she cried out in a girlish laugh. "Kenny! That's what your father always called you ... *Kenny*. What a surprise! I'm so happy to meet you. Your father told me so much about you, and in only what ... six weeks?" She laughed. "Where is he, by the way? He told me he'd be here three days ago. Hope it's not something I said." She smiled again, but then her demeanor turned serious as she began internalizing the meaning of the word *was*.

"Oh no ... *was?* You said Walt—was —your father?" She paused. "You're kidding me. Please tell me you're kidding."

I took a deep breath, held it for a few beats behind pursed lips, then said flatly, "My father died three days ago."

She looked at me as if trying to gauge my sincerity ... as if I might be playing with her. She took a step backward, then turned completely around like I was going to tell her this was all a joke. That maybe Walt was here with me and watching the whole charade play out from a seat across the room. "You're teasing me, right?" I didn't respond. She turned to her left as if to leave, then swung back towards me. "You're not!" This time she turned in a complete circle, her face going pale as her hands flew to her mouth. "Oh no," she cried. "What happened to Walt?" Her lashes grew heavy with tears that glistened in the fluorescent lights.

"I've got to talk to you," I said. "But not here."

"No!" she sobbed. "You can't be right. You're lying to me."

I leaned in closer. "Considering where we are and who could be listening, it's probably not a good idea to make a scene. You know what I'm telling you, right?"

She looked around, tears now noticeably lining her face. She nodded, and, in a quieter voice, asked, "What happened?"

"He was on his way to see you. Did you read, or hear about, the plane that went down in San Francisco last Monday morning?" She nodded dumbly. "He was a passenger on that airplane."

"Ohhh no!" Her hands again flew to her mouth, and she collapsed into a chair at the table next to me … quietly sobbing. I was beginning to think this Lipkin woman was legit. Hard to fake this kind of reaction in front of a complete stranger. "And to make matters worse, Walt was the one targeted."

Her distress was noticed by one of the bouncers at the bar. I saw the guy looking at me as he maneuvered his way through the tables, his right hand in his coat pocket. I quickly leaned over to her and whispered, "I have to talk to you about my father. Can you get off early?"

Her head nodded in slow motion, her body still quivering with emotions. "Give me twenty minutes," she said between sobs. "I'll meet you in the parking lot out front."

She stood and, drying her eyes, walked toward the bouncer who, by this time, was only two tables away. He placed his arm around her paternally and spoke softly into her ear. She shook her head, saying something to him in return. The bouncer cast a glance my way that said, "Lucky you, chump." I acknowledged him with a slight nod.

I saw Delgado taking in the scene from a table a few rows back. As soon as Lipkin and the bouncer were out of sight, he came over and sat down. "Hey, man! I can't leave you alone for ten minutes without you getting yourself in trouble. I was just waiting for the bouncer to come over and start hassling you. I could've taken him out in less than twenty seconds. I hate guys who try to bully you with their size. But inside? Inside, most of those guys are as soft as little girls."

"That was the Lipkin woman."

"Yeah. I figured. You obviously told her about your father."

"I did. She didn't take it well. She's either the finest actress who ever graced a strip club stage or was genuinely torn up to hear about him." Delgado nodded, sipping at his Coke. "I'm meeting her in the parking lot in twenty minutes. She's taking the rest of the night off. She has an Uber coming. I'm leaving the car for you." I passed him the keys. "Once we get there, I'm going to get the key she has to my father's house and call you to come get me. Shouldn't take long. No later than one o'clock, for sure. Then we can both get our butts over to Coronado."

"Works for me, Mac. And while you're gone, I'm thinkin' of spending some quality time with Tiffany. She's starting to look darn good to me 'bout now."

"Yeah, I can tell. But remember two things: one, she's young enough to be your daughter; and two, I'm going to be back here about the time the owners call the police and get your squabbily butt arrested for molesting minor children."

"Thanks for being so honest," he chuckled, taking another sip of his Coke. "A question for you. What happens if this Shira woman doesn't have the key to your house in San Francisco?"

"Then you get a room somewhere. She and I will be having a *come to Jesus* talk."

# CHAPTER 20



I glanced at my watch as I saw Shira Lipkin exit the far door of the Magic Kitty. 11:30. I'd have to hurry if I was going to meet up with Delgado at 12:30. The taqueria was still open for business, though no sign of customers. Why wasn't I surprised? The two Mexicans sat outside their front door watching as I met Lipkin at the bottom of the stairs. Even though I wasn't concerned, I internally registered a caution flag.

She smiled wanly at me as she drew near, the puffy eyes indicating her sorrow hadn't been faked. She wore a short black leather skirt and a cream-colored blouse under a knee-length black leather coat. The three-inch heels on her boots brought her close to eye level.

"Is your ride here yet?" I asked, looking down at my watch.

"Yes." She pointed to a beige-colored car at the far corner of the lot. "I've been working here at the request of your father for a little over six weeks now. In case you haven't noticed, this isn't what you or I would call the upscale part of town. Driving home alone every night after work would be asking for trouble. You wouldn't believe how many creeps find out where you live by tracking your license plate. I ended up renting a small bungalow about three miles from here. Your father was adamant that I carry a weapon. He didn't have to ask twice as I've carried a weapon almost every day of my life since I was nineteen years old. I ended up vetting every Uber driver in the area until I found one that allowed me to carry. I now take the same Uber to and from work every night. He's parked right over there."

I looked back as we walked toward the Uber. The two Mexican dudes were still staring at us.

"Don't worry about them," Lipkin said dismissively. "They're not going to harm me ... or you."

I nodded, but still remained hyperaware of my surroundings as I opened the car door for her.

"I want to apologize for losing my composure in the club," she said, sliding across the backseat. "I was selfish. Only thinking of myself. I'm so sorry about Walt. A tragedy if there ever was one. I loved him like I loved my own father." Once seated comfortably, she turned toward me, and, with a renegade tear running down her cheek, said, "I want to thank you for coming all this way to tell me about Walt. I ..." she hesitated while reaching into her jacket pocket for another tissue. "I've known your father for a good while. We worked together on a few drug cases over the past few years." She let out a deep sob.

"Are you okay?" the Uber driver uttered. He was an older fellow sporting a white turban over a matted black beard and mustache that I instantly recognized as Pakistani.

"I am. There's nothing to worry about. Thank you for asking, though."

"Same address?"

"Yes," she said, as we both settled into the back seat. She waited for the driver to pull into the street, then asked me, "Are you in San Diego often?"

"Now and again," I answered. "As of right now, I live and work near DC." I looked out the side window. "I spent most of my life in the military, so didn't get a chance to visit the West Coast as often as I'd wanted. In any case, I probably wouldn't have come to this place with my father."

"Why not?"

"Strip clubs aren't my favorite places to spend money."

"Then you're different from most of the men I've met ... even in Israel."

"Then you're meeting the wrong guys." I said, settling into the back seat while staring out into the darkness. "I don't know about *your* service in the military, but I've seen a considerable number of naked people in my life." I paused, looking out the side window. "Some because explosions had burned away their clothing along with half their bodies. Some because their captors stripped them naked before doing things to them you couldn't even imagine." I turned back to her. "I've seen naked bodies without arms. Some without legs. Some with their guts spilled all over the ground. Some without heads. Truth be told, unless I'm with the right person, naked bodies don't get me all wound up.

"And just so you know ... I didn't come here to see you with your clothes off ... or on, for that matter. Since I can't bury my father, I'm really here to get the key you have to my house in San Francisco. Once I have it, I'll be out of your life forever."

"That's it? No plans for a memorial service? No getting to know the families of the other people who died with your father?"

I turned toward her and said, "I'm afraid not. Believe me, I don't mean to sound harsh or diminish in any way what you felt for my father. It's just there are things I have to do in relation to his death, and, unfortunately, I don't have much time. Under ordinary circumstances, I would've done this differently. Unfortunately, these *aren't* ordinary circumstances." I looked out the car's front window. "How far are we from your house?"

"About fifteen minutes," she replied, taking a deep breath as she turned her face toward the window. "You're a lot different than your father, you know? He was a warm and caring person who softened as he got older. You? You've still got a long way to go."

I didn't respond, thinking maybe she didn't know my father as well as she thought. On the other hand, maybe she had me pegged from the get-go. Maybe killing people for a living visibly destroys your humanity. Under the present circumstances, however, I wasn't in the mood to ponder the psychological or philosophical ramifications of any of it. I closed my eyes, leaned back in the seat, and was rewarded with ten minutes of sleep before the Uber pulled up at her house.

# CHAPTER 21



Rinaldo Ruiz answered the phone on the first ring. From the series of clicks that greeted him, he knew exactly who was calling.

"Sorry to disturb you," the voice said. "I know I told you we'd no longer be doing business with you, but something came up."

"Like?"

"You have a strip club in San Diego named the Magic Kitty, correct?"

"Yes. So?"

"Your club manager, Jairo Esteban, and a woman who is either a bartender or a stripper named Shira Lipkin, were informants for the now deceased DEA agent, Walter McArthur."

"We know all about McArthur, but what's this about Esteban?" Ruiz barked into the phone.

"He's an informant," the man said.

Ruiz stared at the woman lying seductively next to him in bed. No longer in the mood, he got up, put on his robe, and sat at his desk so he could talk to the gringo calling from somewhere in California. "Why didn't you tell me sooner? Did you think I couldn't handle it?"

"Not at all. It's just we choose not to tell you everything that our intelligence apparatus unearths," the voice answered smoothly. "You know our deal! You have the assets to eliminate people we can't, and in return, we give you certain information we think you should know while at the same time not compromising us. This particular situation was a case we thought we could manage. And we did until the Walt McArthur fiasco. Now we have people, including his son, snooping around. We're going to have to clean up around the edges, Mr. Ruiz. We've got reasons for not wanting either the woman, who we believe still works for you as a stripper, nor the son of the recently deceased Walter McArthur, living past daybreak tomorrow. McArthur's son, in case you didn't know, is at your club as we speak. If you can get rid of them both tonight, we owe you."

"I'm more disturbed about Jairo Esteban," Ruiz said. "The culero ran four of our clubs in San Diego, and you're telling me he's working for you behind our back? I gave him everything he ever wanted. Kept his women in four different clubs so he'd always have one near when he felt the need. And look how he repays me. There is no loyalty anymore. His family will pay dearly."

"Do with Esteban what you wish; it's the female and the younger McArthur who concern us the most. They know too much, and we can't trust either of them to simply let the older McArthur's death slide by without retribution."

"You've got your problems, Señor, we have ours. I'll tell you what I will do. If you are right about the younger McArthur being at our club with a stripper, I will personally deal with both of them tonight." There was a pause, then, "Tell your boss he owes us a big favor."

"I will. And for you, my friend—just make sure you get the woman. We think she might be an Israeli plant hired by the older McArthur, and we've already taken care of the older McArthur for you. We're just not sure where, or if, she fits into all this, so just being alive she presents a problem. And now the younger McArthur is involved with her, and therefore both have to be eliminated."

*Perfect,* Ruiz thought. *Esteban and McArthur are coming to us.* "Don't worry. I will have my men take care of both of them tonight. I'm glad you called."

Ruiz peeked over his shoulder at the girl squirming sensuously in his bed. Blowing her a kiss, he gestured that he'd be with her shortly. Picking up the phone, he called the Magic Kitty. "I have a job for you, Ernesto," he said, recognizing the voice. "And Juan, too. You have to do it tonight. I will not accept failure."

"Si, Patrón."

"You have a puta there by the name of Lipkin?"

"Si, Patrón."

"She works for our enemies. I want her dead."

"She left a few minutes ago, Patrón. With a gringo."

"Perfect. Kill them both. Tonight! And Ernesto ...you know Señor Esteban is at the club tonight, correct?"

"Si, Patrón."

"I want him dead, also. He's talking to the American Federales. You need to make an example of him. Have Juan get a soldier to go with him to kill both the puta and the gringo. I want you, my friend, to kill Esteban personally. And his entire family. Show the world what happens when our own betray us."

# CHAPTER 22



The Uber dropped us off at Lipkin's house at 11:45 p.m. I was going to have to make this a quickie if I was going to meet Delgado back at the club before it closed. She lived in a two-bedroom house in a modest suburb east of San Diego. Like most homes in the development, it was defined by a patchy front lawn that ran some twenty yards from the house to the street. Ten-foot hedges separated the property lines. A cement walkway ran along the right-side hedge all the way to the front door. Metal wind chimes hanging from the front porch tinkled in the soft breeze that floated through the neighborhood that night.

"I have a dog," she said, as we climbed the four steps to her front door. "His name is Buck. He's a pit bull who's been with me for over two years. Ever since my husband died. Just so you know and understand, he is very protective of me. So don't get too close to either of us until I properly introduce you." She searched her purse for the key.

"Have you and the dog lived here long?"

"This is our fifth month living here. Even given that timeframe, Buck is still kind of skittish around visitors." She placed the key in the lock and opened the door.

I heard a deep growl and glanced downward. Standing in the middle of the entrance hallway, illuminated by the streetlamp, was a large beige and white pit bull, brow furrowed, teeth bared, and staring directly at me. Like he was sensing a meal.

"Shush, Buck," she commanded, bending down to take hold of the dog's collar with one hand while the other stretched upward for the keypad that would turn off the alarm. Accomplishing both, she stood and flipped on the light while motioning for me to come forward. "This is Buck," she said, "my protector. But don't worry ... he'll get used to you as soon as he knows you mean me no harm."

"I can only hope his sixth sense is working."

She gave a soft laugh. "Just walk slowly and you'll be alright." She knelt and hugged the animal, who didn't quite know whether to be happy about having her home or to do battle with the stranger in the room. Shira cooed in Buck's ear. "He liked Walt," she said over her shoulder, "so, in theory, he should like you. Walk over slowly and offer your hand so he can smell you." I did exactly as she asked, not wanting to have to kill the dog if he attacked me.

Buck sniffed me diligently for about half a minute and

then, apparently deciding I wasn't a threat to his mistress, trotted past me into the living room. "Congratulations," Shira said to me. "You passed the Buck test with flying colors. So, while you're here, let me show you around."

She set her purse on the small table in the hallway and walked into the kitchen. "Can I get you coffee or maybe a drink of something stronger? I have beer in the refrigerator and gin in the cupboard. Personally, I'm going to have a cup of tea. I've got a carafe of day-old coffee if you don't mind it being reheated."

"Thanks, but no need to fuss. Just the key and I'll be gone."

"Oh, for goodness' sake! Lighten up, will you? I won't bite … I promise." She paused. "I can just tell you're wondering about the relationship your father and I had. It's written all over your face. Do you want me to tell you about it? It's not nearly as complicated nor smarmy as you might think."

I shook my head, slowly tapping my fingers on the countertop. "Really, I can't stay long." I paused, then said, "Tell you what. After that one cup of coffee, I'll take the key to my San Francisco house and be out of your hair. I really have no need to know about you and my father."

She shrugged her shoulders in a *suit yourself* sort of way, then placed both my coffee and the water for her tea in the microwave. When both had finished heating, she passed me my cup and I followed her into what obviously was a sunroom, though in fact was the house's original living room. On the wall over a small fireplace hung a large eucalyptus wreath.

"Forgive the surroundings," she said. "I hadn't planned on

living in this house for very long even when your father was alive." She paused, then pointed to a white brocade sofa that had seen, even to my untrained eye, better days. "Why don't you sit there," she said, while settling herself into the wing-backed blue chair across from me. I smiled. Between the two of us, there was no doubt who had the better seating arrangement.

After sitting for a few moments, she rose and went across the room to close the drapes on the sliding glass door that led into the backyard. "No use giving nosey neighbors something to talk about," she said as she curled her feet back under her.

Not knowing where to go with that, I leaned back into the sofa, sipped my coffee quietly, and glanced at my watch.

"I know what you're thinking," she said, breaking the uncomfortable silence between us. "And if I can convince you of one thing during your fifteen-minute coffee break, I want you to know nothing ever went on between your father and me."

I responded with a polite nod. Just then, Buck stirred in the corner— head up, ears cocked. A low growl escaped his throat. Scrambling to his feet, he sprinted into the hallway towards the front door.

"Buck! What is it, boy?" Shira said, uncurling her legs and standing. I, on the other hand, was already up and moving. "Keep quiet," I whispered to her, trying to fix where Buck heard the noise. "Stay right where you are." I quickly followed Buck toward the front of the house. Just as I reached the hallway, the dog turned and burst past me back into the sunroom. At the sliding glass door, he stopped and bared his teeth, saliva glistening in the light of the lamp by Lipkin's chair. Then I heard what Buck had heard. Footsteps on the patio.

"The light," I hissed. "Kill that light." She was way ahead of me, yanking the cord from the wall socket. Since the kitchen light was still on, the room hadn't gone completely dark. "You have a gun?"

"Of course I have a gun." she murmured angrily. "And I can use it." I quickly followed her to her bedroom where she pulled out a Glock G-26 from her nightstand drawer. "Nice piece," I said. She nodded, but didn't comment on the weapon.

Just then we both heard rustling noises coming toward us from the front of the house. "Sounds like we have another visitor," she whispered, nodding toward the front door.

Quickly assessing our options, I said, "Okay ... station yourself at the front end of the hallway across from the front door. If someone comes through that door, can you shoot them?"

"Hey, stop treating me like I've never been in this kind of situation, okay? I was in the Israeli Mossad for over fourteen years" She went quiet, then said, "I'm used to shooting people."

*My kinda lady*, I thought with a smile, as I retrieved a wire hanger from her closet.

"Are you going to be okay with just that?" she asked.

I nodded and unwound the hanger wire. "SEAL training 101," I whispered. "A wire hanger can be just as fatal as a knife." I slowly turned toward the back of the house, listening as the lock on the sliding door came free. I then heard the patio door slowly slide open, wondering why the guy wasn't overly concerned about the noise he was making.

Buck's growl, lower and more menacing now, agreed with me that the guy from the back of the house had already breached the patio door. I also heard some noise outside the garage. The conclusion I came to was the more noise the intruder made jimmying the back door slide, the more Lipkin and I were supposed to panic and try to escape out the front door, directly into the sights of his buddy who was no doubt lying in wait near the garage.

*Thank goodness these guys are amateurs,* I thought as I straightened the wire hanger, its tip now protruding a little over four inches between my index and middle finger. I quietly slipped out the bedroom and back into the sunroom.

As the god of war would have it, my adversary saw me first, and, with a smile creasing his lips, brought his Glock up to firing position. But, as so often happens in cases like this, the god of war can be fickle. Unbeknownst to the dude in the sunroom, I was armed not only with a wire hanger, but with a pit bull named Buck who, wasting no time, jumped the gunman just as the guy's weapon came into firing position. The guy was just a tick slow as Buck's jaw clamped down on the shooter's forearm. From the scream he emitted, I knew the power of that jaw had just snapped the dude's right ulna bone in half. I did have to give the guy some kudos. Even though he had to be experiencing severe pain in his right arm, he still had the chutzpah to transfer the Glock to his left hand. Fortunately for me, his reaction time had slowed just enough to allow me to cleanly punch the four inches of wire hanger I held in my right hand, into, and through, the shooter's neck. On its way through, it fortuitously punctured his carotid artery. Almost immediately, his eyes went wide with surprise, then clouded over as a stream of arterial blood turned Shira's comfy blue chair into a sea of crimson.

I picked up the dead man's Glock from the floor, checked to make sure there was one in the chamber, and headed quickly toward the front door.

# CHAPTER 23



"Shira," I whispered as I moved in behind her. "Can you tell me what's happening outside?"

"We've got movement in our front," she answered quietly. "Hold on, we're about to go dark." Her arm snaked around the corner and flicked off the kitchen light, plunging the entire house into darkness.

I inched my way past her to the front door. Buck had stationed himself to my right, his low growl a warning that we still had company outside.

It was then I heard what Buck and Shira heard ... a soft scraping sound along the outside wall of the house underneath the kitchen window. I took a step back and aimed my gun at the front wall, following the scraping sound the intruder made as he inched closer to the front door.

"Mac!" a voice said softly through the door. "It's me ... Vinnie. I know that it's you in there. Open up."

"Vinnie!" I said, breathing a deep sigh of relief as I quickly unlocked the front door. "Get your butt in here. We've got a dead man in the living room."

"That's not the only dead guy we've got," Vinnie said. "His partner is on the driveway about twenty feet from where you are standing." Turning to Shira, he said, "I remember you from the club. And when I saw you and Mac getting in the Uber ... and then these two pieces of manure running to their car ... it didn't take long for me to figure you and Mac could probably use my services."

"You figured right," Lipkin said with a smile. "It's good to have you here."

"After you guys left in the Uber, and I saw both of these guys jogging back to their car, I didn't have to be the smartest guy on the block to figure where they were headed. Mac ... I told you I was going to watch your back, remember? And I did!"

"I'm in your debt, my friend. Mucho thanks!" Looking down, I said, "You sure gave that hombre a nasty head wound."

"Yeah, I know. And I really didn't plan on doing all that damage, Mac. Unfortunately, he didn't leave me no selection. He had a gun in his hand, and I had to break his wrist or he never would have let it go." A satisfied smile creased his lips. "Then, once I had the gun, he still fought me ... so I smacked him upside his head with it. This time, he went down like a stone in water. I honestly didn't think I'd hit him that hard, but in the final analysis, the only thing that mattered was he went down and stayed down. You can tell I wasn't all that disappointed."

"What say we get back into the house." I said, "Much warmer in there."

Once inside, I turned to Shira. "What happened here tonight? Did these two bozos really come here to kill you?"

"Not just me, Mac," she said, "but you and Vinnie, also." She sat down at the table. "Maybe they thought my skimpy outfit wasn't skimpy enough. Or I wasn't good enough to even be a stripper at the club." She laughed. "Hey, I've been here for close to six weeks now, and all I've done is take drink orders and listen carefully to what the other women talked about."

"And what's the owner's name?" Delgado asked.

"Esteban. Jairo Esteban," Lipkin replied. "He owns four clubs in San Diego. In my short time here, I've heard a lot of the girls swear he's a member of the Mexican Mafia." While pushing an errant strand of hair off her face, Lipkin turned to Delgado and asked, "Can you pour me a cup of coffee? And, if you know where to look, there is some Bailey's in the cupboard above the carafe. Might as well finish that, too."

"Absolutely." Delgado said. "You want coffee, Mac?"

"No thanks, Vin, I'm good." I turned my attention back toward Shira. "I have to ask ... did you work for my father?"

Maintaining eye contact with me, she replied, "Well ... not *for* him – but *with* him. You already knew that I'd been a Mossad agent for the past fourteen years. When my husband was killed in that firefight in Al Aqsa three years ago, I was given a six-month bereavement leave. That leave lasted two months before I got back to being a Mossad field agent.

"You might think this strange," she continued, "but one of

the many things I admired about your father was how thorough he was at combing through my background. Our first sit-down together was the one that lasted over six hours—mostly from your father telling me about me." She paused. "Your father even came to my husband's funeral after he was killed in a battle with the Brotherhood. He also met my two younger sisters, both of whom he personally financed for a year in drug rehab."

"Can you tell me what you know about this fellow Esteban?" I asked. "My understanding was that my father included him in his circle of friends because of his aversion to drugs."

Lipkin took another sip of Bailey's, then said, "Your father and Mr. Esteban happened to be on the same page as it pertained to drugs ... though for Esteban, his aversion to drugs came primarily because he had this notion that drugs were bad for his business. His real business, by the way, was nude dancing. I happened to be there one night when Esteban told the dancers that if he ever caught them using drugs, he'd fire them on the spot. And this from a guy who willingly pimped out his girls. Go figure!"

"How long ago did Esteban stop giving drugs to his women?" I asked.

"About Esteban? I'm not really sure," she said. "I only worked for him for something like four weeks. Your father tried to talk me into working undercover for Esteban full-time, but it so happened it was my first week at the club, so I declined."

"Would you mind if I changed the subject for a minute? I've always wanted to get a straight timeline of my father's death." I picked at a few of the blood flecks spotting my shirt, then asked Lipkin, "When exactly were you at my house in San Francisco?"

Lipkin jerked back, her eyes hardening as her voice went flat. "Where did that come from?"

"Well, you were there, weren't you? At my house?"

"Yes, I was—and actually *in* your house. But what's that got to do with anything?" Her eyes narrowed. "Please don't tell me you think there was something going on between me and your father?" She hesitated for minute, then said, "Come on ... you've got to be kidding! In all the time I knew your father, I visited your house in California exactly ... twice." She pointed two fingers at me for emphasis. "And what? You think I was intimate with your father during those two visits? Let me tell you something straight out—slowly and in front of anybody you'd care to bring forward." She paused, then looked me straight in the eye and said, "No ... We ... Were ... Not ... Lovers!" She leaned back in her chair and said, "Not physically, at least."

"And that means exactly what?" I asked.

She went silent for a moment, then reconnected eye contact and said, "It means I loved your father ... but in a completely different way than you think. I loved him like I loved my own father. Probably much like you loved your own father." She nodded and went silent once again.

I acknowledged the silence, then asked, "Did you take the key from my house?"

"Yes, I did," she replied. "Your father gave me the key to the house long ago ... so, and I quote, 'if I ever needed to R&R in San Francisco when you weren't home ...'" She paused, then said, "The swap was reciprocal. He told me I could stay at his house anytime, and I told him he could stay at mine in Tel Aviv anytime. Did that mean we were sleeping together? No, it did not. In fact, he never, ever slept at my house. Not once. Because if he had, he would've found himself sleeping with Buck, not me."

"And where is the key now?" I asked.

"That key is in my purse and will see the light of day when you actually ask me for it back before we land in Oakland."

# CHAPTER 24



I called the police about the Lipkin house break-in, and they promised to be there within the hour. Delgado had already driven off in Lipkin's car with Buck in the back seat and Mateo Fox's body rolled up in a blanket in the trunk. His job was to deposit Fox's body in a deserted land dump somewhere in Compton, then come back to the Magic Kitty and wait for me and Lipkin to finish talking to the police.

Before the police arrived at our door, Lipkin and I rehearsed our stories. Since I had the credentials and, more importantly, was an out-of-town male, I led off by giving the police my credentials which, hopefully, would save Shira and me a ton of time.

Both police officers took their seats directly across from us at Lipkin's kitchen table. They spent the first ten minutes filling out their paperwork— names, addresses, phone numbers, and who to call if Shira and I decided to leave town. Once they had all the pertinent information on us, they settled back into interrogation mode.

Hoping to short-circuit that process, I asked the officers to please allow us to give them our names and credentials and tell them why Lipkin and I were sitting across the table from them. After the two officers looked over our credentials, they glanced back up at us and said, "Looks like you two are good to go. We'll get the paperwork filed later this morning, and send it over to you."

"Thank you, gentlemen," I said. "We're hoping both Agent Lipkin and I will be able to catch a few hours sleep before meeting with Admiral Moore." I paused, then said, "In case you or your people are at all interested in what we're doing here, it was my father who the cartels murdered when they blew up the airplane in San Francisco last week."

That essentially ended the interview. Both officers were obviously tired and sympathized with me over my father's death.

The first thing I did after they left was call for a taxi to take Lipkin and me to the Magic Kitty. Next, I called Vinnie, who had already made it back to the Magic Kitty after dumping the body he carried in his car from Lipkin's house to a vacant lot in Compton.

"We're on our way to you at the Magic Kitty," I said. "Be there in fifteen minutes."

"You're in for a surprise," Vinnie said. "We got police officers running all over the place. The parking lot has so many lights on, it looks like a football stadium at halftime; except, of course, for the yellow crime scene tape strung across both entrances. The police forced me and Buck to park a block away. I wasn't sure what was going on, but after what happened at Lipkin's place, I'm thinkin' it's a good chance they're probably related."

"Where's your new girlfriend, Tiffany? Can she tell us what the heck is going on?"

"I told her to sweet talk some cop into escorting her back to her locker. I'm sure you've noticed how good she is at persuading males to do what she asks?" Vinnie chuckled. "In fact, at this very moment, I can see her across the parking lot working her magic on one of the younger cops." Vinnie paused a beat, then said, "Hey, hold on just a second ... Tiffany's on her way back, but without her gear. Let me find out what's happening. I'll call you back."

"I'll still be here," I replied.

I could hear muffled talking between Delgado and Tiffany. A few minutes later, Delgado was back. "Okay, here's the skinny, Mac. Turns out the owner of the club got himself offed sometime earlier this morning."

"The owner?"

"Yeah. That Esteban dude we were talking about at Lipkin's place."

"He was killed at the club?"

"Yeah. A cop told Tiffany they tortured and then executed him. Gotta tell ya, Mac, these guys play hardball."

"Then you better watch yourself, Vinnie. Reserve a hotel room at the airport for both you, Shira, and the dog, and then have someone at the front desk make a noon flight reservation for both you, Shira, and the dog to San Francisco. When you get to San Francisco, grab an Uber to my house. You remember the address, right? And you still have the key I gave to you, correct?"

"Of course," he answered.

"Then get that lady and her dog safely to my house, Vinnie. I'm counting on you. In the meantime, the rest of us will be on our way to visit Admiral Moore in Coronado."

# CHAPTER 25



I walked into the Naval Special Warfare's *Development Group* office in Coronado at 0900. Stinger, FT, and Wolfman were already seated.

"Look what the cat just drug in," Stinger said as I entered. "When did you show up, Mac?"

"I arrived in San Diego last night around 9:30 with an old friend of mine ... actually, an old friend of *ours* from the Teams ... y'all remember Vinnie Delgado, don't you? Even though he retired a few years back, I'm sure you guys still remember him as a great teammate and one tough hombre. He's already put his house in order, and just last night I hired him as the second newest member of Red Squadron. Sorry I couldn't run this by you guys first but, given the circumstances Vinnie and I just went through, I thought he would be a perfect teammate."

"Hey, Mac," Wolfman said. "I want you to know that I, for

one, have nothing but good feelings towards Vinnie." He paused, then said, "I served with him in SEAL Team 4. Have to admit, he could be over-the-top volatile at times, but he's just the kind of stand-up dude we all need … and want … in times of danger. And besides, the volatile ones are the guys you can count on to watch your back in a fight. He retired what … three or four years ago? Maybe even five. I can't remember."

"Closer to four," I said. "But volatile or not, he still can kick butt and take names with the best of us." I took a breath, then said, "Again, as far as I'm concerned, he's just the kind of guy we're looking for."

Every head in the room was nodding in the affirmative as Admiral Moore walked into the room lugging a briefcase full of papers. "Thanks for coming, gentlemen," he said, placing his briefcase under the desk. "I'm sorry, but, as usual, it turns out I don't have much time. The President just called a special meeting having to do with those Mexican cartels trying to blanket the US with fentanyl. As of right now, it's the numero uno drug of choice for Americans as young as fifteen and as old as forty-five or fifty. When we last spoke, I mentioned we had successfully opened a connection with the President of Mexico regarding what Red Squadron could bring to the table if he needed a buffer between him and the cartels."

"But all for naught, Sir, if I remember correctly," I said, looking directly at Moore. "Didn't the Mexican President flat out refuse to authorize US Special Op troops on his soil?" I paused a moment, then said, "Has he changed his mind?"

"For some reason, it's beginning to look that way, Mac," Moore replied, a smile creasing his face. "Early this morning, President Ortiz-Gil called the White House and actually apologized for refusing to allow American Special Op troops into Mexico. He told us that as long as we could provide plausible deniability, he'd turn a blind eye to a small squad of specialized American troops helping to eliminate, or at least control, the cartels."

"And a small squad to him means exactly what?" asked Wolfman.

"Squad to him means however many people we want it to mean," Moore replied, placing both of his hands flat on the table. "As a result of this offer, the President, with a gentle nudge from yours truly, authorized the Department of Defense to hire Red Squadron under the heading, Classified Consultant Group."

"You've got to be kidding, Admiral," I said. "Our Team is going from combatants to consultants? You sure you want to do that?"

"Don't worry about the consultant designation, Mac. Everybody on both sides of the border knows what a Consultant Group does ... and how it works."

"And their president has authorized us to form a squad of American Special Op troops to carry it out?" I asked.

"He's told me personally that he would turn a blind eye to our numbers as long as they don't exceed fifteen."

"That's good to hear, Sir. We now have Vinnie Delgado, and a female combatant whose name is Shira Lipkin, with us today. Both are exactly the kind of warriors we want and need."

"I remember Mr. Delgado, but haven't as of yet met Shira Lipkin," Admiral Moore said.

"She's exactly the kind of combatant we need, Sir," I said. "She spent close to fifteen years in the Mossad before starting to work part-time with us. I've worked with her before and can attest that she's an extraordinary special operator."

"Well, then, let's get both of them operational as quickly as possible," Moore replied. "I'll send them everything they'll need to get operational while they're in San Francisco. Let me tell you, however, that when we get into one of these *brief* meetings, there's no telling how brief that meeting, or any meeting for that matter, will be. I'll suggest you guys grab some coffee in the mess, and I'll instruct my N-1 to put together the paperwork you'll need to get back to San Francisco. Everyone good to go with that?" All heads nodded in unison. "Then let's get our asses in gear."

Moore closed the folder in front of him and stood. "As you plan strategy, gentlemen, I'm going to presume your first target will be the Tormenta cartel."

"Rest assured, Sir, that the Tormenta piece of the equation has already been scheduled!"

"Good. That'll give the President the additional cover he'll need for our operations in Mexico." Moore grabbed his folder, turned toward us, and said, "One thing I can promise you people. You're going to be swamped, but you're also going to enjoy every minute of the ride."

"I can guarantee, Sir," I said, "that Red Squadron is looking forward to taking that ride with you."

# CHAPTER 26



"Change in plans, gentlemen," he said with an edge to his voice. "Assemble in my office immediately."

Twelve minutes later, the four of us, minus Vinnie and Shira who were already on their way to San Francisco, were seated around the Admiral's desk. "Have you heard what's been going on in this neck of the woods these past few days?" Moore asked, wanting to get the backstory firmly entrenched in our brains.

I glanced over at my compadres ... blank stares all around. "Looks like we haven't, Admiral. Mostly been drinking coffee and waiting for you to call and fill us in."

"Well, turns out there's been some big-time drug deals going on in the SF Bay Area ... smack in the middle of where you guys are staying. Just got a message from SOCOM that the entire area has come under some kind of attack that, as of now, is being classified as biological."

"Biological? Oh, come on ... you've got to be kidding! You're telling us that San Francisco is, at this very moment, under some kind of biological attack?"

"We've got the evidence," Moore said. "It's looking as if the two largest drug cartels in Mexico, the Tormentas and the Nuevo Pueblos, have buried their hatchet and are preparing to flood our shores with fentanyl." He paused. "I'm guessing you're all familiar with fentanyl?"

"We are, Sir," I said. "And as of this moment, we're all wondering what the heck is going on. You're telling us that the cartels have centered their attack in Northern California, and are using fentanyl as their drug of choice?"

"That's exactly what they are doing, Mac," Moore said, "but, as it turns out, the users have discovered a new and improved fentanyl. It's the drug that is going wild in today's market, and as of this very moment, has become the most lethal drug in human history. If you can believe it, I'm being told that fentanyl is one hundred times more potent than morphine."

That little tidbit changed the temperature in the room, but before any of us could reply or ask questions, Moore told us to gather up our gear. "You're scheduled to be at Miramar Naval Air Station in forty minutes," he said. "I'll be giving you a call as soon as you're airborne." Moore stood and started to walk out the door, but he hesitated and turned, saying, "Just so you know, forty-seven people have already died of fentanyl poisoning in and around the San Francisco Bay Area in the past two hours. Another 172 have been hospitalized." He paused for a moment, then said, "Your job, gentlemen, is to get a handle on what is going on up there in our own backyard ...

and then report back to me pronto. Are you clear about that?" We all nodded in assent.

Once in the air, the Cessna copilot handed us headsets. "You'll be able to hear and talk; but just so you know, the system doesn't allow you to talk over each other. Follow the rules and you'll have a peaceful flight."

I immediately connected with the Admiral. "We're in the air, Sir. Can you fill us in on what the heck is going on in the Bay Area?"

"It's pretty grim, Mac, and getting grimmer by the hour. The Center for Disease Control in Atlanta messaged us earlier today to tell us another 112 people died either sniffing or eating fentanyl. So far, the total death toll has reached 159 people." Moore went silent for a moment, then said, "And you can bet by the time you land in Oakland, that number will be exponentially higher."

"This whole scenario is hard to believe," I said. "And it's due almost exclusively to the cartels flooding our country with that fentanyl garbage?"

"I've talked with people who've been tracking this drug for the past three years," Moore said. "They've come to the conclusion that fentanyl is now the most dangerous drug to hit the streets in our lifetime."

"How the heck did that happen?" I asked.

"Fentanyl, it turns out, is a synthetic opioid that is now being produced in laboratories," Moore replied. "The experts tell us it's very similar to morphine—only fifty to a hundred times more potent. The synthetic opioids now being peddled on the streets will not only get you strung out but will actually kill you."

"Thanks for that information, Sir," I said. "And before you go ... just so you know ... within the next five to six hours, there'll be six of us living at my house in San Francisco. And on the payroll, lest you forget." I laughed, then said, "I think by now it would be helpful for you to have all our names handy. I'm sending you the cheat sheet version. The ones you already know – retired SEALs Stinger; FT; Wolfman; and me, plus retired SEAL Vinnie Delgado and former Mossad agent Shira Lipkin."

"When will you be arriving?" Moore asked.

"I'm thinking our ETA at Oakland will be close to seven," I said. "And just so you know, Sir, I've already invited both Vinnie and Shira to become active members of Red Squadron. I've known and served with Delgado on the battlefield. He's a great asset. And now that I've come to know the Lipkin woman, I can testify that she's a keeper. And again, just so you know, I double-checked her status with the Israeli Mossad and heard nothing but good things about her. Not surprisingly, she's now on our payroll."

"I'm with Mac on this one, Admiral," Stinger added. "I don't know the Lipkin woman all that well, but I did serve with Vinnie Delgado the year before he retired from the Teams. He's a tough, stand-up dude."

"And I can attest to the Lipkin woman," I said. "My father got to know Shira Lipkin and worked with her on and off for a number of years. I want everyone to know that in the short time I've been around her, I'm convinced she'll be a valuable addition to our crew. Just so we all know, she served fourteen years of her life as a Mossad agent. My father got permission from her superiors to work with her on a number of short-term undercover assignments the DEA was working on, mostly in the Southern California area. Unfortunately, being an undercover asset also assured us that no one alerted her to the fact that my father had been killed. It's the reason Vinnie and I went to San Diego in the first place—to meet her and find out firsthand whether she was friend or foe. After seeing her in action against the two assassins that were sent to kill us, I can attest that her skill set fits in perfectly with our Red Squadron."

"You have my permission, Mac," Moore said. "Please give both Vinnie and Shira my best."

Our plane from Southern California arrived in Oakland at 7:10. I called Vinnie to let him know we had landed. He not only told me that the Admiral had called the house to welcome both him and Shira to Red Squadron, but that he also had sent a small cargo plane full of goodies that should already have landed on SFO's north quadrant runway.

"The old man must have called in some favors," I remarked to Wolfman as we watched a C-23 Sherpa land and taxi to where we had parked our car. After Sherpa's crew unloaded two medium-sized wooden crates into the back of the Suburban I'd rented, the plane turned around and took off. An hour later, we were parking the Suburban in my garage and unloading six extra-large Round Table pizzas plus a case each of Sierra Nevada IPA and Modelo. Thanks to the Admiral, it was promising to be a good night.

# CHAPTER 27



After watching the gringo's house for the past five hours, Ernesto Calderon called Ruiz to tell him it was not only the puta, the short gringo and a large dog who had settled into the San Francisco house, but in the last twenty minutes the tall gringo along with another three men showed up. All warriors, too, by the looks of them. "What do you want me to do?"

Ruiz went silent for a few moments, then said, "Too much confusion, Ernesto. As of this moment, they have the advantage. We'll deal with them another day." He hung up and called Victor Serna, telling him that Jairo Esteban was no longer among the living.

"Excellent," Serna remarked. "You're to be congratulated."

"I can only hope," Ruiz replied. "We eliminated Esteban, but unfortunately, missed the younger McArthur. He is still among the living, and my people are telling me it looks like he is now taking up residence in a large San Francisco house along with a group of his own people."

There was a long silence before Serna spoke. Ruiz had experienced this particular silence many times before, so he knew what to expect.

"Rinaldo, how long have you and I been together?" Serna asked, his voice having traveled from neutral to borderline venomous in a span of seconds.

"Many profitable years," Ruiz answered, attempting to deflect the onslaught he knew was coming. "And many more on the horizon, Ángel" He cringed, knowing from long experience how ugly Serna could get when infected by certain moods. Unfortunately, there was nothing he could do about it. On the bright side, as quickly as the mood settled upon him, it could fade just as quickly. Ruiz could only hope this time it would fall into the latter category.

"So, why is this happening?" Serna snarled. "Why do we have defectors like Esteban when we pay them so handsomely? Why is there no loyalty?" His voice began to rise in intensity. "And this McArthur person? Why is *he* still alive? This is not acceptable, Rinaldo. I keep control of my people. If they screw with me, I chop their balls off in front of their wives. And then decapitate their children and place their heads on poles alongside the highways. They soon learn."

Ruiz thought he heard a change in Serna's tone which, he hoped, meant the burner inside the man was petering out, or, even better, completely turning itself off. Fortunately for him, it was the latter.

A much calmer Serna now declared, "I want to visit you,

my friend, on the American side of the border. It is so peaceful there, and I've had so many bad dreams lately. They frighten me. Maybe we can get together and my dreams will be more peaceful, eh?"

*"Please, no"* Ruiz thought to himself. He was not in the mood to dispense psychological advice to his friend, especially one so volatile. Serna once cut out the tongue of a therapist he'd hired because he didn't like the advice she gave him. Ruiz cherished his tongue and remembered things like that.

"I'm thinking of coming to The Casa along with our dear friend, Diego Velasquez. Can you handle both of us?" Serna asked with a chuckle.

"With pleasure," Ruiz replied. "When would you like to come, Ángel?"

"Tomorrow, my friend. Can you arrange it?"

Ruiz shivered at the thought, but, with a controlled smile, assured Serna he could. "You will fly, of course?"

"Of course."

"I will prepare the Casa for you, my friend. It will be good being with both you and Diego."

# CHAPTER 28



"Welcome to my humble abode," I said to Stinger and Wolfman as they walked into my house. "And look here," I said. "Shira and Vinnie have been good enough to prepare the dining room table for the food that we're bringing in via Admiral Moore's largess."

As we all settled in around the dining room table, I said, "I'm sure most of you have already heard somewhere down the line that I was born in this house, right? And that I lived here until my mom and dad decided to split when I was seventeen? My mom died seven years ago ... God rest her soul ... and it took almost all of those seven years for my father and me to finally reconcile. Unfortunately, my father was killed ... actually murdered ... in the airplane he was on that blew up close to here."

I paused, then said, "Okay, enough of this ghoulish

business. My father can wait. We've got some very important issues to chew on. Time to get serious."

The chatter in the room quickly went silent. "The first thing on our plate is Admiral Moore's idea to split Red Squadron into two teams: Team Alpha would be headquartered on the East Coast, and Team Beta on the West Coast. As far as I'm concerned, his proposal is a non-starter." I looked around the room. "Anyone care to comment?"

"I think that the Admiral had hoped to form us into an eight-man squad," Wolfman said. "To me, it sounded more like a business decision. I'm not sure the Admiral fully appreciates the damage the six people now sitting in this room can do as a unit."

"Agreed," I said. "Last time he looked, our squad consisted of four of us doing battle in the Hindu Kush. Since then, we've added both Vinnie and Shira to our crew."

"The first thing we've got to tell the Admiral," Wolfman continued, "is we think it best to re-form Red Squadron into an eight-man unit, with the seventh and eighth warrior spots to be added at our discretion. By putting the six of us in this room together as a unit, all we would need are targets."

"I'm with you there, Wolfman," I said with a smile. Just then my cell chirped. Turned out it was Admiral Moore. "Sorry to call without warning, Mac," Moore began, "but I wanted you folks to be the first to know that Homeland Security just elevated the NSA Threat Level on the West Coast to *Imminent*."

"Imminent? There are six people in this room, Sir. Can I put you on speaker?"

"Absolutely," Moore answered.

"Sir, our people here are all ears. I just finished telling them the NSA Threat Level in the Bay Area just turned Imminent. And Sir, isn't Imminent the highest threat level we have?"

"Mac, as I'm sure you've already heard, parts of the West Coast have already been attacked by an as-yet-unknown terrorist group using fentanyl as its preferred weapon of mass destruction. As of this very moment, I'm looking at 305 confirmed deaths—thirty-four more than there were just two hours ago. The hospitals on your coast are filling up rapidly. This is serious business, Mac."

He went silent for a few minutes as he put us on mute. "Sorry for the interruption," he said, returning to the phone. "I wanted you and your men to know we just concluded an hour-long White House sitrep with the unanimous decision being JSOC and DEA will be given joint operational command over the West Coast until further notice."

"Sir ... it's Mac, here. If I may ask ... why get JSOC involved? From all we've so far been told, this has all the markings of a domestic terrorist attack. And I, for one, understood domestic terrorism to be more a law enforcement issue than a military issue."

"If this were a domestic attack, Mac," Moore replied, "your assessment would be spot-on. But the view held by the Joint Chiefs, at least at this stage in the attack, is that fentanyl is a dangerous opioid that's being peddled in America by at least two Mexican cartels. And they, my friend, have to be stopped ... period! If not, you're talking to a United States military that will respond to them on their own soil."

"A military response in Mexico? This is getting mucho

serious, Sir," I said. "Please know that Red Squadron is locked and loaded and at your disposal."

"That's good to know, Mac. And just so you *also* know, your old pal Gilardi has been named Special Agent in Charge of the entire DEA West Coast operation."

"Gilardi?" I went silent for a few moments, then said, "Well, Sir ... I'm sorry, but I gotta tell you. I haven't been around Gilardi all that much, but the times I have been, he hasn't left me with a good feeling. In fact, I'm surprised he's been so well-received by you folks. Is there a reason for that?"

"One of the senior people at DEA's El Paso Intelligence Center told the White House this morning that Gilardi should be appointed because he's one of only a few agents who has studied the ebb and flow of both anthrax and fentanyl in the country."

I shrugged my shoulders and said, "Well, as you know, Sir, anthrax and fentanyl are two different animals, though I can understand Gilardi's dual interest. My question revolves around his qualifications. I'm trying to piece together his handling of the 2010 anthrax attack with his takeover of the current fentanyl attack. Looks to me like he's just pushing for another promotion, which in my corner of the world would be a huge mistake. My guess is he's trying to relive his glory days of anthrax. That, unfortunately, had to be some twenty years ago ... which makes me hopeful you won't station me, nor Red Squadron, anywhere near him."

"I hear you, Mac," Moore said. "But I'm thinking it'll probably take days to sift through all the evidence we've been accumulating before we can come to a consensus on how to deal with fentanyl. About all we know for certain is there are thousands of Americans, mostly between the ages of sixteen and thirty-something, who are living in close proximity to you in the Bay Area, and who are, at this very moment, most probably ingesting fentanyl ... and dying from it."

"And that's exactly why I think Gilardi isn't worthy of such a high-level appointment," I said. "As far as I know, he's never been in a *real* war ... shooting or otherwise. And it's looking clearer and clearer to me that this attack from the two cartels pushing fentanyl could very well push us into an actual war."

"I couldn't agree more, Mac. Are your people still with us?"

"They are, Admiral. We're all in the living room and we're all mentally locked in."

"Good." Moore went silent for a few moments, then said, "From now on, everything said in this room stays in this room." He paused. "Understood?"

"Roger, that, Sir."

"Good! First off then, the Joint Chiefs have given me the authority to hire Red Squadron to infiltrate the Mexican cartels doing the damage on the West Coast ... with the objective of shutting them down forever. As of this moment, the evidence shows that only one cartel, with Chinese Communist help, is pushing fentanyl as their anchor in the war being waged against the United States."

"And the use of fentanyl, Sir, is important ... why?" asked FT.

"Because, as of this very moment, fentanyl is the most abused, and therefore the most lethal, drug in the world," Moore replied. "The *high* that comes from its use can actually kill people—and by *people*, I mean mostly those in the sixteen to forty-six-year-old age bracket. Right now, fentanyl deaths are at the highest count ever recorded."

The room became so quiet we could hear Moore taking a sip of water. I waited enough time to observe protocol, then said, "A question, Admiral?"

"Go for it, Mac," Moore replied. "Just remember, I've got a ton of things on my plate, so I can't be here with you much longer."

"Copy that, Sir." I paused a few beats myself, then said, "I'd like to focus on only one of the cartels you've already mentioned --- the Tormentas. To those of us who are somewhat familiar with the Mexican drug scene, it looks as though Mexico's two former West Coast cartels have just combined forces into one cartel and are now living the good life by forcing Mexico's second-level distributors to buy the product from the new cartel at outrageous prices."

"Where are you going with this?" Moore asked. "We all know it's a dangerous world out there for both us and the cartels, but to tell you the truth, from where I sit, I'm only sympathetic to the Tormentas." Moore paused, then said, "Because the Tormentas are the ones that will lose the most."

"I've been thinking, Sir, of what would happen if we position the Tormentas into doing their business in an even more dangerous world." I paused, then said, "Why not send Red Squadron into Mexico with the goal of crushing the Tormentas ... top-to-bottom." I poured myself a glass of water, then said, "I'm thinking that Red Squadron could flat-out guarantee you that within the first six months of us being hired, the Tormenta fentanyl business would have been squeezed to death." I stopped, awaiting Moore's response.

"You're forgetting one thing, Mac," Moore replied. "Mexico just happens to be a sovereign country, and—just a guess—probably not too keen on having Americans on their soil squashing their business."

"I'm aware of that, Sir. Believe me, I'm anything but naïve. But isn't it factually true that the two primary Mexican drug cartels import most of their drugs directly from China? And isn't it also factually true that those same cartels want to be selling their China stash to dealers in the States?"

"I'm sure you're right," he said.

"Then we have to do something completely unexpected, Admiral, or we'll find our country awash in fentanyl ... along with an untold number of American corpses."

"Get to your point, Mac," Moore replied. "I've got another meeting scheduled in fifteen minutes."

"I hear you, Sir," I said. "This will take only a minute or two. We all know now that the Tormenta cartel is one of the biggest, wealthiest, and nastiest bunch of bad guys in our hemisphere. In my mind, if you give us the go-ahead, it's that particular entity that my Red Squadron would put out of business ... and quickly. We can, and will disrupt their distribution pattern so that their entire infrastructure will crumble, and if their infrastructure crumbles, so do the Tormentas." I paused, then said, "At least that's how we see it."

"Sounds like you've already planned this out," Moore said with a chuckle.

"Well, truth be told, Sir, we've been working on this for the past few weeks. It's still in its infancy, but we have the outline of a hybrid war scenario pieced together such that we think we could put a huge hole in the Tormenta drug trade."

"I'd like to see the plan in its entirety when you have it finished, Mac," Moore said. "And, after I see it ... I'd like you to show it to Gilardi."

That took everyone in the room by surprise ... especially me. "Gilardi?" I muttered aloud with more vehemence than I intended. "As you are probably aware, Sir, we aren't overly fond of how Gilardi runs his shop. So, if you don't mind, we'd prefer to take orders directly from you. If you're agreeable to that, we'll assign Alex Navarro, whom you spoke to on the phone a few days back, to be our liaison with Gilardi. Just having Nav there will allow Gilardi to be the head of what he is fond of calling his piece of the puzzle. That way, Red Squadron can do its own *piece of the puzzle* and, hopefully, bring down the Tormenta cartel once and for all."

"I've got no objection to anything you just said, Mac," Moore replied. "All I'm suggesting is that you tell Gilardi what you are going to do ... strategically."

"Sir, that's all I needed to hear. We'd be delighted to tell Gilardi that."

"Good! But remember that he's still an asset of ours ... and therefore we still have to put up with him."

# CHAPTER 29



At 11:30 p.m., after the various people now living in my house had already retired to their assigned rooms, I sat alone in my father's office, pouring over some of the electronic correspondence Moore left for us regarding Victor Serna. Hearing a creak, I looked up and saw Shira Lipkin standing barefoot in the doorway next to *Buck*. Her hair was pulled back in a ponytail, and she was wearing a man's long-sleeved blue shirt that barely covered the top of her thighs.

"Sorry to disturb you," she said, "I was on the way to the kitchen to get *Buck* some food. Poor dog—I usually feed him a lot earlier, but with all that's been going on around here, it just slipped my mind. And while I'm in the kitchen getting *Buck's* food, can I get you anything?"

"No, thanks. I'm fine."

Shira returned eleven minutes later carrying a tray with two mugs filled with hot coffee, along with a bowl of dried dog food. "Mind if Buck and I join you?" she asked with a smile.

"Absolutely not," I said, minimizing the computer screen and leaning back into my father's leather chair. "Please, come in." I pointed to the matching leather chair positioned on my left. "Have a seat."

Placing Buck's bowl of food on the floor, Shira walked around the desk and placed the tray with two coffee cups between us. "For you," she said, her mouth curving into a smile as she sat across from me in the leather chair to which I'd pointed.

"Thank you," I replied, raising my cup towards her in a mock salute. "Here's to you and your four-legged bodyguard." I gave a small chuckle as I settled back into the chair.

When Lipkin leaned forward to put her coffee on the desk, the top of her shirt gaped open. Sensing my stare, she innocently pulled the top closed. "Sorry," she apologized. "This was your father's shirt, and the top button is missing." With her left hand, she pulled the opening of the shirt tight around her throat. "As of today, except for a few shirts from your father's dresser, most of my entire wardrobe is hanging in a closet somewhere ... courtesy of the Magic Kitty." She stopped, then said, "even if this was my house and I was not expecting a visitor, I still wouldn't wear some of the clothes the other dancers left in my cubicle. And since Mr. Delgado was in such a hurry to leave that place, I just threw a bunch of their clothes into my carry-on." She laughed, then said, "Hope they fit."

I nodded and tugged at my ear to help bring me back from *fantasy land*. "When I lived here," I said, "my father spent most of his time in this very room. As a youngster, I remember the thrill of actually being invited into this office. And that's what it became known as in my mind—*his office* ... the *original man cave before the invention of man caves.*" I pivoted in my seat and pointed toward the far wall. "It's really a shame," I said. "The only things left in his office were two thoroughly banged up filing cabinets, along with, as you can see, a big hole in the wall where his safe once lived." I looked at her and smiled. "And let's not forget these two chairs we're sitting in."

She surveyed the room, then said, "I am so sorry, too. In hindsight, I can now see why my key became so important to you. You were thinking the key may have been used by them, whoever the *them* were, to let themselves into your house?"

"Well, that's still a distinct possibility. And please forgive the way I treated you at the club. There were, and still are, an assortment of loose ends surrounding my father's death." I took a deep breath. "For example, who was it that authorized placing the bomb aboard the airplane my father was on? I'm guessing it was the same people who then ransacked his house after the plane blew up."

She nodded. "I'm just now beginning to understand why you were all over me regarding the key to your house. But when you think about it, if it hadn't been for that particular key, we would probably never have met."

I glanced at her, wondering if she was just teasing me in her own flirtatious manner. The smile that framed her lips certainly looked flirtatious. At least I hoped it was ... but in any case, I wasn't about to complain. "I hope you didn't think I was rude putting you in my father's bedroom," I said, trying to bring both of us back to some kind of manageable equilibrium. "I only did that because of its private bathroom."

"That was thoughtful of you," she replied, again flashing a smile. "I really appreciated it. In all my so-called adventures, I can honestly say I've never lived in a house with five men ... with me being the only female."

"I have no doubt that, with your Mossad background, you are quite capable of taking care of yourself ... no matter how many guys are in the house." I chuckled then leaned back in my chair and asked, "Tell me what it's like to be a Mossad agent."

She hesitated a moment, then said, "Well, first and foremost. it's a job. Much like yours, I imagine. I've been at my job now for close to fifteen years, though I did take a two-month leave of absence three years ago."

"What ... you got burned out? That pretty much happens to all of us."

"Didn't happen quite like that, unfortunately. I thought you knew! My husband, Randy, and three other Mossad agents were given a task to capture, or kill, if need be, a man named Tamir al Abid. This *al Abid* fellow was the chief of logistics and weapons procurement for Hamas. As such, he oversaw the transfer of anti-tank missiles from Iran to the Hamas forces in Gaza. Since he was the operative in charge of targeting Israel, Tamir was fingered to be eliminated."

"So, they went and eliminated this guy?"

"Exactly," she said. "At 3 a.m. the morning of January 19th, 2021, Randy and his crew of three were in the Al Bustan Rotana Hotel in Dubai quietly wrapping the door handle of Room 205 with a soft, hand-molded, breach explosive."

"Uh-oh. I can see that this is not going to end well."

"You're right. It didn't," she replied softly. "I was told the timed explosive went off as planned ... with one exception.

While the door to the room blew inward as planned, the explosion unexpectedly blew the door's handle backward, hitting Randy in the left temple. They told me he died immediately." She paused. "That, at least, was comforting to hear. After Randy was buried, I took a six-month bereavement leave, which only lasted two months. I just had to forget what happened, so I went back to work."

"And that's when you met my father?"

"Yes. Even though I was two months removed from Randy's death, I was still having trouble emotionally. Not for the first time did I find myself sitting alone in a bar feeling sorry for myself. But serendipitously, this older gentleman came over to me one evening and introduced himself as Walter McArthur, a senior officer in the United States Drug Enforcement Administration." She smiled. "He told me he was in Israel to see if the Mossad would be interested in joining forces with the DEA to once and for all eliminate the scourge of drugs in both our countries. It turned out he already knew about Randy and offered to buy me a drink. We sat there over two hours talking about both of our agencies. Mostly insider stuff. It was fun. Once home, I called the Mossad to check his story. They told me he was a legitimate DEA officer.

"During the next two weeks, we had dinner out every night. He never asked to come over to the house. If he had, that would probably have ended our friendship. More importantly, he never touched me or made any advances towards me.

"I told your father more about Randy's death. I gave him my phone number and then, later, my address. We formed the perfect relationship. I wasn't in the market for a boyfriend or husband, and he wasn't interested in a woman twenty years his junior.

"Over the next three or so months, we got to know each other pretty well. He talked to me at length, and with passion, about ridding America of illegal drugs. I told him about my own father's addiction, and how he once tried to rape me. Walt asked if I could help him accomplish something special for families being torn apart by addiction to drugs … just like mine. He said we could both make a difference in the world. For families. For their future." She dabbed away a tear. "Can you see now why I loved your dad? He was the father I never had."

"Ironic," I said. "My father never let *me* get that close to him. He and my mother got divorced when I was seventeen. I lived with her until I was eighteen. It was then I joined the Navy. Never got a chance to see much of my father after that. I wish now that I'd made the effort."

"I wish you had, too. He spoke of you often."

An awkward silence followed. She looked at her watch and said, "It's getting late. I should get to bed."

I nodded. "Thanks for the talk. You're going to be a big help to us, so don't be disappointed if I keep you."

"I was thinking the same about you," she said, taking one last sip from the mug. She gave me a peck on the cheek, called out to Buck, and left.

# CHAPTER 30



It was shortly after 5:30 a.m. when the first National Guard units arrived in downtown San Francisco and began to deploy. City workers had already started to erect barricades at major intersections to keep the expected crowds of demonstrators at bay. Navarro and I arrived at 5:45 a.m. I made a left turn at Hayes, and another left into Van Ness. Big mistake. By my own count, I tallied more than a hundred demonstrators milling around that particular intersection.

Fortunately, the National Guard had cordoned off the sidewalks on both sides of the street with ropes and barricades in the hope that the opposing sides wouldn't start a riot and begin shooting each other. On one side of the street, sixty or so left-wing crazies were chanting and hefting signs and placards with messages like *Shame on Corporate America* and *Turn America Red.*

"Hey, where are the *Free Huey* banners?" Navarro asked while flashing a peace sign at a demonstrator who quickly gave him the finger. I chuckled and shook my head.

On the other side of the street, the right-wing nuts had also taken over, though given the political profile of the City and County of San Francisco, there weren't nearly as many right-wing crazies as there were in the *Bring Down Corporate America* crowd.

"Take a look at those guys," I said, pointing to the smaller crowd. "They're no different than their partners in crime across the street ... except their shtick wants to portray this attack as a definite sign of God's displeasure in *hedonistic* San Francisco." Nav shook his head in humorous disbelief. "Hey, welcome to the City ... with a capital C ... by the Bay, as it is known by the press."

"Yeah. Isn't it weird how soon we forget what a nut case this city can become at times?"

"And look ... the press is already out in force," I said, counting almost as many news reporters in the crowd as demonstrators.

By the time we arrived at the Phil Burton Federal Building, the National Guard had already established its command post. Looked to me like they had at least two hundred or more troopers milling about, every one of them wearing a *Level A* Hazmat Suit and carrying a Sig P226 in a side holster. It was also apparent that each trooper was wearing a bulletproof vest under their Hazmat Suits.

As we exited the elevator on the twentieth floor, Navarro saw his old friend and partner, Bill Murray, standing to the side of the crowd. Calling him over, Nav introduced me.

"Heard a lot about you," Murray said with a smile as we shook hands. "I knew your father. A stand-up guy if there ever was one. Sorry he couldn't be with us." He hesitated for a few seconds, then said, "And let me welcome you back to San Francisco ... home, as you know, to Fisherman's Wharf and fentanyl."

"Appreciate it," I said with a laugh. "By the way, what room is the party gonna be in? And do you know how many have been invited?"

"There's a large theater room on this floor," Murray answered with a smile. "They want us police and ex-military, like you guys, to learn the *ins* and *outs* of how fentanyl is marketed, and what it does to people who've already ingested it. We're hopeful you guys can help us find the perps who are distributing it."

As we waited for the escorts, a guy named Jacobson pointed to the glass windows lining our hallway, and said, "Don't you find all this security business rather odd? Like the National Guard being called out to escort us through this building?" He swept his arm wide, then said, "A building, by the way, which they haven't, as of yet, fully secured?" That caused some chuckles from the people standing around him.

Murray smiled, shook his head again, and said, "Take a good look at this building we're standing in. You think it's safe? Come on, people! We're in a twenty-something floor building virtually enclosed by glass." He paused, then, pointing to all the windows that encased us, said, "Hey ... I'm guessing one well-placed explosive would send enough shards of glass coming from those windows to cut us all into little pieces. Which, if you remember, was exactly what happened to the people in the Federal Building in Oklahoma City a number of years back."

"You know ..." I said loud enough for Murray to hear me, "I vaguely remember that Oklahoma City building going down." I paused, counting on my fingertips, then said, "I was, what ... like twelve years old when that happened? Something like that, anyway."

"Hmmm. We all forget what a youngster you are," Navarro chimed in. "Anyway, in case the rest of you were too young to remember the explosion that brought down the Oklahoma Federal Building, 168 people died that day. Unfortunately, most were moms and dads that had their kids with them." He paused, then said, "And guess what? That particular incident so frightened San Francisco's city fathers, it only took them *all of the next fifteen years* to finally decide to put up safety barriers a hundred yards from the building where we now stood."

"Geez, thanks for sharing," I said, patting him on the back. "I feel so much better now."

"Yeah, right!" Navarro replied with a grin. "And, hey ... speaking of sharing, remember that Mexican gangbanger you arrested a day or two ago?"

"You mean that Gallegos punk?"

"Yep. That be him, Mac. He's dead. Got himself kited!"

"Kited?" I paused, then said, "You're kidding me, right?"

"I'm guessing it's gotta have something to do with you and your friend here," Murray said, pointing to Nav and me just as our DEA escorts arrived. "What we're hearing is this Gallegos dude didn't fulfill a jail contract that had been given him. That's a *no-no* in his world." Pointing to me, he said, "Hate to tell you this, my friend, but you've got some powerful enemies for being so new in town."

# CHAPTER 31



Less than an hour after the National Guard escorted Navarro and Mac into Gilardi's office, Victor Serna, Diego Velasquez, and Rinaldo Ruiz were settling into the *Casa Moraga's* large living room in Borrego Springs.

"Thank God for Borrego Springs, eh, Rinaldo? How long have you owned it?"

"I purchased the land in the early two-thousands," Ruiz replied. "One hundred acres. It's been good to both me ... and us, eh?"

"And don't forget," Serna replied, "it was you who kicked me in the butt to get my okay to buy this land ... and for next to nothing, too. Now, with the buildout of the Hacienda and fourteen rooms for our closest friends, it's worth what? Close to five or six million dollars?"

"At least," said Ruiz. "And from my standpoint, it's the

remoteness and the hospitable nature of the surrounding topography that makes this the perfect spot for us to either relax and/or conduct business."

"Couldn't agree more," Serna said. "No one pays much attention anymore to the fact that we can actually do business on this side of the border."

Ruiz smiled to himself. It had taken a number of years for him to convince Serna that this land would be a great purchase. The day Serna gave him the thumbs-up, Ruiz purchased the original acreage under a shell corporation owned by his aunt. In order not to draw attention to the site, Ruiz took several years constructing what turned out to be an eight thousand square foot, ten-bedroom, ten-bath, hacienda, complete with a ten-bed dormitory for Serna's bodyguards. A seven-foot wall of sand-colored plaster concealed the reinforced steel core surrounding the hacienda. Serna ended up christening the site *Casa Moraga* in honor of Gabriel Moraga, a member of Juan Bautista de Anza's expedition.

To solidify the anonymity Serna and Velasquez required, Ruiz promised the owner of a small airport six miles to their north a yearly stipend of $20,000 to allow Serna and assorted friends to fly in and out of the compound at their leisure. Along with his financial generosity, Ruiz also offered the owner of the airport another kind of stipend— if the owner ever mentioned the name Serna to anyone outside of Ruiz's immediate circle, he would be immediately killed along with his family. It was an offer the airport's owner couldn't refuse.

～

THE GOLD CLOCK on the mantel said it was three minutes to eight. Sinking back in his chair, Serna silently looked west at the Laguna Mountains that protected Borrego Springs from the marine influence of the Pacific Ocean seventy miles to the west. For some reason, Serna's mood had changed. While Ruiz was used to his mood changes, this one caught him by surprise.

"I've been thinking," Serna said. "Isn't it your job to locate and recruit local talent?" He paused, then said, "It's obvious to me you don't have enough men to take care of business here. And worse, the ones you already have are proving not to be very reliable." He paused again. Ruiz took a deep breath, knowing what was coming next. "I'll give you kudos for killing that old man, McArthur," Serna said. "But his kid? Come on! Why is his kid still alive and kicking? How come he wasn't part of the original package?"

Serna went silent for a minute before saying, "Tell me … how hard could it have been to kill McArthur's kid?" He paused to light another cigar. "Our organization is starting to look foolish, Rinaldo. The people on this side of the border will need a reminder of the danger awaiting them if they ever cross us." He took a sip of his drink, then looked at Ruiz. "Do you have any suggestions as to how we can recover?"

"First of all, Victor, allow me to say I'm sorry if you think I've let you down. Nothing is further from the truth." From the very beginning of their relationship, Rinaldo used an old, and surprisingly effective, ploy to keep Serna's fiery nature in check. "You are my oldest and best friend," he said, "and we've been through many, many good times together, and there is nothing to stop us from making those times even better." He paused, then asked Serna if he had heard the latest news.

"Of course not," Serna responded. "I've been so absorbed in our own business that I can't pay much attention to other people's business." He paused, then said, "Okay, what's happening in the rest of the world that I should know about?"

"Well, there's been what the newspapers are calling a *terrorist attack* in Northern California. So far, it's been pretty much contained to the San Francisco Bay Area, but it's starting to spread quickly. At least that's what the press is saying."

"Terrorist attack? ¡Mierda!" Serna cursed. "How can that be? None of *our* people have ordered a *terrorist* attack! Somebody is off the reservation, my friend, and we've got to find out who. This has got to stop, Rinaldo."

"Couldn't agree more, my friend," Rinaldo replied. "The word is that it's an Al Qaeda thing."

"How come that information hasn't been transmitted to us? To me?" Serna said, angrily pounding the table. "Hezbollah certainly would have told us!" His voice rose in anger once again. "I let them use our courier systems into the United States, and this is how they repay me? Mark my words, Rinaldo, heads will roll. They don't respect us anymore. But by the time I'm through with them, they'll either do what I tell them, or I'll have their children's heads cut off."

# CHAPTER 32



Navarro and I were escorted to the private offices of what Gilardi called Task Force 64. "Thanks for coming, gentlemen. Have a seat." Turning to Navarro, he said, "I haven't had the pleasure of meeting you. I understand you bring law enforcement credentials to Ken's new agency."

"That I do," replied Navarro. "And thanks for inviting me."

"You and Mac are welcome here any time," Gilardi replied. "Allow me to fill you in on where we are to date." He clasped his hands together and rested them on the table in front of him. "First, as you can imagine, ever since Homeland Security raised its fentanyl threat level to *Imminent,* my office has been deluged with phone calls—everything from federal and state agencies to what seems to be every news outlet on the planet. So, if I have to interrupt our conversation periodically, you'll understand why."

"No problem," I said. "We live in that world, also."

"As of three this morning *California time*, the Governor, in conjunction with Homeland Security, activated California's Emergency Preparedness Center so other Governors nationwide could get the latest news and information on the dangers posed by the new drugs, especially fentanyl. And while I was at it, I insisted fentanyl be classified as a *Weapon of Terror* in order to highlight the seriousness of what's occurring on our streets.

"I also made mention of who to contact, if they, or anyone under our auspices, fell ill. Implicit in our activation is whoever knows who's behind these attacks is duty bound to tell us. Our Governor has, thank goodness, instructed all citizens in the San Francisco Bay Area, which for a time was the epicenter of this attack, to shelter in place. The City's law enforcement departments, along with the National Guard, will try to keep everyone off the streets until they determine how fentanyl, along with its companion drugs, are being distributed."

The phone on Gilardi's desk rang. He held up his hand for quiet as he took the call. A few minutes later, he hung up. "That was Homeland Security calling with an update," he said. "Four hundred and fifty-nine deaths so far in California." He paused, then pounded on the table. "And rising, for God's sake. Reports are now filtering in from Nevada, Arizona, Oregon, and Washington State. Bad stuff, man."

"Has any group claimed responsibility yet?" I asked.

"No," Gilardi replied, "but where I come from, this has all the earmarks of an Al Qaeda operation. No entity I know of could conduct something this big. I'm absolutely positive that we'll be getting a communiqué from them soon."

"An attack using fentanyl?" I exclaimed, shaking my head. "Unbelievable! As a SEAL Team, we were trained on what to do if attacked by chemicals like Sarin, or Tabun, or Phosgene. Those were ones we thought the douchebags would use if they decided to come after us chemically."

"Exactly," Gilardi replied. "The thinking was that a biological attack would be far too complicated for those idiots to manipulate. Precisely the reason the people who should have known better never considered something like fentanyl. They honestly never thought it was that powerful."

"I hear you," I said. "I was personally told fentanyl was too old-school for sophisticated players like Al Qaeda. They were either just flat-out wrong ... or were trying to steer us away from that stuff. The question now is ... what to do about it?"

"The first thing we're going to do," Gilardi said, "is set up a command center in the next room. That way, data will be current all day and night within five-minute intervals. I'd like you and Navarro to give us a fresh pair of eyes. Tell us what you see. Maybe together, we can actually catch these SOBs with their pants down."

"Both Nav and I had some experience with fentanyl a year or so ago," I replied, "but certainly not as much as you guys have had lately. In fact, before fentanyl became such a popular commodity, no supposedly *sophisticated* agent treated the drug with much respect." I paused, then said, "The world soon learned."

Gilardi responded with a chuckle. "And as long as we're going to be working together ... please call me Bill, okay?" Both Navarro and I acknowledged him with a nod. "You're also invited to a seminar on *everything-you-ever-wanted-to-know-*

*about-fentanyl.* It's mostly for the local police departments but will also be a big help to all of us. If nothing else, you'll get to meet our team. We'll convene at 10:00 a.m. sharp. It would be good to have you there with us."

"Thanks for the invite," I said. "Nav and I could use a fentanyl refresher course."

# CHAPTER 33

TASK FORCE 64, FRIDAY 9:00 A.M.

We entered the conference room and found a seat. Dr. Leslie Coombs, head of the Infectious Disease Department at the University of California in Berkeley, had already been introduced and was standing at the podium ready to tell us all about fentanyl.

Coombs was a tall, angular woman in her fifties whose gray hair was pulled back behind her head and kept in place with a blue, dolphin-shaped barrette. Behind the half-glasses that were perched precariously on her nose were eyes that told the story of harried days and sleepless nights.

"I'll try to make this short and sweet," she began. "I've been up most of the night looking at the data surrounding the opioid *fentanyl*. As most of you already know, fentanyl was used in the old days as a powerful pain reliever. How powerful you ask? Well, try one hundred percent more powerful than morphine."

She cleared her throat, moved some papers around on the podium, then looked out into the audience. "Historically, fentanyl has been around since the early '70s. By the late '70s and early '80s, however, an illicit form of fentanyl became available on the street." She paused, then added, "as early as 2007, the DEA had identified over 1,000 deaths associated with illegally manufactured, non-pharmaceutical fentanyl."

"Dr. Coombs?" a fellow from the back asked. "Forgive me. My name is Michael Kim. I just got here and hope you haven't already answered my question. I read somewhere that if you caught the fentanyl drug early enough and treated it with massive doses of antibiotics, it wasn't all that deadly. Is that correct?"

"An excellent question," replied Coombs. "We are trying to keep up with the ways fentanyl is being mixed with other drugs. The problem facing us is that fentanyl itself is an extraordinarily powerful man-made drug that can be, and is, mixed with virtually every other drug in creation to make new drugs. As we speak, there's a fentanyl coming out of China that's considered the most dangerous drug ever produced. Its high potency is especially dangerous as it transports the user from extreme alertness to extreme drowsiness, and from there to overwhelming respiratory confusion ... and then death.

"The lucky ones will have severe breathing problems, then go into shock. About half of them will die. So, the answer to your question is ... fentanyl is extraordinarily lethal, and most of the people who use it will end up dying from it."

Dr. Coombs answered another six questions from the crowd ... and then scheduled herself a fifteen-minute break.

Taking advantage of the free time, Navarro and I walked back to the command center with Gilardi, where he passed us off to Agent Jackson who opened a computer terminal and booted it up for us.

"I'm going to show you a film so you can get an idea about how fast things are moving here," Jackson said as he fiddled with the machine's mouse. "This was the data we had as of this morning at 5:30 a.m. Remember, what I'm showing you now is almost one hundred percent fentanyl data from Northern California. You guys ready to go?"

Navarro and I both nodded. Jackson dimmed the lights and the screen came alive.

Fentanyl Poisonings: Friday, 5:30 a.m.

Reported Cases: 448

Reported Deaths: 213

"Now take a look at this," Jackson said, bringing up the next slide. "This is the newest data as of five minutes ago."

Fentanyl Poisonings: Friday 8:00 a.m.

Reported Cases: 1923

Reported Deaths: 778

Geographical Distribution of Reported Deaths as of Friday, 8:30 a.m.

Reported Deaths from Fentanyl Poisonings:

243 deaths in California's Penal System;

135 deaths in the City of San Francisco;

106 deaths in the City of San Jose;

[Reported deaths in the Los Angeles area are on hold.]

378 deaths reported in San Diego;

105 deaths reported in Washington State.

"That's it," Jackson said with a shake of his head. "Looks like it's gonna be a bad day after all." Turning to Navarro and me, he said, "Don't you find it curious that even in this short amount of time, we're getting death reports from not only California, Nevada, Oregon, and Washington State, but now from Arizona, for God's sake ... and even Idaho. How the heck did all that happen?"

"I've absolutely no idea," Navarro responded. "Whoever is spreading this would have had no way to cover so much ground in such little time. It simply doesn't compute."

"And let's not forget the Los Angeles stats that went offline more than thirty minutes ago," I said. "They haven't, as far as I can tell, been put back into our overall tally." I hesitated, then looked over at Navarro. "Nav's right," I said. "The big mystery in all this is how can an Al Qaeda cell of two or three people, or even ten people, for that matter, do this much damage over such a large area in such a short amount of time?" I paused, then said, "The answer is *they can't*. And, to make all this more complicated, our group is being called back to San Diego."

Jackson started to reply when his cell phone interrupted. "Sorry about that, gentlemen," he said as he hung up and started to escort us out of his office. "You'll have to come with me. The President is about to tell us what is really going on. We can finish our conversation later."

We followed Jackson back to Gilardi's office. His Task

Force 64 members were already seated around a big-screen television where the President had been carrying on a news conference for a little over twenty-five minutes. His goal was to reassure the nation that terrorists who spread fentanyl and other dangerous drugs will not only be caught, they'll be subject to swift American justice. He told the nation that most of what is known about the spread of fentanyl in the United States points to the Mexican cartels. He paused, then said that if his investigation finds that the United States is being attacked by a state-sponsored entity, he would authorize an immediate military strike, or strikes, against the offending nation state, or states.

Applause and fist bumps from the Task Force 64 group greeted the conclusion of the President's address. It took Agent Jackson another twenty minutes to herd the whole group back to their command center.

# CHAPTER 34



Just as Navarro and I sat down in Gilardi's office, my phone chirped. I went out into the hallway so as not to disrupt anyone. It was Admiral Moore calling from his plane, presently about hour and a half east of San Diego. "We just crossed into Arizona," he said with no preamble, "and found out both Victor Serna and his partner, Diego Velasquez, are staying with Ruiz at his *Casa* in Borrego Springs. I'm calling you so we can arrest all three of those dirtbags in one fell swoop."

"That's great news, Sir," I said. "I'll get my people ready. Will leave Shira here with Navarro. Any chance your name could get the rest of us a flight to Coronado ... say at eleven or thereabouts?"

"No problem. I'll get it done. I'm coming in from the East,

so my plane will beat the one you are on by about twenty minutes ... give or take."

"Perfect," I said. "You can take us with you to Coronado."

Once airborne, I remembered we were going to need someone who carried a federal badge in order to arrest both Serna and Velasquez while still on American soil. I called Gilardi to see if it would be possible for him to meet us in Borrego Springs. He told me he was way too busy and only had one spare agent, a fellow named Torres. He gave me Torres's phone number and told me that he'd have all the credentials he'd need to arrest Serna and Velasquez. Told me it was the best he could do on such short notice.

I was going to end up stashing Torres on the helo with us no matter what, but truth be told, I was more focused on getting the six of us on the ground in front of Ruiz's private Casa in early afternoon than the six *plus one* we'd get from having Agent Torres riding with us.

THE CALL CAME at 11:15 a.m. on one of the twenty-two burner phones Rinaldo Ruiz kept at the Casa. He called them his "phones for all occasions."

"The Feds know that both Serna and Velasquez are spending time with you at the Casa," the voice said. "Trust me ... you've got to get them both out of there quickly, or they won't be leaving ... ever!"

"How do you know this?"

"You've made too many mistakes, Rinaldo ... that's how I

know. The Americans are, at this very moment, selectively monitoring your phone calls. From now on, be careful who you are speaking to on the phone."

"I'll sue the United States government," Rinaldo spat. "They have no right to monitor my phone. I'm a citizen of the United States. I'm an attorney. There's such a thing as attorney-client privilege in this country."

"Yeah, right," the voice *hissed* derisively. "The Feds will have a drone over your Casa within the next three hours, maybe less. Get Serna and Velasquez out of there now ... and by car. The Feds already have the air corridors covered."

"Consider it done," Rinaldo said, none too cheerfully.

"For the information I just gave you, we're asking a *quid pro quo*. We've asked this of you at least twice before, Mr. Ruiz, and you failed us both times. This time, failing is not an option." There was a long pause, then, "Do you understand what I'm telling you?"

Ruiz thought of his recent talk with Serna about being jinxed. He sighed. "Yes, I understand. Whatever you want me to do ... it will be done."

"We've sent you a written plan that will guide you in getting Serna and his friend out of the country. You'll have it in your hands within the next five minutes. Follow it step-by-step with no deviations. Do you understand? We'll have our people nearby to make sure you do exactly as we tell you."

"I understand," Ruiz said, seething under their yolk of superiority.

"We hope so. Now get both of your guests out of there. I'll call back in ten minutes to make sure you've put the plan into action. And by the way, have you ever met the Navy SEAL Ken McArthur? Though he goes by Mac."

"Never."

"You're about to in less than an hour," the voice said. "Unless you get your sorry butt in gear right away, this McArthur fellow will be putting Serna and his bodyguard in a jail cell right next to yours."

# CHAPTER 35



The six of us walked into the Admiral's office at 1:05 p.m. carrying our gear. Looking tired from his cross-country flight, the Admiral leaned back in his chair and waited until we were all seated. Pointing to the storage trunk in the corner, he said, "Don't know what you brought for clothes, but since I'm in the habit of knowing the kind of outfits you like, I took the liberty of supplying them. By the time we get to Borrego Springs, you'll be at least loaded for bear ... each of you will be carrying an MP7 with three forty-round clips. The only way you'll be outgunned is if they have a small army out there waiting for us ... which they don't."

"We're thinking you'd prefer us take Serna and whoever he has with him, as prisoners. Am I right?"

"Absolutely! If nothing else, it would sell better to the press if we captured him and his cronies. It's my hope they won't force us into a battle."

"Speaking of battle, Sir, I just received a call from Agent Torres. Says he'll be landing here with his gear in ten minutes."

"Tell him he's gonna miss lunch, but we'll still treat him nicely."

AFTER GETTING Agent Torres in the copter with some leftover food, we took off. Our group was locked and loaded and sitting in an AH6 Little Bird on the way to Ruiz's Casa. "Okay, listen up, people," Moore shouted over the rotor blades. "We've got a fifty-minute flight in front of us. In case you didn't get the agenda, we are here to capture two of the most wanted men in our hemisphere. Together, they're responsible for supplying about seventy percent of the fentanyl drug our people ingest. In his speech, the President mentioned how many of our youth have died so far by using fentanyl. I forget the exact numbers, but it's somewhere north of six thousand."

"Six thousand?" I muttered aloud.

"At the very least," Moore responded. "Normally an attack of this nature would bring about a military response, but because of our historic closeness to Mexico, the President requested, and received, a meeting with Mexico's President tomorrow afternoon.

"And where does that leave us, Admiral?" I asked.

"Same place as we are now, Mac. The President is hedging his bets publicly because he knows he's going to be asked to respond in ways that are demonstrably different than before."

Moore took a sip from his water bottle, placed it on the seat to his front, and extended his palms upward. "We're after the big cats, and every now and again some of those *cats* have dared to have a vacation of sorts on our side of the border." He smiled and said, "Just recently, we were told that two of those Mexican *cats* are vacationing in Borrego Springs. Today is going to turn out to be a special day, gentlemen. We're actually going to arrest the three of them for daring to be so bold." He chuckled, then said, "How 'bout we take a peek at our target?"

He sat and fiddled with his laptop until he brought up a picture of a Mexican-style hacienda. "This is the Casa Moraga," he said. "Just so there are no surprises, I wanted to give you a picture of the layout before we land."

"I'll be darned," Wolfman exclaimed. "You call that a Casa? Man, this guy's compound looks more like an army base."

"The locals have been telling us over the past several years that there's been considerable activity here," Moore replied. "Big parties; expensive cars coming and going; loads of armed men patrolling the perimeter. Gunfire. And, not surprising, some deaths!"

"And none of us were invited?" FT said, shaking his head. "How very rude of them."

Moore smiled. "So true, FT, so true. But as of this moment, we've reason to believe there are only three people in the Casa: Rinaldo Ruiz, who actually owns the place; his good buddy from childhood, Victor Serna; and an old running mate of both of them ... a guy named Diego Velasquez."

"You got a drone on them?" I asked.

"Yes. For the past twenty-five minutes," Moore replied.

"Unfortunately, we're getting only one heat signature from the ground. Hopefully, that *one* will belong to Serna."

"How'd you find out that Serna was in Borrego?" Delgado asked.

"He's a hard nut to crack, but we knew Ruiz lived in La Jolla, so I asked our SIGINT friends to zero in on him. We needed to get him back on radar, anyway. It took us a few days, but it produced dividends immediately. Earlier today, for example, they cracked a call Ruiz received last Thursday from Serna. Both, along with old friend Diego Velasquez, were making plans to meet up at the Casa, and they did exactly that. If everything had gone right today, you'd actually have had a chance to meet all three of them up close and personal."

With Moore's assistance, we finalized what we hoped would be our plan of attack. "The Bird will land right in the middle of the Casa's courtyard," he told us. "From there, we'll follow SEAL procedures to affect a takedown in a hostile environment."

"Just so we're clear ... are we there to capture or eliminate?" I asked.

"Like I told all of you," Moore said, "you are here to respond to whatever is necessary for us to maintain *our* safety and the safety of *our* crew." He paused, then said, "Unfortunately, while it looks more and more like our banditos have vanished, we'll still use SEAL procedures for our own safety." He looked up. "Y'all ready to go?" There was silence. "Then, gentlemen," Moore said, "it's showtime!"

# CHAPTER 36



Little Bird got airborne in San Diego just as Victor Serna and Diego Velasquez parked their car in the garage of a small house on Andrade Avenue in Calexico, California.

"An hour and a half, old friend," Diego said with grin and a satisfied nod. "We actually shaved three minutes off our best time."

"Three minutes? Imagine that," Serna said, eyebrows elevated. "Are you pushing on me to increase your already bloated salary, Diego?"

"I can only hope, Patrón," Diego said with a smile. "I can only hope."

Before they got out, Serna turned and placed his hand on Velasquez's shoulder. Narrowing his eyes, he said quietly, "Diego, I know I've mentioned this before, but I'm very, very serious about you not calling me Patrón. I know you use it both in respect and in jest, but you, me and Rinaldo have been friends for too long for you to even pretend to be my servant. Not even in jest. Do you understand what I'm saying to you?" Serna remained silent until he saw Diego's head nod from the front seat. "Good. Let's not forget that, okay?" He opened his water bottle, took a long drink, then passed it forward. "Finish it, my friend."

The garage door had been closed for ten minutes before Serna and Velasquez exited the vehicle. Having witnessed the sloppiness of other cartels, the waiting was a safety measure they had adopted a few years earlier to detect the *wrong eyes* in their place of business. Using retinal and facial recognition software to gain access to the tunnel, they walked exactly 400 meters before they came to the light rail system that would deposit them in Mexicali.

"Times have certainly changed, eh, Victor? Every time we travel like this from Mexico to California, I can't help but remember the first grocery store we opened in Guadalajara. Remember that one? Our first dip into money laundering?"

"How could I forget? Those were suffocating times," Serna said, shaking his head at the remembrance. "Almost nine years ago now, Diego. Can you believe it?" He snorted. "The only memory I have of that house was how small it was."

"That's my memory, also," Diego said. "Since I'd been stuck in jail for a few years, I had absolutely no experience in how quickly these homes filled up with our money." He laughed. "Remember how you commissioned that architect to come up with a secret addition to the house so you could expand without having to move?" He shook his head from side-to-side, sighing heavily. "That idiot thought he could fool us by building a house so small that we'd soon have to expand. Making him a little richer and us a little poorer."

Serna took another sip of water from the bottle. "If I remember correctly, that poor man lost his life in a hit-and-run accident within a week after building that tiny, tiny house and expecting us to live in it." He smiled and shook his head. "They never learn, do they, Diego? They just never learn."

Twenty minutes later, the two of them settled into an Escalade that had been waiting to drive them two hours to San Felipe. "Can you believe the garbage spouting from the mouth of that gringo?" Serna said. "I simply can't listen anymore." He reached forward and changed the channel. He could already feel the inside of his body contracting. That darn dream! It was driving him insane. He had to tell Rinaldo about it. He would know what to do.

SERNA AND VELASQUEZ had been in Mexican territory for over two hours before Little Bird flared and dropped into the courtyard of the Casa Moraga. The squad fanned out and even though there were no hostiles in front of them, they set up a defensive perimeter. Into that vacant perimeter walked Rinaldo Ruiz.

"What is the meaning of this?" he demanded. "Who do you think you are attacking my home like this?"

I made a hand gesture for the men to spread out and scour

the premises. Turning to Ruiz, I said, "My name is Ken McArthur."

"I know who you are, Mr. McArthur. My name is Rinaldo Ruiz."

"And I know who you are also, Mr. Ruiz. You're the man whose friend murdered my father."

That stopped Ruiz for a few beats before he gathered his composure. "Ah, yes," he said. "Regrettable! But don't feel so privileged. Victor Serna has killed many fathers. If I were you, I'd be worried more about your own life than that of your deceased father. The only thing you can do for him now is to join him. My advice to you is to forget Señor Serna."

I swallowed an urge to shove the barrel of my rifle down his throat. "We'll see, Mr. Ruiz. We'll see."

"Dry hole," I told Moore after our crew had searched the hacienda. "Ruiz swears that Serna and Velasquez have never been to the Hacienda. He's making noises about suing us for profiling him because he's Mexican."

"Throw enough stuff against the wall and look what happens," Moore said with a laugh. "Hey, why not have Ruiz talk to Agent Torres? Mexican to Mexican. That should quiet him down."

"It hasn't. He's with Torres now, and I can still hear him ranting and raving about taking us to court for violating attorney-client confidentiality laws. He contends we spied on him while he was talking to Victor Serna ... who, he says, is his client.

"Well, I'll at least give the guy credit. He's got cohones." I paused, then said, "Okay, let's wrap this up. It's a dry hole. But, on a more positive note, both Admiral Moore and Rear Admiral Vaughn will be waiting for us in the Blockhouse in less than an hour."

# CHAPTER 37



In ordinary business parlance, the Blockhouse would have been known as a *conference center*. It was, after all, a place where meetings were held in classroom-style rooms under one roof. While this Blockhouse had meeting rooms, no one at NSWC called it a conference center. It was a steel-encased, 4,000-square-foot structure built three stories underground. The place where you'd want to be if the country ever suffered a nuclear attack.

"Do you believe this?" Wolfman uttered to me as three armed guards escorted the six of us into the Blockhouse. "Where do these guys come up with the money to build a needless hunk of cement like this."

"You got me, Wolf," I said. "All I can say is ... let's hope all this is really necessary."

Our escorts led the six of us through a foot-thick steel door to an elevator that took us down three stories and deposited us outside a long row of what looked to be conference rooms. Another set of armed guards appeared and escorted us to the conference room where the two Admirals sat waiting.

We took seats around a large conference table. Open laptops sat plugged in at charging stations next to our seats. Four large flat-panel screens lined the opposite wall. In the front corner sat a printer.

"Look at all this hardware," I said.

"Must be where the big boys hang out, huh?" FT whispered to me as we took our seats.

"I guess we should be honored," I whispered back. "I'll bet not many of our pals even know this place exists, let alone been in it."

"Guess we're just the lucky few," he smirked.

Admiral Moore called the meeting to order and introduced Rear Admiral Roger Vaughn to the group. I'd heard of him before but never had the chance to meet him. He was a short man built like a multi-purpose bowling ball—big round arms, big round legs, big round chest, and big round hips. He had a ruddy complexion, and short whitish hair that lay in patches across the top of his head. He was a SEAL, and, within that community, was known as a no-nonsense commander, a stand-up guy who, it just so happened, was also the commander of the Advanced Force Operations for the Joint Special Operations Command. AFO, as it's known, has the responsibility of targeting all clandestine operations undertaken by Special Ops troops, as well as those Special Operators who work off-book. It soon became clear to us that in the past twenty-four hours, Red Squadron had been re-classified as *off-book*.

"Please sit," Vaughn said, as he shuffled through the papers in front of him. "The President, as I'm sure you've already heard, has *not,* as of yet, signed off on any ground operations in Mexico, especially those conducted by Special Op units of the United States military. He has permitted us, however, through back channels, to degrade the cartel leadership as we see fit."

"Excuse the interruption, Sir," I said, "but what does *as we see fit* mean in the real world?"

"*As we see fit* means the Admiral, and/or myself, can activate Special Forces troops like you people to complete clandestine missions anytime and anywhere." He paused, then said, "Is that well enough explained?"

"Couldn't be any clearer, Sir," I said with a smile and nod of my head. "But just one thing ... we happen to be short one of our comrades."

"Won't make any difference in our plan one way or the other, Mac," Vaughn said. "We're talking here about infiltrating just two of you into Mexico to free a woman of interest. Her code name is La Voz – *The Voice.* We need to get her out before either Serna or Velasquez finds out where she is currently hiding ... and kill her."

"Who recruited her?" Delgado asked.

"Mac's father did," Vaughn replied. "Both Serna and Velasquez put together a scheme making it virtually impossible to compromise her whereabouts. It combined a sophisticated encryption system with a software program initially designed by the US Navy to protect highly sensitive data transfers used by the military."

"But when dealing with Serna," he continued, "the first thing we had to get used to was realizing he's absolutely paranoid about his own safety. For him it makes perfect sense. He's not only watching for those *we* send after him, but also for how many other cartel 'brethren' will be on the lookout to grab his territory. And that's to say nothing of people in his own cartel wanting to move up. Victor Serna learned a lot about those minefields when he first went into business. It's those minefields that *have* made him extraordinarily paranoid."

"What about communication?" I asked. "Is SIGINT on him?"

"They tell me he's really hard to track," Moore replied, "but thanks to this *La Voz* woman for converting to our side, she's made our task infinitely easier. Just as an example ... for the last six months, we got to read every message Serna sent through La Voz. Unfortunately, it turned out neither Serna nor Velasquez used La Voz as a cutout in any of their preparations to kill your father. Instead, it was the DEA in Oakland who got the message from one of *their* plants, a fellow code-named Munoz. And he, poor man, was caught trying to deliver that message to the people aboard that plane. Serna butchered that dude."

"Where is this La Voz woman now?" Delgado asked.

"In a small town in Chihuahua named Batopilas," Vaughn said. "We had her go to ground, hoping Serna wouldn't find her before we could send a rescue team for her." Turning to Moore, Vaughn said, "We need to launch that mission immediately if we are to get her out alive. The what, why, and how is up to the Admiral here."

"Well, the *why* is the easy part," Moore said. "First, since La

Voz was one of Serna's favorite women, she just happens to know more about him than maybe any living person on the planet ... making her invaluable to us. Second, she's now gone to ground in an effort to escape him. Both Serna and Velasquez have tentacles in every corner of Mexico. If he doesn't know where she is by now, he will know within a very short amount of time. Then she'll be tortured and killed. Serna has already murdered half of her family. Let me tell you ... for what this woman has sacrificed, we owe her big time." He paused and looked over at me. "In my view, Mac, this is a mission absolutely crafted for Red Squadron. We've actually set up an extraction zone for you. Please look at the computers in front of you."

All eyes focused on the screens as they came to life.

"Batopilas is a village more than a town. Population is a little under a thousand people, including children. It lies in the hills about 300 miles northeast of Culiacan. At one time, Serna had a base of operations there. He abandoned it two or three years ago."

Moore paused, then said, "I'm thinking two operators can handle this mission. In my view, Mac should be one since La Voz knew his father and would be trustful of him. And as you all know, in these kinds of scenarios, trust can be essential."

"If it has to do with rescuing a female, Mac knows I'm his guy," Delgado said, getting a chuckle from everybody in the room.

"I'll have a private jet at North Island at 0500 tomorrow. You'll be in Parral by midmorning."

"Fine by me," I replied. "Vinnie? You up for it?"

"Of course, Bro. Let's do it."

"The jet will take you to Parral, a city about 150 miles east of Batopilas. Because both locales are in the mountains, I've asked officers I know at the Mexican Naval Infantry base in Hermosillo to get you a driver. They're sending a young Marine named Emilio Hernandez to pick you up in Parral. He'll drive you both to and from Batopilas. He knows exactly where to pick up our lady friend."

"Where do you have us staying tonight?" I asked.

"Here, of course. You two should have La Voz back to us by first light. And if you want to expand your military armaments before you go, you have my permission."

# CHAPTER 38



Vinnie and I made our connection with Emilio Hernandez in Parrel. He was a bear of a man, not what you'd imagine as a Mexican Naval Infantry guy. He stood well over six feet tall and had to go at least two-twenty. When he volunteered to drive, I looked over at Vinnie who simply shrugged. "Be our guest," I said.

The road was narrow and twisty as it dropped through the mountain passes of the Sierra Madres from Parral's 5300-foot elevation to Batopilas' 1500. Both Vinnie and I noticed Hernandez seemed wary, and it showed in his attitude.

"This is bandit country," he said. "Very dangerous."

"We thrive on *dangerous*," Delgado said with a chuckle. "And either of us can drive if you want to rest,"

"No, Señor. It's not the road that makes me nervous." He

drove another mile or so before he pulled off to the side of the road and extracted a black cloth from his back pocket. He tied it, handkerchief style, over his nose and mouth. "When we do these kinds of missions," he said, "we usually wear some kind of facial covering. We're dealing here with the cartels. Make no mistake … these people are butchers. First, they come after your families." He paused, then said, "And once they have finished with them, they come after you."

"You're doing the right thing, Emilio," I said. "People like you have to stand up if the world is going to rid itself of the cartel curse once and for all."

"I'm a soldier, Señor. And, like my comrades, I have to be careful." He let the thought sit a moment, then said, "Lillianna Martinez, for example. They killed her family. Now they're after her. We have to protect her."

"Understood," I said. "Tell us about her."

"La Voz?" Hernandez asked. "I thought you knew."

"We knew the name *La Voz* but never heard her real name until this very minute. What's her story?"

"At one time, Señor, she was Victor Serna's girlfriend. It turned out he didn't treat her as she had hoped, so she turned on him. It was then that she contacted us."

"Hell hath no fury, huh?" Delgado replied with a laugh. "I know because I've been there, done that."

"Both Serna and Velasquez somehow found out she was working for the gringos," Hernandez said. "A man named Walter McArthur."

"He was my father," I said. "Victor Serna murdered him."

"Oh, I'm terribly sorry, my friend," Hernandez replied.

"He's done the same to many of our families." He rolled down the window and spit. "¡Mierda! He came after Lillianna Martinez, too. Raided her house one night when he knew she wasn't home. Wanted her to know he was the *Ángel de la Muerta* and would be coming for her, too. But not that particular night. That particular night, he came after her family. His men butchered her grandmother, her father, and her cousin."

"How safe will she be here in this town?" asked Delgado.

"No matter who you are or where you are, Señor, no one is safe in Mexico ... period!" Hernandez answered. "Too many people are indebted to these, how you say ... *these butchers*."

"As good a saying as any," I replied.

"A man like Serna? He pretends to be Santa Claus. Everyone loves Santa Claus, right? If you're poor, he gives you money. Sick? He'll provide a plane to get you or your family to a hospital. And then he'll pay your doctor's bills. When your child gets baptized, he sends a gift. Do you need a well in your village? He wires money and hires workers. He's a hero to many, many people, Señor. They even write songs about him. Ballads are sung in coffee houses that praise him. *Narcocorridoes* they are called! What's never mentioned in the ballad is, if you don't do exactly what he tells you to do, he will butcher your entire family in front of you ... and then butcher you."

THE SUN HAD REACHED its zenith by the time the three of us arrived in Batopilas. We parked under a tree that had seen better days. The temperature gauge in the car told us it was over a hundred degrees outside. It seemed hotter.

"Does it ever cool down here?" Vinnie asked, his shirt plastered to his upper body, even though the car's air-conditioning was blowing full blast.

"Maybe to thirty-six," Hernandez answered with a smile. "Or as you gringos would say, *ninety-eight*."

"And where exactly are we supposed to meet Señorita Martinez?" I asked. "The quicker we can get to her, the quicker we can get her out."

"Amen to that," replied Vinnie. "But to be safe, let's wait an hour or so before we make the rendezvous. If Emilio is right about Serna's reach, even this tiny village may have too many eyes."

"I'm right about Serna," Emilio said. "You'd be wise to be wary. My people told me we'd find Señorita Martinez on the other side of town, in a small cabin at the bottom of the barranca, near the river. When we get there, I'll pull us off the highway and hide the car in whatever brush is available. From there, the three of us will have just a short hike to where she's hiding."

"How far is a short hike?" Vinnie asked.

"No more than half a mile, Señor. She's taken up residence in an old pulqueria."

"And what exactly is a *pulqueria*?" Delgado asked.

"It's a tavern, Señor. These little towns used to be famous for making *pulque*—an alcoholic beverage made from the maguey plant. Maguey is plentiful in these mountains, and at one time each village had its own pulqueria. The richer ones had two or three. The government cracked down on the beverage ten to fifteen years ago. You can still make it, but it's illegal to sell it unless you're a government-approved tavern. *Government-approved* means they take most of your profit. But in these mountain villages? You can rest assured everyone living here still makes their own pulque."

"And the Señorita has taken up residence in one of those government-sponsored taverns?" I asked. "Doesn't sound too safe to me. Does it to you, Emilio?"

"It is safe," he answered. "At least … I hope so. The tavern we're talking about here has been intermittently open and closed for years. For the past few weeks, my friends tell me it's been open for a few hours a day."

Vinnie and I did as Emilio told us … we pulled out our ski masks and covered our faces. Making sure our MP7s were locked and loaded, the three of us began our slow walk toward the cabin.

"How many people, would you guess, are aware of this particular pulqueria?" Delgado asked.

"People who live in the area would know of its existence," Hernandez answered. "But the chances of anyone finding it open would be remote. My superiors told me La Voz has been here a week, and as far as we can tell, no one knows she's here. Batopilas is truly, Señor, the far end of the earth."

"You feeling a little uneasy about this?" I whispered to Vinnie.

"Being careful is all," Vinnie whispered back. "*Remote* can be a good thing, or it can be a *burial ground*. I think we should at least spread out as we walk this path. It's only 2:15. We have plenty of time."

Fifteen minutes later, we found ourselves within thirty

yards of the pulqueria. There was no light spilling out from the inside. *A good sign,* I thought, as Vinnie and I moved off the path and into the bordering brush.

"You speak the language, right?" I whispered to Hernandez. He nodded his head in the affirmative. "Good! So, when you get to the door, make sure your hands are out in front of you so La Voz can see you are not armed. Be sure you tell her who you are. We don't want her shooting you." Hernandez smiled but remained silent. "Vinnie and I will stay in the brush line. He'll circle to your left while I do the same on your right. Once she opens the door and we're sure it's safe, we'll break cover."

We moved out. Hernandez was already on the pulqueria's steps when Delgado looked over and saw a red laser dot flitting over Hernandez's back. "Emilio ..." was all he could yell before they heard a shot ring out. Hernandez stumbled forward a few steps, then crumpled on the porch. The echo hadn't yet died before we heard a woman scream from inside the house.

Delgado's warning to Hernandez had also given away his position, and within seconds bullets began to pepper the brush around him. There were two shooters. I instinctively knew that Vinnie would quietly crawl deeper into the brush to his left. The one who took out Hernandez was off to my right. He was the closest and therefore would be the first to die. While I circled around him, every wiggle or fidget Delgado made in the underbrush would hopefully elicit random gunfire which would allow me to do my thing in complete stealth mode. Both Vinnie and I now knew we were facing only two bandits ... and amateur ones at that. But we were taking nothing for granted. Both of us were acutely aware that amateurs with guns could kill you just as quickly as professionals with guns.

It took me the better part of five minutes to find shooter number one. He was lying prone on a slight rise about forty yards from the pulqueria, trying to pinpoint where I was hunkered down. I was inching to my right when another shot rang out. Closer to Delgado. His MP7 immediately answered with two quick bursts.

Delgado and I had been in situations just like this before. We both knew what to expect from each other. Vinnie's first burst was designed to fix the position of the shooter to his left and to keep him there while I eliminated the dude on the higher ground to my right. I toyed with the idea of stealthily sneaking up on the guy and slitting his throat, but the thirty-yard distance between us convinced me I didn't have the time nor the inclination. Instead, I went prone, raised up on my elbows and sighted in. My two-shot burst blew open the side of the shooter's head.

With the first gunman now down, it only took Delgado a few minutes to take out the second shooter who had stationed himself in the brush near the cabin's front door. I signaled to Vinnie to cautiously work his way toward the cabin. Once we both neared the front door walkway, I could make out the body of Emilio Hernandez. Most of his body had crumpled on the front porch. Not knowing whether another dude was in the cabin, both Vinnie and I slithered up to the side window. We lucked out. The entire house was a one-room cabin, and La Voz was now its only living inhabitant.

Vinnie kicked in the front door just in case there was a sleeper agent inside. There wasn't. Only La Voz! She was naked from the waist up and tied to a chair in the middle of the room. Even though she had been gagged, blood drooled from her mouth and her left eye was swollen shut. What looked like razor cuts on her left breast were sure signs her captors were going to slowly carve her up. Vinnie got a damp towel and began cleaning her wounds as I helped free her from the chair.

# CHAPTER 39



The two of us spent the next hour attending to her injuries. "Nothing really serious here," I said to her, though both Vinnie and I knew that plastic surgery would be a certainty in her future. More importantly, however, the three of us instinctively knew that getting back to civilization in one piece was not going to be easy.

"What're our options, Mac?" Vinnie asked. "You think we could take Hernandez's car back to Parral?"

"Not likely," I said. "It's a six-hour trip at the very least. I'm guessing both Serna and Velasquez now know we're in this village. If I'm correct, they'd also know which mountain pass we'd take to get to our friends. We'd be finished off before we got halfway down."

"Maybe Lillianna knows a place in this town where we could 'borrow' a satellite phone," said Vinnie. "I'm sorry to have to say this, but the only way I see the three of us making it out alive is if we can reach someone in the outside world who could come and get us." He turned to Lillianna. "Is there anyone in this town that you know and/or trust?"

"Unfortunately, no," Lillianna said in remarkably good English.

"I'm disgusted with myself for not packing a satellite phone," Vinnie said. "Are there landline telephones here?"

"Of course," Lillianna said. "The couple who owns the grocery store in this town have one. I saw the symbol on their door. As a rule, if there is one phone in a small town, there will be more."

"Are you well enough to help us find a phone?" I asked.

"Who will you call?"

"I'm thinking of officers in the United States Navy. In San Diego, California, to be exact."

"If we find a phone in this town, I'll make the call," she replied. "It won't work otherwise."

Delgado slid over next to me and whispered, "She's right, Mac. What if there's no one in this town that speaks passable English? She could be a big help to us trying to maneuver through the language barrier. Also, her known association with Serna might be a bonus. At least she'll know how to get past any inquisitive exchange operator."

"There will be questions," Martinez assured us. "And one more thing—we should walk to town. The clank or rattle of a car this time of day will only draw unwanted attention."

"Sounds good to me," Vinnie said.

"Me, too," I said. "But before we get into town, let's get

Emilio's body into his car. We're going to have to come back for him later."

It took us ten minutes to wedge Emilio into his car. The walk into town allowed us to check how many homes actually had telephone lines. I counted twelve.

"A wealthy community," Martinez said.

"Which house should we choose?" Vinnie asked.

"The second one," she said, pointing to a house a quarter mile away. "It's the most remote. Fewer people will hear their cries if they refuse to help."

"Okay. Here's what we have do," I said. "First thing is to peek in every window. If there are children in the house, we'll pass it by. And oh, by the way, can you handle a gun?"

Martinez smiled and nodded.

"I figured you were no stranger to firearms," I said. "Here's a pistol we took off one of Serna's men." I released the safety and handed the gun to Martinez. "Okay, remember ... we don't want to shoot anybody today. Too messy ... and way too noisy. But we do have to make people think we mean business. You understand what I'm saying, right?"

"I know what I'm doing," she replied as she instinctively worked the slide, making sure there was a round in the chamber. There was, so she switched on the safety. Vinnie and I were impressed enough to give her both a head nod and a thumbs-up.

The first two houses had two or three children. We passed them by. The third house had two bedrooms and a phone. Perfect for what we were looking for. I quietly opened the door leading to the living area, which featured a desk with a chair in one corner, and a large sofa upon which two people sat while watching a small television.

"Tell them we work for Serna," Delgado whispered.

"I don't need any coaching," she shot back.

"Well, then," Vinnie said, "let's just get it on!"

The frightened couple followed Martinez's every instruction, both in placing the call and then handing the phone back to her. Turned out it wasn't as easy to connect to the United States as we had hoped. Martinez fixed that by dropping Serna's name each time she encountered resistance. Problem solved. In what seemed like an eternity, Martinez handed me the phone. On the third ring, Moore answered.

"Admiral Sir? It's Mac. We're in Mexico and we need your help to get us out ... preferably alive."

# CHAPTER 40



I stayed on the line listening as Moore contacted his counterpart in the Special Forces unit of the Mexican Naval Infantry. Between the two of them, they came up with a plan not only to extricate us from Batopilas, but also to deliver Hernandez's body to his unit in the Mexican Navy.

As we were leaving the house, Martinez turned to the couple and invoked Serna's name while at the same time pulling her index finger across her throat. Message delivered!

"Okay, let's giddy-up," I said. Checking that our weapons were locked and loaded, we walked back to Hernandez's car and carefully carried his body to the clearing near the chapel. We settled in for what we knew would be a one-to-two-hour wait for the helicopters.

Lillianna Martinez sat on the ground next to Vinnie and me. "Are you going after him?" she asked.

"You mean Serna?" She nodded. I hesitated a minute, then said, "In case you didn't know, Serna murdered my father. So, the answer is yes. I *am* going after him. It's payback time." I leaned back against a tree stump. "That's one of the reasons we came to get you. We heard you knew him well and could help us find him."

"I lived with him for two years," she said. "I know his likes and dislikes. His habits." She paused, then said, "I also know from personal experience what a hideous monster he can be." She snorted a contemptuous laugh.

"Help me here if you can," I said. "Why does a guy like Serna, who's made millions and millions of dollars in the drug trade, act as if he's scared to death by his own shadow? Except for his yacht, the M-40, I hear he lives a frugal and solitary life."

"Two or three years ago, that would've been true," she said. "But new competitors have entered the trade in the past few years. The thought now is it's better to live ten or fifteen spectacular years in the trades and then be killed by a rival gang, than living a lifetime in the trades and never stepping foot out of their mansions. The young ones now go to the nightclubs in their Porsches and Lamborghinis ... some even in Bentleys, for goodness' sake. They even post pictures of themselves on social media. As a consequence of their not taking care of business, some of the younger ones are no longer among the living."

"And you think that will happen to Serna?" I asked.

"If he's not careful," she said, blotting her forehead with a wet handkerchief. "Don't misunderstand me! He's still a monster, but not like he used to be."

We all turned our heads to the faint whir of a helicopter approaching. I gave everyone a thumbs-up. "You said you knew

Victor Serna's idiosyncrasies. Care to share them with me? I'm going to be up close and personal with him any day now."

"Well, for one, he loves gourmet food. A year or so ago he started asking me to find the most elegant restaurants in Mexico. It didn't matter to him where they were located. If he found a five-star restaurant worthy of him, he would take his helicopter, land on the restaurant's property, send in his bodyguards to confiscate all cell phones, and then spend the next two or three hours eating and drinking. He would order the most expensive items on the menu, thank the other diners for being so patient, pick up their tabs and leave." She smiled, then said, "Always to applause, by the way." She hesitated as we all looked skyward to follow the helicopter as it circled us on its final approach.

"It used to be random," she said, as we picked up our gear. "But now, he's got a routine. He spends most of his time between Culiacan, Cabo San Lucas, and his yacht, which is berthed a wee-bit south in Colima. He distributes his women between those three places. You know what his biggest expense is these days? Most people would guess his yacht or the ten helicopters he has access to. But I can tell you for certain it's neither. His biggest expense is Viagra."

# CHAPTER 41

NORTH ISLAND, EARLY EVENING

Stinger, Wolfman, and FT were waiting on the tarmac as Vinnie, Lilliana Martinez, and I deplaned on North Island. Once we cleared the aircraft, Stinger took me by my arm and pulled me close. "We've got a big problem, Mac," he whispered, "Shira Lipkin has gone missing."

"Gone missing? You're kidding me. Gone missing where?"

"Gone missing ... like in *kidnapped* gone missing."

"You've got to be kidding!"

"I wish, Mac," Stinger said. "Last evening, Nav's wife and Shira Lipkin went shopping on Pier 39 in San Francisco. Shira excused herself to find a restroom. She never returned. Just vanished."

"It was Serna's group that kidnapped her, Mac," Wolfman said. "We've already received a communiqué, and Moore already has us flying back into Mexico. So, there's nothing to do but get our butts back on that plane."

Once airborne, we all huddled in the back of the aircraft. "Before you read their long-winded rant, Mac," Stinger said, "let me go over what we already know. First off, they must have followed Shira and Navarro's wife from their house last night to the stores on Pier 39."

"How'd they know she was at Navarro's?" I said angrily, still trying to make sense out of what happened.

"She stayed at Navarro's house, Mac," Stinger answered. "Somehow they found out where she was staying."

"Remember that gangbanger, Gallegos?" Delgado asked. "That dude knew not only where Nav lived, but also knew where you lived."

I thought for a minute, pursed my lips, then slowly nodded my head. "Yeah. My bad. Too many people knew where I lived. From there, it was easy to find out where Nav lived. Sorry ... this one's on me. I gotta do better about keeping my mouth shut."

"So, as of now, Serna is telling us he not only knows where *you* live, but also where *Nav lives.*"

"I should have known those idiots would follow us," I mumbled, slamming my hand on the tabletop.

"So far, Mac, none of us have mentioned her kidnapping to the police," Stinger said.

"The police aren't our worry," I said. "Let me see that communiqué!"

"It's long and rambling, Mac," Stinger said. "Just let me give you the Reader's Digest version." He picked out the communiqué that would make the most sense to us. "Their manifesto says they have Shira Lipkin stashed in a cabin in the Culiacan Mountain range."

"Dammit," I said. "That's just where we came from."

"This is all just a ploy to get under your skin, Mac," Wolfman said. "The communiqué says he doesn't want to kill Shira, but he will if you don't play ball with him. They're obviously gonna want you to come and get her. Alone, of course. They told you not only where to find her, but how to get there. Nice to be playing with amateurs, huh?"

"Their fatal error number one," I murmured.

"They're actually telling us if you, Mac, come alone, they'll take that as your solemn oath to stop hunting Serna and Velasquez … especially in Mexico. They're also telling us they have a small army watching the Lipkin woman, so … if you come to rescue her with *your army,* they will not only kill her, they will graciously give us the coordinates where we can find her dismembered body."

"Culiacan Range, huh?" Vinnie asked. "And they claim they have a small army?"

"That *small army* of theirs is about to get chewed up and spit out," I said. "And you can make a bet with me right now … there's not one of them that's gonna make it out alive."

"Amen to that, Mac," FT responded. "Serna's guys know for sure that we'll be coming for them, but they won't know how many we'll bring nor what avenues we'll take. They'll think that knowing the countryside as they do will give them a distinct advantage. I'm guessing they'll station people on every trail they think we'd use to get to their hideout."

"I'm betting they'll think we'll come tonight," I said. "And I, for one, would like to oblige them. But we aren't going in blind. We need the Bird. Can we get Moore to supply us with one?"

"Already done, Mac," Stinger replied. "The first thing I did when I read the manifesto was call Admiral Moore. He delivered the Bird at three this morning, along with the communication gear and more ammo for the 7's."

# CHAPTER 42



Ernesto nodded and picked up the burner phone from the table. "We'll be lucky to get any reception in this area," he said, looking at the cellular status displayed on the screen in front of him.

As he waited, Ernesto again thought through the preparations for Mac's arrival to free the *puta*. Earlier that morning, he had cobbled together a vest stuffed with explosives. He knew it would be at least a day, possibly two, before the gringos showed up. It was only then that he'd put the vest on the girl and stake her out in the clearing that fronted the cabin. *A reversal of roles*, he thought with a smile. *I'll be in the cabin with the woman and the remote when McArthur and his gringo crew will be trying to sneak in and rescue her. As soon as either McArthur or one of his gringos wraps his arms around the puta, I'll blow them both into bloody chunks. It'll be an appropriate payback for McArthur murdering his Magic Kitty friend, Juan, at the puta's house. As the gringos are fond of saying,"* he thought with a smile, *"payback's a mother!"*

Ernesto held up his hand for quiet, hoping his phone call would go through. It did.

"Señor McArthur? I'm glad it was you who answered. My name is Ernesto. You probably remember me from the Magic Kitty, eh?"

"How could I forget a scumbag like you?"

"I can tell you, Señor … that is not a good way to start our conversation. Especially when you have so few chips on the table, and I have so many." He paused, then said, "I want you to know we have your woman here. She's a real beauty. And so soft. She's been dancing naked for all of us, and I can tell you from personal experience, Señor, that she loves to be touched. And, as you can well imagine, we do touch her a lot." He went silent for a few beats, then laughed aloud. "We've all played with her, Señor. I was hoping we'd be able to call and tell you not to pick her up until at least tomorrow, but, alas, our bosses tell us that won't be possible." Vinnie walked over and put his hand on my shoulder.

"But Señor Serna knows you are not stupid. And because he is generously giving the puta back to you, he knows you will go away and leave him forever alone. I'm, in fact, calling you at Señor Serna's request to tell you to come and reclaim her. She'll be waiting for you in this very cabin. However, if you don't follow our instructions, Señor Serna told me he will not pay for her funeral. Nor for yours." He laughed and hung up.

"Okay, everyone," Stan said, taking control after Ernesto

hung up. "Pay attention ... all of you! We can't afford any screw-ups." He paused, making eye contact with every person in the room. "I'm next to certain that not many of you have ever been in a remote area like this, to say nothing about going into battle for the first time. And even though the official sunset in these mountains is a few minutes before nine, you know it will be close to complete darkness by eight-fifteen. Like us, our adversaries will only be able to see where they're going through the night vision scopes on their rifles. While most of us will be stationary, the people coming after us will have to walk through the tangled brush at the same time as looking through their night vision glasses. That will slow them down considerably. They won't know where you are until you start killing them." He paused, looked at his watch, and said, "It's midafternoon, gentlemen. I'm counting on the gringos being dead by midnight."

Each of them was then given a specific area to cover with orders not to engage in a firefight until the gringos themselves reached the cabin.

# CHAPTER 43

CULIACAN MOUNTAIN RANGE, SATURDAY
EVENING

I pounded my right hand on the table as Ernesto hung up. "Couldn't have hoped for anything better. They're going to use Shira as bait, hoping it will entice us to show up early."

"Then let's not disappoint them," FT replied through pursed lips. "I can't wait to get either my hands or my sights on those SOBs."

We all dressed in full battle gear and placed our locked and loaded weapons in the back of the SUV next to the RQ-20A Puma that Admiral Moore sent to us. From working with the Bird in Pakistan, we embraced the Puma like an old friend.

It was after eight in the evening before we reached the Culiacan Mountains. It was closed, as we knew it would be. Various shades of darkness had already settled on the land as Stinger drove the SUV as far into the mountain range as he dared, then maneuvered the vehicle so it slipped deeply into the tree line.

Opening the hatchback, Stinger and I pulled out the Puma. As in Pakistan, he got the job of operating it.

"Come on over, guys," I said. "Stinger is going to show us what we'll be facing."

"We've already got the GPS coordinates," Stinger said, "so we already know where the cabin is that's holding her. Just know we're in for a hike." He outlined the general area on his screen. "The *Puma* is already there." Motioning for us to come closer, he pointed at the screen saying, "Looks like we got a big problem." He paused, then said, "These other dudes picked themselves a great spot. The overhead foliage around there is so dense we have no other alternative than to go in blind." He paused and shrugged his shoulders. "Granted it's not a favorable equation, but it's all we got."

"But the Puma can pick up heat signatures, right?" Delgado asked.

"It can," replied Stinger. "But with the brush being so dense in the area, it's going to be nearly impossible to pick out exactly where the shooters are stationed until they have us in their crosshairs."

"Let me pass something by you," FT said to me. "Didn't we read somewhere this whole area used to be owned by a timber company?"

"That be true, FT," I replied. "So?"

"They were here like thirty years ago, right? And now it's so overgrown with trees and shrub-brush even the Puma's cameras will have a hard time mapping the terrain."

"And your point is?"

"I'm getting to that, Mac, hold on." FT paused, turned to Stinger, and said, "Can you show the footage the Bird's camera took from the time we sent it skyward to where it was over the territory with the heat signatures?"

Stinger looked at me quizzically. I shrugged my shoulders, then said, "Let's make this quick, FT, okay? We're wasting precious time."

Stinger pushed a few buttons and stepped out of the way so we could see ground images float by. "Okay, stop it there," FT said. Moving closer, he pointed to the screen. "There ... see the tiny ribbon on the photo?" He traced it with his index finger. "What do you think it is?"

"I'm not sure," I replied. "You tell me."

"It's an old logging road, Mac. Hasn't been used in like forever. But look," he pointed to a particular section of the tree line, "it hardly has any canopy."

I came closer to the screen. "This is unreal," I said softly. "How in hell did you ever find that, FT?"

"I was playing with my phone on the ride down here and found a site that showed the logging roads that were staples here many moons ago. This one kinda stuck out at me."

"FT, my man," I said. "You are a godsend." I turned and motioned for the crew to come take a look. As they huddled around the screen, I slapped FT on the back. *"Praise the Lord and pass the ammunition,* boys," I said. "FT found us *the road to heaven.*"

The road to heaven ended up sending us on a short two-mile hike that emptied out on the backside of the cabins, not even close to the route Serna's "small army" expected us to travel. Since our new path to the cabin had less of a canopy, the

Puma showed us the road that passed within a quarter mile of the cabin.

"We'll be coming at them from a direction they never expected," FT said. "And if the Puma had to fly above even parts of the canopy, it would still pick up the heat signatures of anyone waiting for us near the cabin."

"Put on your night vision gear, people," I said. "We can take it slow and easy down this road. Time just became our friend."

# CHAPTER 44



"Past nine," Stan said, looking at his watch. "Time to dress her, Ernesto."

Lipkin was under a blanket tied to the bed. Ernesto pulled the blanket off her naked body and untied her.

"Get up," he said, grabbing her arm. She tried to stand, but the drugs she'd been given to keep her in a twilight sleep hadn't worn off. She stumbled then slumped to the ground.

"I'll take care of her," said Ernesto. "It's time for all of you to get in your positions." He looked over at Lipkin and laughed. "Unless of course, you want to watch what I do to her."

"Cal and I are getting sick and tired of you, Ernesto," Stan said in a not-so-friendly tone. He'd been sighting his rifle through the window but now brought it slowly back around until it was aimed directly at Ernesto's forehead. "You keep thinking about poontang, you idiot, and you'll get us all killed. Just forget about her, okay? We've got a battle in front of us that we've got to win. We'll be fighting at least one ex-Navy SEAL. Maybe two or three for all I know. I've been around SEALs for a long time and know one thing for certain. If you don't respect them, they'll eat your skinny butt for dinner. So, forget trying to show what a stud you are, okay? She's not impressed, and neither are we. Just do your damn job! If you deviate in any way, I'll have your cohones chopped off and hung on that tree out there." He paused. "Comprende?"

Ernesto stared blankly into the barrel of Stan's rifle, nodded once, then reached down and pulled Shira to a sitting position, struggling to get her arms through the vest. Once secured, he connected the two wires. The green light on his remote blinked, confirming the connection had been made. Then he slipped the serape over her head, shielding the four pounds of explosives and two pounds of ball bearings sewn into the front and back of the vest. He stepped back and took a deep bow, hoping Stan would admire his work. "The lamb," he said, patting Shira's head paternally. "The wolf will not be able to help himself." He took her by the arm, lifted her to a standing position and walked her out the front door of the cabin. "*Madre de Dios*," he swore as he shoved her forward. "Such a beauty. What a waste."

The rest of the men followed Ernesto out the door and into the clearing. "You all know your jobs, right?" Cal asked. The men nodded. "Good. It's time to take your positions. You'll probably have to wait a few hours before those guys get here. My instinct tells me they probably won't come until close to midnight. Maybe later. Remember, though, you're going to be fighting a highly trained, dangerous unit of professionals. Your only advantage will be one of surprise. They won't know where you are. If you don't fall asleep, you just might live to see another day. Another day, by the way, that will make us all a lot richer. Be sure to send compliments to Señor Serna."

"But remember," Stan interjected, "let them pass by you *without you* making a sound. We don't want individual gun battles going on. Cal and I will be at your nine and three o'clock positions on the hill above you." He pointed. "Ernesto will be in the cabin playing with his explosives." A few of the men chuckled. "Better if we herd them all into the clearing before we engage. That way, we'll take them all out together. Much cleaner, and infinitely more efficient." He paused, then said, "And safer for all of us."

Stan let the others disperse, then walked back to the cabin and waited for Ernesto to finish trussing up Lipkin in the courtyard.

"We need to talk a minute," Stan said as Ernesto returned to the cabin and sat on the bed where Lipkin had been held. "Let's go over the plans again, okay? Just so you know, tonight is about killing McArthur and everyone he brought with him. But primarily McArthur. I know you want to test out the suicide vest the girl is wearing. So do I. But if any of us get a free and clear shot at McArthur, you're not only cleared to take it, you're ordered to take it.

"And finally, keeping the girl alive is not an option. She betrayed Serna's operation in San Diego, and you all know how Señor Serna deals with people who betray him. You don't want to be one of those. When we shoot McArthur, you're going push the remote in your hand to kill the girl. Understood?" Ernesto was clearly not happy, but nodded.

"Cal and I will be halfway up the hill. We'll have enough separation between us to have two interlocking fields of fire. If one of us happens to miss the shot, the other will take it." He stepped out the door and motioned for Ernesto to follow. "We're pretty sure McArthur will be coming from that direction." He pointed east. "He'll no doubt have two or three men with him. After he finds the cabin, just know he may go to ground for an hour or so to see if one of us gets spooked and makes a noise." He walked to the corner of the cabin. "He'll come up behind us here. We won't have a shot at him until he clears the cabin on the other side." Walking to the front door, he said, "We'll wait until he gets around to the front ... here by the window. You'll hear him, Ernesto. Don't get spooked. This guy's a professional. You make a mistake with him, and he'll cut you in half."

When Ernesto smirked, Stan got close to his face and whispered menacingly, "Don't laugh, my friend. You have no idea who you're dealing with here. Do what we tell you and you'll get a chance to live long enough to rape other defenseless women."

The two men left and hiked into the tree line. "Let's not get too far up," Cal said. "These night scopes we have aren't the best. Too bad you couldn't have requisitioned night goggles."

"Couldn't take the chance," said Stan. "I would have had to fill out paperwork. Instead, I ended up going the internet route. Even online, though, the high-tech stuff leaves too much of a fingerprint. It's why I bought these. They're second-generation, Vietnam-era scopes. Russian-made. No infrared capabilities, only ambient light. But I figured, what the heck. If it was good enough for the Russkies back in the day, it should be good enough for us. As long as McArthur stays directly in front of us, we'll be good to go."

"Let's hope! And after we get him, the first thing I'm gonna do is shoot Ernesto. Put him and what's left of the woman's body in a shallow grave somewhere in these mountains and be done with the both of them."

"Works for me, pardner," Stan replied with a smile.

# CHAPTER 45



"That FT found this path was a miracle, Mac," Stinger said, holding the viewer from the Puma in his hands. "You're gonna have to give that boy a raise."

"Hey ... I can assure you his raise is the number one issue I'm focused on," I replied with a chuckle.

"Yeah, I know! I know! But seriously, Mac, thanks to him, we're not looking at anything more than a turkey shoot. We won't have a dense forest canopy looking us in the face, and the Puma's infrared will pick out the squirters. It's really all we'll need."

"Then let's get going," I said. "We've got to get Shira out of there and back home."

We launched the Puma through a small hole in the trees and leveled it out at thirty feet above the timberline. Stinger guided it southwest toward the target. Three minutes later, the first red image showed up on his tablet screen.

"Puma found the cabin. Take a look," Stinger said, passing me the tablet. Its outline was clear because it retained heat from the bodies who occupied it during the day. We could even tell where the door and windows were by the heat escaping through them.

They watched as someone dragged what no doubt was Shira Lipkin out of the cabin and tethered her to a small tree in the middle of a clearing. That person then walked back into the cabin.

"Remember, that *hoss* is mine," I whispered. The other four nodded their heads in unison.

"Take a look at this, boys," Stinger said, pointing out six infrared signatures taking different paths to the trail they expected us to be on.

"They're doing us a big favor," Delgado whispered. "Marking the spot where they want to be buried."

We watched the two heat signatures walking together up a small rise fronting the clearing where Shira was now tethered.

"So, they got one guy in the cabin," I said. "His job, I'm guessing, is to shoot me as I come into the clearing to get Lipkin. Two guys are stationed on the hill above the cabin. Their job is to kill any of us who gets through the other six shooters."

"We'll take out the six dudes first," Delgado hissed. "They're in for a big surprise."

"It's unfair fighting such amateurs," FT said with a smirk. "But, hey, I ain't complainin'."

Stinger ran the Puma in concentric circles from the cabin

outward. It didn't take long to find the two shooters who left the cabin together lying prone on a hill about fifty yards above and west of the cabin.

"All bandits accounted for, Mac," Stinger said. "We got one guy still in the cabin. The rest are scattered."

"We're fortunate you found the other way in for us, FT," I said. "Thanks a heap. Otherwise, we'd have been walking right into their sights about now." I turned to Stinger and said, "Before you bring the drone home, could you make one last pass over the cabin? Something I saw has my danger meter twitching."

"Sure thing, Mac," he answered. The drone outlined the cabin on the screen, along with the heat signature of who we supposed was Shira.

"We're assuming it's her, right?" I asked. They all nodded. "Okay, then let's plan this out. They'll want us to have directions to the cabin, so they'll light her up in the clearing. Doesn't change anything for us. The Puma has already pinpointed their positions."

"Looks that way," Stinger said. "She's the bait."

"Yeah, that's what makes me nervous. Anything strike you as odd about her heat signature?"

Stinger refined some of the tablet's resolution. "You're right, Mac. Her signature is a little brighter than the others. What would account for that?"

"We saw the same signature in Iraq, remember? The dead dog on the road glowing bright red?"

"Son-of-a-B, Mac! You think they got her wired up with explosives?"

"Wouldn't put it past 'em, would you? But, in any case,

better safe than dead."

I gathered the men around me. "Here's what we're looking at. As you saw from the drone, we have nine shooters scattered around with nothing else on their minds but to kill us. If it were only them, this op would be a piece of cake. But they have Shira, and it looks like they've got her wired."

"Which means one of the nine has the kill switch," Delgado said.

"Right, Vinnie," Stinger replied. "Probably the guy inside the cabin."

"Exactly what I'm thinking, too," I said. "Otherwise, there'd be no use for him to be there. A wasted soldier."

"I'll bet it's because they've got a pretty unsophisticated detonator," Delgado said. "Not much range."

"We're on the same page, Vinnie," I replied. "So, he's the guy we have to make sure we kill before he detonates the bomb. Our storming the cabin ain't going to get it done. He'd hit the switch as the last act of his worthless life."

"Fragging him would present the same problem," Wolfman said. "Lobbing a grenade through the window would still offer him a second to hit the switch."

"Even a death twitch would be all it would take," I said, "so we don't have too many options. The best bet as far as I can see is for FT to shoot the dude."

"Tricky one, Mac. But if you can get him to come to the window, his time on the planet will expire," FT replied.

"Perfect," I said. "To get him to show himself, I'm going to walk slowly across the clearing toward Shira. I'm hoping the guy in the cabin will come closer to the window to see how close I get to her before he detonates the explosives strapped to her. You'll get one shot, FT. Just one. Has to be an instant kill. Can you do that?"

"Not only can—but will."

"I have every confidence in you, my man," I said. "But as a backup, in case the guy doesn't present you with a shot, I want Vinnie down by the cabin, too. Depending on what kind of shrapnel they've packed into her vest, even if it goes off when I'm only halfway through the clearing, I'd still be toast. So, Vinnie, on the off-chance I do get halfway across the clearing, and FT hasn't yet taken out the guy in the cabin, drop a frag on him. I'm counting on you to hold on to that puppy as long as you can before lobbing it in. The longer you can hold it, the longer Shira and I get to stay alive."

"Good thing you're one of my favorite people, Mac," Delgado said, flashing what he considered an angelic smile. "For most people, I'd only hold it for two, maybe three seconds. For you, I'll count to four."

"I was just hopin' you could count that high," I responded with a smile and nod of my head. Then, turning to the others, I said, "FT, before you get the pleasure of blowing the cabin dude's head off, I want you and Wolfman to take out the six who are waiting on the outlying paths. You want Stinger to send the Puma back so you can have real-time intel on their location?"

"I'm fine with what we already saw," Wolfman said. "They shouldn't be too hard to find, and even easier to take out. They won't be expecting us to come at them from behind." FT nodded in agreement.

"Vinnie ... you and Stinger take out the shooters on the

ridgeline above the clearing. Their top gunslingers will be positioned there."

"Roger that, Mac," Stinger answered.

"Comms check," I said. "Microphone and earbuds." Stinger whispered into his microphone, and they all nodded. "For each person you take down, click once on channel two. When we've counted to eight clicks, let's re-form around the backside of the cabin. Especially you, Vinnie. I'll be expecting you in the brush on the east side of the cabin. Then we'll get serious about taking out the guy in the cabin." I looked around. "Questions?" Silence. "Then let's get this over with and go home."

# CHAPTER 46



CULIACAN MOUNTAIN RANGE, SUNDAY 1:30 A.M.

I worked my way to a spot at the edge of the clearing ... less than a click east of the cabin. Luckily, there was enough brush to make sure I was invisible to the shooters on the ridge.

From my spot, I could clearly see Shira. She was on her knees, sitting on her heels. Almost like praying. The pose reminded me of a picture my mom showed me when I was a child. In the picture, a pilgrim was kneeling at the shrine of Our Lady of Fatima, a holy place in Portugal. The difference in the pilgrim's pose was Shira had her arms tied behind her back and a rope around her neck while wearing a vest filled with explosives.

I heard a click in my ear. Then another. Two down. *Just a bit longer, Shira,* I thought. *Hang in there.*

During the next ten minutes, I heard four more clicks. Five

minutes after hearing the last click, FT and Wolfman joined me.

"Any problems?" I whispered.

For the sake of silence, FT held up six fingers, and Wolfman gave the thumb down.

I bumped fists with them and then directed FT's attention to a point across the clearing opposite them. "Anywhere along there," I whispered. "As long as you can get a clear shot into the cabin window. But take it slow getting in. The two guys on the hill are still in play." No sooner had I said that, we heard another click. I smiled. "Sorry, guys," I whispered. "My bad. Now only one in play."

FT checked his weapon, positioned his EOTech scope on the MP7, then nodded. "Good to go, Mac," he whispered.

"As soon as you hear me talking to Shira," I whispered directly into FT's ear, "get ready. I'll already be out in the open. Remember, if you don't get him by the time I'm halfway across the clearing, Vinnie will frag him through the window. And then ... well, then we'll just hope for the best." FT nodded and quietly slid to his left. It was then I heard the eighth and final click in my earpiece.

Breathing a sigh of relief, I waited a few more minutes to make sure FT was in position, then stood and moved into the clearing. "Shira," I called out.

Shira Lipkin jumped like someone had hit her with a taser. She shook her head and tried to stand, but stumbled, rebelling against the tethers that bound her.

"Shira," I said. "Be still!" I could see her entire body trembling. "I'm coming to get you. Don't say a word."

"No," she shrieked. "You can't." Her voice cracked. "You don't understand. Don't! Please!"

"Shira," I said as soothingly as I could, given the rage I felt. "I'm all by myself. They promised me if I came alone, they'd let you go." I was talking loud enough to make sure the guy in the cabin heard what I was saying. "I did come by myself, just like they told me. Now I expect them to let me take you home."

"No. Don't come any closer. I don't want to go with you. Don't you understand? Please. Go away."

I kept walking. I noticed the serape, and said, "I'm glad they gave you a coat to wear. Keep you warm and covered. That was nice of them." I again talked loud enough for the shooter in the cabin to hear. "I know they gave you even warmer clothes to wear underneath the blanket. These mountains can get chilly." I was trying to let her know I knew she was wearing something under the serape. But I also knew she probably had no idea what I was talking about. As it turned out, it didn't matter.

The sound of an MP7 spit into the quiet night air. Five hearts in that clearing skipped a beat, but then ... nothing. A peaceful and welcoming silence enveloped the camp.

I ran over to Shira. "It's all over," I said, holding her trembling body next to mine. "You're safe, and I'm here to keep you safe." I slipped the rope from her neck and untied her hands. Before taking her into the cabin, I laid her back on the ground and raised the serape. My spirits rose considerably when I noticed the suicide vest she wore was definitely homemade. Even at that, though, I slowly and carefully disconnected the wires lining the vest. I'd seen hundreds of them during my SEAL career and had nothing but respect for the damage they could do. After carefully removing the vest, I carried Shira into the cabin and laid her on the bed. FT and Wolfman followed me in. Seeing Ernesto's body on the floor next to the back wall, they smiled. "Nice shooting," was the extent of their conversation.

Delgado entered the cabin and went straight to Ernesto's body. He was lying against the back wall, the suicide vest's detonator switch lying ten feet to his right. FT's shot had pierced Ernesto below his right eye, causing him to fall backward and allowing the detonator switch to fly out of his hand. Delgado quickly picked up the detonator and laid it gingerly on the table.

Stinger arrived last. "Mac, I think you better take a look at this." He placed two wallets on the table. "They're from the two bodies on the hill." I opened them. Staring back at me were the IDs of DEA Special Agent Michael Gray and DEA Special Agent Brian Jackson.

# CHAPTER 47

**CULIACAN MOUNTAIN RANGE, SUNDAY 5:30 A.M.**

"Let's hurry and finish this up, okay?"

"You going where I think you're going?" Vinnie asked. I remained silent. "If you need company," Delgado said, "I'd gladly come with you."

"Thanks, Vin. I appreciate the thought. But my *come to Jesus* talk with Gilardi is gonna be a personal mano et mano dust-up."

THE NEXT TWO hours were spent sanitizing the area. We picked up as many spent shell casings as we could find, then collected all the weapons and IDs from the dead bodies. We buried Gray and Jackson in shallow graves next to the cabin to hopefully keep the animals away until their colleagues came and retrieved the bodies. Knowing that Serna didn't much care whether *his* men were buried or not, I told my group to leave their bodies where they fell, knowing full well that after the forest animals had finished with them, none would be identifiable.

Because Shira was still wobbly and hadn't yet fully shaken off the effects of the drugs, the five of us took turns carrying her the three and a half miles back to where we stashed the vans. An hour and a half later, we parked our vans in the two adjacent Culiacan homes that Admiral Moore had rented for us. In another half hour, I was on a plane to San Francisco.

At exactly 11:19, I pushed my way into Gilardi's office unannounced, threw the two wallets on his desk, and said, "What the hell did you do?"

"Hey ... wait just a minute!" Gilardi said with acidic sharpness. "Who do you think you are barging your way into my office like this?"

"These ..." I said, pointing to the wallets, "allowed me to barge into your office, you SOB." I paused, then said, "Open them up."

Gilardi reached down and flipped one open, did a double-take, and opened the second one. "Where did you get these?" he demanded.

"Don't be playing games with me," I uttered through clenched teeth, "or I'll come across this desk and rip your arms out. These were the men you sent to kill me and my crew after you kidnapped Shira Lipkin."

"I have no idea what you're talking about," Gilardi replied angrily. "I sent those men to San Diego a number of days ago to help Agent Torres interrogate that Mexican lawyer you guys rousted in Borrego Springs."

"You're a lying sack of manure, Gilardi. How do you think I got these?" I slammed the wallets with my open hand. "The two men who owned these wallets, *your two men*, are lying side-by-side in graves next to a cabin in the Culiacan Mountains."

"I don't know where you got these wallets, but I'll find out," he snarled. "Take a seat."

"Thanks, I'll stand."

"Suit yourself," he replied with an icy smile.

He sat and dialed a number, all the while shaking his head disgustedly. When no one answered, he hung up and dialed another. After a few minutes, he hung up again.

"Neither answered. Let me call Torres." He went quiet for a few moments, then said, "Pete? Thank God. It's Bill. I'm here in the office with Ken McArthur. Are Brian and Mike with you?"

Looking up at me, he shrugged his shoulders and shook his head, then said into the phone, "Yeah. I've been trying to reach them, but they don't pick up." From the look on his face, I could tell he didn't like what he was hearing. "And you didn't call me?" Once again, Torres's response didn't please him. "I wish you'd have let me know, Pete. Get your butt back here pronto. Call me when you get in. I'll wait for you at the office."

Gilardi hung up, stared at the badges and IDs for a long moment, then looked up at me with a bewildered look. "I..." he stammered. "... I don't know what to say. Apparently, Jackson and Gray never made it to San Diego. They told Torres that I had changed my mind, and reassigned them to another project, and that they were to take over Ruiz's interrogation." Gilardi shook his head. "I don't understand any of this. You said a cabin somewhere in the mountains outside the city of Culiacan?"

I nodded.

"I know that cabin. It's actually one of ours." He shook his head. "I honestly don't understand any of this."

"You were one of my father's best friends," I said, leaning forward and putting my hands, palms down, on his desk. "Did you have him murdered, too?"

Gilardi violently shoved his chair back and stood, his lips pursed—his neck and face flushed red with anger. Placing both hands on the top of his desk, he leaned forward toward me and growled, "Now, wait just a minute, you first-class jerk. Who do you think you are walking into my office and accusing me of something like this?" He paused, then, in a quieter tone, said, "I loved your father. I would have done anything for him." He pursed his lips, then pointed to the wallets on the desktop, "I know this looks bad. But believe me, I'm telling you the truth."

"We'll see," I snapped.

"If it means anything to you, I plead guilty to not being savvy enough, or on top of my crew enough, to see that those agents were dirty. It was my responsibility ... and I failed. I'm ashamed of myself for that failure of leadership. But you have to believe me when I tell you I'm innocent of any complicity in their actions."

"We'll see," I snapped again.

"If there's a silver lining in all this," Gilardi murmured, "we at least know the leaks came out of this office and we know who leaked them."

"We'll see," I whispered, as I turned and walked out of his office. Even before reaching the car, however, my mind had shifted back to Culiacan and disrupting Serna's freedom.

# CHAPTER 48



"It goes to show you, Rinaldo, we're slipping," Serna said into the phone as he swiveled in his chair at the sound of the patio door sliding open. He smiled as the dark-haired woman entered from the pool, water droplets trailing down her half-naked body. Putting the receiver to his chest, he snapped his fingers at her, pointing to the humidor sitting on the ornate black walnut credenza to her left. Pulling a cigar out, she seductively walked toward him, rolling the tip of the cigar on her bikini bottom where it disappeared between her thighs. "I'll call you back, Rinaldo," Serna said, replacing the receiver and pulling the girl to him.

❧

THREE HOURS LATER, Serna called Ruiz back. He'd already instructed Diego to drive the girl back to wherever she came from while he used the tunnel system to make it back to the hacienda on the hill.

"Where were we, my friend?" he asked.

"I think you said to me we were slipping," Ruiz answered through a mirthless laugh. "And then you *did* slip ... with whoever you had in there with you."

"I didn't slip," Serna snapped back. "Merely having a little recreation." He paused. "And it's none of your business what I do."

"But it is *my* business to ask what you're doing to *our* business. And it's not a matter of slipping; it's a matter of becoming *soft*. You're living too much of the good life, Ángel. You've got to start paying more attention to *our* business ... yours and mine. And, if I might say so, less attention to the putas."

Serna yawned. From where he now sat, he could see the city stretched out beneath him in the distance. Most people knew he lived in an expensive house in the hills of Culiacan. Only Ruiz, however, knew of the tunnel that Serna had built to connect his casa in the hills with a small, undistinguished house purchased in the flatlands by one of his shell companies. Once finished, not only did Serna enjoy the luxury of the hacienda on the hillside, he also got to quietly frequent the epicurean and sexual delights in the Culiacan flatlands.

Serna knew Ruiz was right, though. It was time to get back to business. But he wasn't about to let Ruiz dictate to him. "I seem to remember a friend of mine getting the nickname El

Rhino for an activity that had exactly *zero* to do with business. Maybe *that* person should not be lecturing me at this moment, eh?"

"*That* person grew up, Ángel. Unlike the person he's now talking to." He let the words sit for just a moment, then said, "But enough of this bickering. It doesn't get us anywhere. You and I have to stop the bleeding."

"I've made some mistakes, Rinaldo. True enough. But my biggest mistake was I became way too nice. Like with that puta Lillianna. When she turned on me, I should've killed her right then and there. But no! I let her live so I could make her suffer by first killing her grandmother and whoever else was in the house that night."

"Speaking of that particular puta," Ruiz said, "how did we end up losing her?"

"I must have missed something," Serna replied. "I had three of my best men grab her. They had her in the cabin in the wilderness. Taking their time killing her. Then, somehow, all three of my men died when that McArthur fellow and one of his comrades showed up at the cabin."

"Another snafu, Ángel, on our very doorstep today. Ernesto texted me yesterday that our men had the trap set to finally kill McArthur and his comrades. I haven't heard from him or any of the six men that were with him. Skilled men, Ángel. Along with two gringos. Not a word from any of them." He paused, then took a deep breath. "I met this McArthur fellow in Borrego right after you left. I could tell that he and the men with him were a different breed. Professionals, Ángel. And now they're coming for us."

"Let them come," Serna spit. "Half of Mexico has been after me for the last twenty years. I've beaten all of them, and I'll beat all these gringos, also."

# CHAPTER 49



Even though I was still fuming from Gilardi's meeting, I forced myself to put it behind me by calling Navarro to see how Shira was holding up.

"Good to talk to you, Mac. Shira's here, as you no doubt know. She's in her room. Want me to get her?"

"No, that's okay. Was wondering if I could come over and have a quick visit with you guys, and Shira?"

"No problem, Mac. I'm sure she'd love to see you."

"Not sure how much time I have, but I do know Red Squadron's positioning itself to do away with Serna once and for all. Can you and Kathleen take Shira and Buck while I'm gone? She's been traumatized by all this, so needs some soothing care. Thought you guys might be the medicine she needs right now."

"Absolutely," he replied. "Come over anytime. Plan on staying for dinner if you have the time."

"Perfect. I'm not scheduled out of SFO until 9:15 this evening."

It was after two by the time I reached Navarro's house. Kathleen met me at the door. Turned out Shira was still in bed.

I took the opportunity to bring Navarro up to speed on what happened to her in the Culiacan Mountains and my confrontation with Gilardi.

"What's your gut feeling about him?" Navarro asked. "I've always thought the guy was just a little west of slimy."

"Amen to that, my friend." I paused for a minute, then said, "I'm hoping he's clean, but I'm still going to be wary of him until he can prove he had nothing to do with my father's death or sending his agents to kidnap Shira and kill me. I do have to give him props, though. He looked and sounded genuinely sorry for what happened. He also took full responsibility and had an answer for everything that happened. Even went so far as using this episode with Gray and Jackson to clear up the issue as to who might have leaked to Serna the time of my dad's flight."

Navarro nodded and then changed the subject. "It was a terrible thing that happened to Shira, Mac. These kinds of experiences, as you know, can leave scars. I don't expect they will with her because she strikes me as a pretty tough lady, but you never know."

"Take care of her, okay?"

"Kathleen and I will, my man. You can count on it."

We all made pleasurable small talk over dinner and then retired to the living room where Navarro successfully embarrassed me by telling stories about when I was a kid. Shira sat next to me on the couch taking in every word.

"Memory book material," she said, scrunching closer.

I smiled at her, then looked at my watch. "I hate to intrude on this Mac-bashing party, but I've still got a plane to catch in an hour and a half."

"I think we should let these two have a few minutes of alone time, don't you?" Kathleen said, tugging on Nav's arm. He looked over at me with a *sorry, it's not my fault* look.

"Hey, you guys stay right where you are," I said to Nav and Kathleen. "I'll walk with Shira to the front porch."

"Isn't this just too cute," whispered Nav to Kathleen, with enough volume so Shira and I could both hear.

Shira laughed. "This is like Mom and Dad leaving us alone after our prom date," she said with a smile. "I know you have to leave, but I wanted to thank you again for last night. *All* of last night." She paused, then pulled me close and put her head on my shoulder. "Especially for risking your life to come get me. That will stay with me forever."

I pulled her even closer to me and whispered in her ear. "The best thing you can do now is forget all about it. Chalk it up as nothing but a nightmare. You won't have as many scars that way."

Putting her arms around my neck, she said, "Remember when I told you in San Diego you weren't anything like your dad? I was wrong." She kissed me full on the lips, then whispered in my ear, "Take care of yourself. I need you to come back to me."

"I can't think of anything I'd rather do."

# CHAPTER 50



At 0900, Red Squadron and I were seated at a large oval table in a meeting room attached to Moore's office at NSWC. I was surprised to find Lillianna Martinez there also.

"Glad you people could make it on such short notice," Moore began. "I wanted to fill you in on what's happening in our nation's capital." He paused, then said, "As you know, not everyone in DC is in favor of going after the cartels. But the President is still one hundred percent behind us. For him, what's going on in Mexico has broader national security implications than just the drug violence. We know for a fact Hezbollah is looking for ways to smuggle nuclear material into the United States to assemble a dirty bomb. Some of the cartels, including our friends in the Tormenta cartel, are allowing them free passage into America via their drug highways.

"The border with Mexico is approximately 2,000 miles long. The last President who tried to do something about the border issue could only get about 600 miles of fence built before they voted him out of office. The fact is, even if we could fence the entire stretch, we'd still only stop some of the smugglers. And it wouldn't take a handful of people with fissionable material to cause untold damage to this country. This President's overall strategic objective, therefore, is to so cripple the cartels so they won't be capable of supporting groups like Hezbollah ever again. It's why we're talking here today. Your responsibility will be to eliminate, or at least seriously degrade, the structure of the Tormenta cartel."

"And about time, too," Delgado spit.

"You've all met Lillianna Martinez," Moore said. "She's the closest thing we have to somebody inside Serna's organization. Her insights are not only invaluable, but those of you who've already worked with her know she's one tough lady. It's the reason we have her here today."

"Thank you for the having me," she began. "Most of you have heard my story, so I won't bore you repeating it. Just know I spent over three years in close contact with Señor Serna. I know him well. In my experience, there are only two ways to stop the cartels. The first is to kill their leaders, like Victor Serna. But the problem with focusing on killing guys like Serna is someone else will take his place, and that person might be worse."

She paused and took a drink of water. "The second way to stop the cartels is to portray them as weak. I was with Victor Serna long enough to see that his power comes from ordinary people being afraid of him. And they're afraid because neither the local nor federal authorities can protect *ordinary* people from the cartel's violence. What you must do is make him look weak. Give him no place to run or hide. When you do that, ordinary people will not fear him as much. The bottom line here is when he runs out of places to hide, he and the Tormentas will be finished as a major force in Mexico."

"Is there a specific button we could push that would make him look weak?" I asked.

"Victor Serna has a house in Culiacan and a yacht in Manzanillo," Martinez answered. "Of all his possessions, I can tell you firsthand that those two have the highest symbolic value. His yacht, however, is the most visible sign of his power and wealth. I've been on it many, many times, and he's told me over and over how invincible he feels there. That no one can get to him. If you asked me where to attack him, I'd choose the yacht, hands down." She took a sip of water, then said, "If you take that from him, within a year he and the Tormentas will be finished as a major force in Mexico."

"Please take a moment to look at the computers in front of you," Moore interjected, taking advantage of a lull in the questioning. "We have pictures of both targets. We'll let you guys choose which one to take down first."

He brought up photos of Culiacan. "As you can see, it's a fairly good-sized city. Has close to nine hundred thousand people."

"Yes, but his house is on one of the most desired bluffs in the city. Eight bedrooms and eight baths. Serna calls it his playground. It's his pride and joy. He spent a year building it."

"How many guards does he have in the house?" asked Wolfman.

"When I was there, four or five at the most. But now there are at least eight full-time guards ... and these guys do not mess around."

"We're positioning a Big Bird over Mexico," Moore said. "We'll have updated pictures by tonight."

"What's Serna's pattern when he's at the house?" FT asked. "Where does he sleep? Does he get up late? And if so, about what time? Are his bodyguards well-armed? Pistols? Rifles? What?"

"It all depends, Señor, on what time of the year it is and who he comes in with." She stopped, closed her eyes, and let out a big sigh.

"Are his bodyguards armed?" FT asked.

"Everyone there is armed, Señor. Most carry automatic rifles. I'm sorry, that's all I can tell you. I don't know calibers very well."

"You told me you think he's there this very minute."

"Yes. I'm sure of it. He likes living there because he can blow off steam at the nightclubs."

The room went silent for a few moments, then I said, "Let's move the focus to the yacht."

Moore brought up the pictures of the central Mexican coastline. He used the cursor to highlight a section of oceanfront property on what was essentially a peninsula between Manzanillo and the small town of Cuyutlán, thirty miles to the south.

"This is Serna's villa," he said, using the cursor to circle a defined plot of land. "Approximately one hundred acres. Nice digs."

"But he never stays there," Martinez interjected. "When

he's in the area, he's on his yacht ... as you can see here." Moore hovered the cursor over it. "It sits moored three hundred meters from land. Only accessible by boat from the dock."

"Obviously for security reasons," said Delgado. "But if we come after him, it makes little difference where he's moored."

"If we follow Lillianna's preference to take the yacht first, when would our first window of opportunity be?" I asked.

"As early as 1330 tomorrow," Moore said. "If you're game, I'll arrange it. You'd be taken fifty miles off the coast and deposited on the deck of the *USS California*, a DDS-capable submarine." Moore looked over at Delgado. "In case they didn't have them in your day, Vinnie, DDS is a Dry Deck Shelter for launching our Mark-11 SDVs."

I looked over at Delgado. "Sir, we'll be training tonight so will get a chance for our rookie colleague here to catch up on all our fancy new toys." I paused, looked at Vinnie, and said, "SDV, by the way, means SEAL Delivery Vehicle, in case you didn't know."

Delgado smiled and flipped me off.

"Any idea how many guards will be on the yacht?" Wolfman asked.

"Not as of this moment. But like I said, we'll have the Big Bird overhead. Her cameras will pick up any movement on the yacht. You'll have the number before you deploy tomorrow night. However, we won't know where they'll be on the boat when you board. You'll have to find them yourselves. But at least you'll know how many you have to account for."

"Are we all good to go tomorrow?" I asked.

"Locked and loaded," Stinger replied, nodding to me.

"I'll tell the *Seahawk* you're a go, Mac," said Admiral

Moore, "and I'll let the Captain of the *California* know that you're coming aboard. See you back here in a couple of days."

As we walked out, I turned to Delgado and said, "Don't know how long it's been since you've had your flippers on, but better get used to them again, pronto. We're going out to San Clemente tonight to practice close-quarter drills. Tomorrow we'll spend some time in the ocean. We've changed technologically and tactically since you were last in the water."

"But the outcomes are pretty much the same, right?" Delgado asked. "I mean ... hey, if I can't cut it, I'll be let go."

"Pretty much."

"Thanks for the opportunity, Mac. I *will* cut it. I'm back to busting bad guys' heads. For me, it doesn't get any better than that."

# CHAPTER 51



Since San Clemente was home to the last of the Navy's live firing ranges, I told the crew to get there as soon as possible. The thirty-five-minute helo ride from NSWC to the Island gave me time to discuss our downrange weapon requirements with Admiral Moore. Being in sync was critical to our success. Once the operation went live, there was absolutely no margin for error.

We spent two hours on San Clemente Island frolicking in *Mother Ocean*. I studied the expected tides and weather in and around the Manzanillo coastline and determined our best choice of entry would be to park our delivery vehicle eight hundred or so meters from the yacht and swim the rest of the way. Swimming eight hundred meters was usually a piece of cake, but I worried about how well Delgado would hold up. On this mission, there could be no room for error. If Vinnie was going to be a hindrance, we'd have to leave him on the submarine. Therefore, part of the two-hour frolic was to gauge his endurance. Thankfully, he passed, so we were good to go.

The *Seahawk* lifted off the island at precisely 1330.

Fifty-two miles and two hours west of San Clemente Island, we fast roped from the hovering *Seahawk* to the deck of the *USS California*. Ten minutes later, we were all sitting in the submarine's galley eating grilled cheese sandwiches and drinking coffee.

"Good duty, huh?" FT said. "I'm thinkin' I could live like this for at least six months a year."

"Good duty until you're sitting on the ocean floor listening to the ping of a missile searching for your sorry butt," Stinger replied. "Me? Given a choice, I'd rather be cold and miserable but have more control over how I die than sitting in one of these cans hoping not to be tracked down by a missile."

An ensign walked in and said, "The Skipper has invited you to his quarters as soon as you are finished eating."

"Glad to have you men on board," said Captain Ron Turner, as we all took seats around a small table in his cabin. "As distinguished guests, I want you to know my crew and I are at your disposal."

"Thanks, Captain. We appreciate your hospitality," I said

as I introduced our team. "You know of our mission, Sir, correct?"

"We do, and we're already communicating with the Bird they've got hovering over the coast. You can look at the comms here, or we can go to the conn."

"If you wouldn't mind, Captain, we'd rather stay here a while," I replied. "It gives the crew a chance to look at the data coming from the Bird. Unfortunately, we still have some planning to do."

"No problem, gentlemen." He called the control room and had the communication from Big Bird routed into the sub's internal system. "I've got to get forward, but you can stay here as long as you like." He went to his closet, pulled out two iPads, and placed them on the table. "Your incoming comms will be directed to channel three ... a secure, password-protected connection." He gave me the password. "The iPads are pre-programmed. All you have to do is turn them on. See you in an hour."

# CHAPTER 52

MARK-11, SEAL DELIVERY VEHICLE

"Welcome to the Mark-11, one of our newest SEAL Delivery Vehicles," I said, as I showed Vinnie around the 21-foot-long submersible. "Launch time is two hours away."

"Pretty cool if you ask me, Mac. I gotta admit, the Navy's come a long way since I left the fold, and that was less than five years ago."

"Yeah. Pretty amazing is right. Just so you know, it's the driver who sits at the controls. Everyone else lies down on these racks. We all breathe through our own scuba gear, though we can tap into the SDV's compressed air supply either in an emergency or for longer missions. Once this puppy gets us to the target, we'll park on the bottom of the ocean and swim to the yacht." I patted Vinnie on the back. "You're gonna find this a hoot, pardner."

We stayed in the cabin for the next two hours poring over pictures sent to us via Big Bird. We all knew, and appreciated the fact, that 1,521 miles due north of our present location, an operator sat in an air-conditioned bunker. On the outskirts of Cheyenne, Wyoming, he pointed the RQ's cameras at a yacht in Manzanillo Bay, Mexico. The operator then sent the pictures electronically to the submarine sitting two hundred feet below the ocean's surface, exactly sixty-two miles off the coast of Manzanillo.

On paper, the mission sounded like a piece of cake: get to the yacht; sneak on board; neutralize the guards; plant four armed limpet mines at strategic places along the hull; find Serna ... and kill him. If by chance he wasn't there, we'd return to the submarine and send the signal for the four limpet mines to explode. They probably wouldn't kill everyone still on board, but should sink one of Serna's most prized possessions.

Unfortunately, sounding simple and being simple were two different animals. First off, we had to overcome the pesky problem of the guards. Taken over the past twenty-four hours at five-minute intervals, Big Bird sent hundreds of photos of the yacht to us, which I then passed out to the squad. We were most interested in the photos showing people. The RQ's cameras identified twenty-one separate individuals. Unfortunately, Serna wasn't one of them. It didn't mean he wasn't on board, simply that he hadn't come on deck in the past twenty-four hours.

We used the photos to reconstruct the crew's watch patterns: there were three of them ... seven guards per watch. We memorized faces and I assigned numbers to each. One through seven had the midnight-to-eight watch. We scheduled them to be the first to die. If we proved stealthy enough, we wouldn't even have to wake the other guards. Most of them would just end up dying when the yacht exploded.

While the RQ photos didn't show the inside of the yacht, they did show all the entrances and exits as well as the angles of the outer decks. We committed those to memory. If a gun-battle did break out, we knew instinctively that those were the places we would use as firing platforms.

By comparing those photos with the manufacturer's specs of the inside of a Delta Marine yacht, we put together a detailed picture of the internal route we would take to Serna's cabin.

At the thirty-minute mark, the squad met under the Dry Deck Shelter hatch to go over the attack one more time. We checked our scuba gear, masks, and weapons. With the predicted tide, we all knew this wasn't going to be a leisurely swim.

"You're the driver, Chief," I said to Stinger. "Let's light her up."

"Roger that," he responded.

"We'll go to ground 800 meters from the yacht," I said. "Captain Turner said lunar illumination would be nil, so we won't have to worry about being seen from above. It's no more than a fifteen-minute swim to the yacht. Wolfman and FT will place the limpets while the rest of us secure our gear to the aft starboard anchor chain." I paused. "Any questions about the boarding procedures?"

When no one responded, I said, "Then let's rock and roll."

~

We launched at 0310. Forty minutes later, we grounded the SDV on the ocean floor a third of a mile from the yacht. It was 0350. The swim, just as I had calculated, took fifteen minutes. So far, so good. A few of the starboard portholes showed light, but the deck itself was completely dark and quiet.

While Wolfman and FT went to attach the mines, I led the others to the stern where we stowed our masks, snorkels, fins, and tanks in specially made bags. We tied those bags to the aft anchor chain. The swim platform was down. Guard number one was sitting there smoking a cigarette, not paying much attention to his surroundings. Two faint coughs from my MP7 sent the guard slumping backward in his chair, the tip of his cigarette starting to burn a hole in his shirt. We weighted him down and silently slipped his body into the water. One down, six to go.

When Wolfman and FT returned from attaching the mines, we all climbed aboard. Each had a specific assignment. Every now and then, I could hear the sound of a shell casing bouncing off the deck. It was music to my ears.

Delgado and I went to find Serna's cabin. It was empty. That was no surprise, but I still had to swallow back the disappointment. I'd fantasized about meeting Serna in person. *Another day*, I thought ... *and soon*.

Delgado rifled through Serna's desk, as I did his dresser, looking for anything of intelligence value. There wasn't much, but Delgado did snag an unopened bottle of Dalmore forty-year-old single malt Scotch whiskey. I could tell he was calculating how much that bottle weighed and it's worth on the open market. When he saw me looking at him, he mouthed ... "Tell no one."

I shook my head and gave him the thumbs-up.

ACCOMPLISHING most everything we needed to do, we collected our gear from the anchor chains, redressed, and swam back to the SDV. We were docked on the *California* by 0600. Before opening the hatch, I punched the control button triggering the mines. A minute later, we all felt the wave as it rolled over us.

# CHAPTER 53



Victor Serna was reading a book but looked up at the television when he heard his name mentioned. On the screen was a picture of what looked like the remains of a yacht, *his* yacht, smoldering in its berth. He grabbed the remote and punched the rewind.

*In a related story, a spectacular explosion rocked Manzanillo early this morning as the yacht of a reputed cartel leader, Victor Serna, blew up and sank at its mooring half a mile from Mr. Serna's villa. No word on the cause of the explosion or of any potential casualties, but reports confirmed Mr. Serna was not on board.*

His scream and the sound of a glass shattering against the wall brought in two bodyguards with guns drawn.

"Patrón. What is it? Are you alright?" one said as the other checked the closet and the outside patio.

"No!" he yelled, his body trembling. "I'm not alright. Get me Ruiz on the phone. Right now. Screw the cutouts. I can't waste time. Call him directly."

"Are you sure, Patrón? No intermediary? What if the Federales are tickling your wires? They'll know you are here."

"Don't argue with me, Jaime. I don't care what they know or what they do. If they come for me, I'll shoot them all down like dogs. I need Rinaldo and I need him now."

"Sí, Patrón." Both guards left the room to make the call. As soon as Serna closed the door, one turned to the other and circled his temple with his forefinger. "Going loco," he said.

The other guard nodded his head in agreement. "The Federales are going to be at his doorstep one of these days. We want to be long gone when that day comes."

"Calm down, Ángel," Ruiz said calmly. "This is not the end of the world. They're showing their strength. Playing with you. Two heavyweights sparring in the ring. It means nothing."

"The snake is being torn apart, Rinaldo."

"What are you talking about," he said. "Speak sense, will you?"

"I am speaking sense. The man in my dream. The giant. He came again last night. This time he held the snake high above him ... like a trophy."

"You told me that before, Ángel, and I said you have nothing to fear."

"Let me finish," Serna said, becoming quieter now. "The giant held the snake above his head and piece-by-piece pulled it apart. My dream, Rinaldo … don't you see? It's coming true."

"Nonsense, Ángel. You should've listened to the shrink instead of killing her, or whatever you did."

"I cut out her tongue first." He paused, "And then I killed her." A small chuckle escaped his lips.

"Well, never mind about her. Calling me like this was foolish, Ángel. You know better. You keep doing stupid things like this, and they *will* tear you apart."

Serna remained silent, then said, "As always, Rinaldo, you are right. I'll call you back through our usual channels."

Five minutes later, Rinaldo's phone rang. "Please forgive me," Serna said. "It was stupidity on my part. Are we secure here?"

"We are."

"As I said before … I get so angry. Not calm like you. Explains why we're such an excellent team, eh? The beauty and the beast."

Ruiz laughed. "I wouldn't go that far, but, yes, we are an excellent team."

"Where and how do you think they'll come after me?"

"We know they have the Martinez woman. Think about what she knows about you. Your habits. Your hangouts."

Serna was silent for a moment, then said, "She was never invited to my mansion, thank God. She knows it exists but has never seen the inside of it. I only let the women whom I'm really attracted to visit or stay in this house. The others come to my house on the flats. The Martinez woman has only been invited to that particular casa."

# CHAPTER 54



Thirty minutes after Serna hung up from Ruiz, Eric Rogers, the Deputy Director of Signals Intelligence at the National Security Agency, was on the phone with Admiral Moore.

"We got a hit you should know about, Sir," he said. "Ever since you picked up that Rinaldo Ruiz fellow in Borrego Springs, we've been monitoring his activities closely,"

"That's good to hear, Eric," Moore replied. "What did you get?"

"Well, your boy's been talking to someone in San Francisco. Not a lot, but enough to concern us. We don't know who it is because the recipient of Ruiz's calls always uses a burner. The guy knows what he's doing, too. One-time use, then destroy ... leaving no record of ownership. But at least we know he's been talking to someone in SF. Thought it might be useful to you."

"Good info, Eric. Thanks."

"There's more, Doug. I saved the best for last." He paused, then said, "Ruiz received a call about an hour ago from Victor Serna's private number. We knew he had one, though we've never been able to trace any direct call to, or from, his casa. Until now. Prior to this, he always routed his calls through untraceable cutouts. Why he didn't use the cutouts this time is a mystery." He paused, then said, "In any case, they talked for about a minute and a half. The conversation came out garbled on our end, but we're working on it. What we do know is Serna called from Culiacan, Mexico."

Moore let out a big sigh. "You and your crew made my day, Eric. We had Culiacan on our radar from another source, but knowing he's there now means we can get on him immediately. When you decipher his conversation, give me a holler, okay?"

"For sure," he said. "Good hunting."

RED SQUADRON WAS BACK in our casas in Culiacan by 1100. By 1130, we found ourselves talking on a secure channel with Admirals Moore and Vaughn.

"The upside is you're going back into Serna's territory tonight," Vaughn said. "You have the right gear for a house breach, right?"

Yes, Sir."

Vaughn showed us updated Big Bird photos of Serna's house in Culiacan on one of the flat-paneled television screens hanging on the opposite wall. "We've had the techs go over these, and there are no substantive differences in either the house or its immediate surroundings from the last photos you saw." He replaced the house pictures with drawings of their best guess at what the house looked like from the inside. "These drawings come from Lillianna Martinez's recollections. No guarantees they're accurate, but so far, everything she's told us has been spot-on."

He turned on the television. "One more thing. You'll be in a city tonight. A big city. Our Marine friends in Hermosillo agreed to let you use their base as a staging area. They'll even supply a chopper to get you to Culiacan. Except for them, very few people know you're in Mexico."

"What about the neighbors?" I asked. "From what we've seen in these photos, you're asking us to breech a *nothing* house in a ghetto part of town ... and hoping Serna is living there?"

"No. What we're counting on is coming at Serna in a way he wouldn't recognize," replied Admiral Moore. "That's why we're sending the Martinez woman with you. She's been to his casa on the hill and already knows of the tunnels that lie underneath Serna's house. "

"How much time do we have before going downrange?" interrupted Stinger.

"We'll set you down in a meadow two klicks from your target. Far enough away so the few people who live around here won't be bothered by the helos. You'll exfil at 0600." He paused, then said, "I suggest you go to the armory now, then get some sleep. It'll be a long night. Good luck. Come home with Serna's scalp."

"Let's make a list of what we need," I said to the group as we returned to the barracks. "It'll help analyze what we'll be facing."

"Good idea," Stinger replied. "First thing I thought of is we'll be breaching a house that will connect us underground with Serna's hacienda. That means we'll not only have to break through a door or two in that house to access his tunnel, but probably face armed guards as we get closer of the hacienda."

"I'm thinking that all we will have to do is huff and puff and the damn doors will tumble down of their own accord," Delgado chimed in.

"You can huff and puff all you want, Vinnie," I said. "I'm guessing heavy wood or maybe even steel might be in our future. Remember, this is one of Serna's properties."

"We should bring breaching tubes, then," Stinger said. "Just in case."

"Good get, Stinger," I said. "I'm guessing a max of three would suffice. We don't want to load ourselves down with stuff we won't be using. And remember, we'll undoubtedly be dark … we gotta be wearing ChemLights."

"Yeah," FT responded. "Wear 'em on our vests, front and back. That way, hopefully, none of us will get shot by Delgado."

"You hope," Delgado replied with a laugh. "But seriously, we haven't mentioned grenades yet. Good possibility we could find ourselves in close quarter combat for some length of time down there. Those puppies could save our bacon."

"Vinnie's right. We should all carry at least two frags and a flash-bang. Agreed?" All heads nodded. "And I want everyone wearing their Molle. Any objections?" Silence. "Then let's get this show on the road." I paused. "And let's not forget the balaclavas ... just in case."

# CHAPTER 55

CULIACAN, MEXICO, WEDNESDAY EARLY EVENING

While I was in the armory picking out the gear for the raid, another small army was also preparing for battle.

In the basement of the house on Calle Abedules in Culiacan, Victor Serna addressed nine of his most experienced bodyguards. "I'm positive they'll come tonight," he said. "You've all had military training. You've even done battle with our own marines in the streets of this city. Tonight, you will do battle with soldiers of the US military."

Someone in the back row spat.

"Exactly," Serna said, acknowledging the gesture. "I'm not sure how many will come, but it won't be any more than we have here in this room. The one thing they cannot afford is publicity. A company of American troops, even though they're technically mercenaries, invading Mexico would not play well on the six o'clock news. No, they'll come in quiet and stealthy, so we have to be wary."

"Why don't we just ambush them outside the house, Patrón, as they come down the street."

"You're way ahead of me, Miguel," Serna replied, smiling. "I want you to take two men with you and occupy the house directly across the street from the one that has access to the real house. Put the owners in the back bedroom and tell them they will be shot if they give us any trouble. When they approach that door, you'll have a clear shot."

"Then why so many of us, Patrón," asked one of the men, "if they all die before they reach the front door?"

"Sí, Patrón. We want to have some fun, too," another said from the back.

"I've been successful in business for thirty years," Serna said, "precisely because I take nothing for granted. My track record is perfect because of redundancy. Always have more firepower than your enemy at the point of attack. Front door. Back door. Makes no difference. Overpower them. That's why you're here. To take them down quickly."

"We won't fail you, Patron," said Miguel. "They won't even reach the front door."

"In case they do," Serna replied, "I want the rest of you to drop back into the basement tunnels. If they succeed in breaching the house, they'll finally end up in the basement. If they breech the basement, they'll find the tunnel entrances. And, when they get into the tunnels, I want them all buried there." He looked over the men. "Miguel has his men. The rest of you come with me. I know just where I want you."

# CHAPTER 56



The helicopter was on the ground for all of forty-six seconds as it deposited the crew and flew back to Hermosillo. We sprinted to the side of the clearing and knelt to sort out our gear, putting on our balaclavas and clipping the ChemLights to our Molle vests, front and back. ChemLights are only visible to the night vision systems of US manufacturers, so theoretically, there was no way one of them could be identified as one of us. At least we hoped.

I gathered the guys around me. "On the flight in we were given photos of the house we'll be attacking. You know what? I'm not worried about those two houses. I am, however, mucho worried about the street we'll be walking up."

"I had the same concern myself," Delgado said. "Any of us who spent time in Iraq will recognize this street. The long and narrow kind, favoring the *ambusher*, not the *ambushee*. Fallujah all over again. Lost a slew of good people there because we weren't careful enough."

"Okay, gentlemen ... you heard Vinnie's concern. From now on, we go slow and easy in case our gear is recognized and all hell breaks loose. Vinnie, I want you to stay with Lillianna. We're not sure anyone is waiting for us, but let's assume they are, okay? The gear we have will tell us when to fire first ... and talk later. That way we'll have a good chance of seeing the sunrise."

WE WALKED CLOSE to a mile through barren fields until we came to Calle Abedules, a street that put us three long blocks from the target house. I signaled a halt and motioned for Vinnie and Martinez to join me. "You know these streets better than any of us," I said to Martinez. "We need your eyes and ears. Vinnie's going to be with you. If you see or hear anything out of the ordinary, pull on his shirt, okay?"

She nodded but also patted the pistol she had in her waistband.

The squad walked single-file on the side of the street opposite the target house. When we were twenty feet away, I saw Martinez pull on Vinnie's vest. I raised my fist for the squad to stop. She came back to me and whispered, "I smell smoke, do you?"

I raised my head to the wind, sniffed and nodded.

"It's coming from that house." She pointed. "I saw a slight wisp of smoke snaking out an open window."

"Could be the owner of the house taking a late-night cigarette break," I whispered.

"No. The owner of the house is Victor Serna. Nobody lives there on his orders." I raised my fist, then pointed for the squad to pull back to the vacant lot we had just passed through. Squatting in a tight half circle, I pointed to the house we had decided on to toss. "Smoke," I whispered.

"Martinez says the house is owned by Serna, and the only people living there will be people we don't like. So, whoever's in there now is not a friend and has to be eliminated before we breach house number two across the street."

"Hold on, everyone," Martinez murmured. "I'm going to walk down the middle of the street, stop in front of that house and start babbling on about something or other. Being a female, and a nuisance, I can do that. Believe me, someone will come out and tell me to go away."

"I don't like it, Mac," Stinger said. "Too dangerous."

"You have a better idea?"

"No."

"I do," Delgado said quietly. "I'll strip my gear, put my Glock in my waistband under my shirt, and go with her. We'd be nothing more than a couple arguing. Since I don't speak the language, it will be a one-sided argument." He paused ... "Like most marriages." He smiled, then said, "If she's loud enough, they'll come out to tell us to leave."

"And then what?" Wolfman asked.

"I'll get belligerent. The dude will come over to get me. He'll leave the door open, and you guys will walk in and take care of business. Me and my suppressor will take care of the dude who's harassing us."

"A risky melodrama," said Wolfman, "but crazy enough to work. And if it doesn't? Hey, all we'll lose is Delgado."

"Thanks," Delgado snickered.

The "risky melodrama" happened exactly the way Wolfman predicted. Lillianna made the fed-up wife routine so completely real that one of the guards opened the door and whispered loudly for them to shut up and move on. When the couple made no effort to leave, one of them stomped out of the house to confront Vinnie. By the time the guard reached Delgado, Stinger and I had killed the two gunmen inside. The slight *pop* I heard while exiting the house was Delgado's message that the business in that particular house had ended. With the three bodies piled in the house, I did a quick recon. Signaling the all-clear, the six of us walked quietly over to Serna's other house.

# CHAPTER 57



Stinger quietly checked Serna's front door for booby traps. "No electronic traps, but the door is reinforced steel. Looks like he was trying to discourage visitors."

"I can imagine," I said with a smile. I walked over to Martinez and whispered, "Go back out on the street. The blast we will make is going to wake everyone. If anyone comes out of their house, be firm. Tell them Señor Serna is doing repairs. He's sorry to disturb them and will generously repay them for their inconvenience. Tell them they don't want to anger the *Angel of Death*. And when you finish, wait for us here. I'll call to give you our extraction point. You know the area well enough, right?" She nodded her head, patted her weapon, smiled, and left.

"Okay," I said, looking down on the door. "It'll take two

charges to breach. FT, that'll be you and Wolfman ... door handle and upper door hinge."

Didn't take long. The explosion blew shards of steel thirty feet into the room. In the small space, the overpressure from the blast blew out the three back windows. If anyone had been waiting in ambush on that floor, they would have either been torn apart by shrapnel or had their head explode from the pressure of the blast.

We moved into the house before the dust settled. I noticed remnants of surveillance cameras everywhere, but the first floor was clear. I nodded toward the stairs leading to the basement. "Any bandit down there is going to be badly concussed," I said. "Even at that, be careful going down. You see anybody, take them out. We aren't here to take prisoners."

As it turned out, there were no prisoners to take on the basement level. "Stairs, Mac. Take a look at this!" I leaned down and followed his gaze. "There's a tunnel under here, for god's sake. I'm thinkin' we should take it slow and easy from here on out. Smells to me like ambush country."

"Could be Serna was here when we breached and took off," Delgado said. "We could be just minutes behind him. I'm for not wasting any more time. We're so close—let's go get the sleazebag and be done with it."

"On the other hand," Wolfman said, running his one free hand through his hair, "this could all be a setup. Could be he and his guys are hunkered down at the bottom of that stairway waiting for us."

"I'm inclined to be with the Wolfman on this one," I said. "I think he wants us to come after him. Ambush city."

"Looks that way to me, too," said Stinger. "But we're not

going to shy away from the *ambush* part. We're the big boys here, playing around with amateurs."

"Well said," I replied with a smile. "Tunnels do put us in a dangerous environment though, especially when we're the ones stalking. As you well remember, a big advantage those guys have is firing down the tunnel that we're walking in and killing us with ricochets off these rock walls."

"You don't need to go any further, Mac," FT whispered. "Y'all laughed at my insistence on bagging an EOTech from the armory along with my MP7." He smiled. "Well, who's laughing now? Turns out this baby is thermal." He lovingly patted the top of the sight. "With this in my hands, I'll be able to see the heat signatures from the sleazebags way before they see or hear us."

"Then you be da man, FT," I said. "And take Vinnie with you as your backup."

"Cool, Mac. Thanks," Delgado said. "Let's get after it, FT."

"We're going to drop a flash-bang down the stairs before you go," I said to the two of them. "Soon as it goes off, get your asses down there. Any dudes waiting close by will be so disoriented you'll waste them easily."

"Can't wait," Delgado said, walking over to the stairs while pulling a grenade out of his vest. "Ready?" FT nodded and Vinnie dropped the flash-bang into the tunnel. "Flash out," he yelled. We all closed our eyes and put our hands over our ears. Anyone within twenty yards of detonation would experience disorientation, confusion, and loss of coordination ... and finally death as we shot them.

As soon as the flash-bang detonated, Delgado and FT

bounded down the stairs. We waited for their "all-clear," but instead heard the rhythmic cough, cough, cough of FT's and Delgado's MP7's being fired.

"You guys good?" I yelled down.

"Yeah," FT yelled back. "Had light bulbs strung out down the tunnel here. Vinnie and I cleared them. We're good to go."

# CHAPTER 58



We all huddled to get our bearings at the base of the stairs. "Good move to put out the lights, Vinnie," I said quietly with a nod.

"Thanks, Mac," he whispered back. Pointing to a tunnel junction thirty yards to our front, he said, "Around the curve there, those tunnel lights are brighter than I expected. Believe me, we're on a well-traveled path."

"Whoever was responsible for digging this tunnel knew exactly what they were doing," Stinger added in a low voice. "This whole corridor is well ventilated. I know because I worked in the mines like this as a teenager in Pennsylvania."

"We're clear ahead, Mac," FT murmured, looking through his EOTech sight. "Can we take off these masks, now? Hard for me to see through the sweat."

"Okay. Everyone who's uncomfortable in a mask, dump it and then move out," I said.

The tunnel we were in was so narrow it forced us to walk single-file. FT led the way. At the bend where the tunnel lights got brighter, we stopped to allow FT's EOTech to recon for us. To our right was an opening the size of a small refrigerator. To our left, the tunnel looked wide and welcoming, but too well-lit to make me feel secure.

"Take a look-see to our right," I whispered to FT.

He nodded, knelt, and swung his MP7 around the corner. "Nothing much, Mac. Just that small-ass opening."

"Okay, check out the one on our left."

FT crawled forward and scrutinized the larger opening. He elevated his hand, pointing his thumb in the air.

"I wanna see where these tunnels lead," I whispered to the group as we squatted together. "I'm going to take FT with me and explore the tunnel on our right. You guys hunker down. We'll be right back."

"Take your time, Mac," Stinger said. "We're in no particular hurry. I'm pretty sure if Serna planned to escape, he'd be long gone by now. If he's going to stay and fight, he'll want to meet us in a tunnel of his own choosing. He knows them a heck of a lot better than we do."

I gave Stinger a thumbs-up as FT and I crawled through the small opening. Once inside, the tunnel expanded enough for us to stand, though not without stooping. The tunnel was about five feet high, with a dim light bulb every thirty yards or so. We walked maybe twenty-five yards before we found ourselves splashing through dirty, shallow water, the smell of which was horrific.

"Whoa!" FT whispered. "Are we in the city's sewer system?"

"Gee, how'd you guess?" I chuckled. "Just think, if you were chasing someone, would you want to come through here?"

"You gotta be kidding," FT said. "In this stench, even first-rate dogs would have trouble following the perps."

"Yeah. Nothing here we need. Let's get back."

At the very moment we turned, we heard an MP7 engage —two shots in rapid succession, then a solitary one a moment later. FT and I broke into a run.

# CHAPTER 59



Victor Serna had been awaiting word from his guards, hoping that McArthur and his band had been killed in the tunnel. But he dozed off, and the dream came again. His nightshirt was soaked. He called Diego.

"Are the gringos dead yet?" he asked, though instinctively knew they weren't. His dream told him McArthur was still alive and, worse, that he was near. "Give me an update, Diego."

Velasquez gulped and cleared his throat, knowing what the outcome of this conversation would be. "We haven't heard from the three shooters in the house. We think they may have taken off … or are dead."

"You've got to be kidding." He paused. "And the tunnels?" he asked.

"The gringos have just entered the tunnels. What are your wishes?" Serna took a seat at his desk. He mentally traced the tunnel from his house in the flats to where he was now sitting overlooking the city of Culiacan. He wondered how close McArthur was. *The giant in my dream*, he thought. *Tearing me apart piece by piece.*

"How many soldiers do we still have, Diego?"

"Thirty-two," he answered. "Not all of them are still here, of course."

"Of course. Do you think all are loyal?"

"Most, Patron. But not all."

"But some are more loyal than others, eh?"

"Sí. That will always be the case no matter how many we have."

"How many are in the hacienda right now?" Serna asked.

"There are twenty-six still in the hacienda plus three in the tunnel."

"I want you to leave now, Diego. I want you to pick out twenty-two of the best soldiers still with us. Tell them I will pay top dollar for their service, along with a six-month contract. During that time, I will take care of their families also. Once you have collected them, move them to El Mesa Cocoyole. You know where I'm talking about, no?"

Velasquez replied in the affirmative.

"Good. Tell them they are not to tell anyone, not even their families, where they are going. Tell them if they have loose lips, their families will die in front of them. But if they are loyal to me for the next six months, I will double their pay and reward their families for their service. This, of course, applies to you, too, Diego. Can you do that, old friend?"

"Sí, compadre."

"I'm leaving tonight. I want you to prepare the airplane."

"Are you sure?"

"We have discussed these many times, have we not?"

"Sí."

"Then do it. The plane will leave in exactly one hour. You know what to do, right?"

"I do," Diego replied, a knowing grin framing his lips.

"And one more thing. Bring me the three soldiers still in the tunnel."

# CHAPTER 60

CULIACAN, 3:00 A.M.

When FT and I made it back to the portal, we pressed ourselves flat on either side of the opening.

"It's us," I yelled out. "Is everything okay? What's happened?"

"We registered two heat signatures, Mac," Stinger said. "Fortunately, we popped both of them. We were waiting for you to get back before we moved out. It's safe to come ahead. We've got zip to our front."

We slithered through the opening, trying to keep as low a profile as possible.

"You guys smell awful," Delgado chuckled.

"We do? Never even noticed," FT replied.

"What happened here, Vinnie?" I asked.

"I was keeping an eye on the side-tunnel, Mac. Curious as to how far it went. As you saw, it goes straight for about fifty yards, then turns right through another small opening. I peeked through that opening. Two guys were walking toward me, casual like. Just jabbering away like they didn't have a care in the world. Both were armed, both oblivious to the fact that they weren't alone. They both died."

"We heard you fire three times."

"Yeah, I had to shoot the second guy twice." He shrugged. "Just losing it, I guess."

"Let's go see the effect of those bad shots," I said with a grin.

We moved out, still in single file. As we got closer to the bodies, the tunnel widened out enough for us to walk two abreast.

"Let's get these bloated bodies out of our way," I said. "Then take a careful look-see as to what's in front of us."

What was in front of us was three hundred yards of open tunnel. "I'm not surprised," I said. "This part of the tunnel connects with Serna's hacienda up ahead of us. Which of you guys have the SAT phone?"

"That be me, Mac," Wolfman said, coming forward while pulling the phone off his vest.

"How's the reception down here?"

"Don't know. Haven't tried it yet."

"See if you can reach Moore. I have a question for him." I looked at my watch. 0315. I walked back to Delgado and whispered, "Vinnie, we've got to be at the LZ no later than 0500. I need you to get back to the first house we entered and collect the Martinez woman."

He nodded. "On my way, Mac."

As he stood, I leaned in closer and said, "And wear your mask." Delgado smiled, gave a swift salute, and was gone.

"We're going to take this slow," I told the team as we began the three-hundred-yard incline we hoped would lead to Serna's house. "It's just too inviting," I said. "Start looking for tripwires."

As we came closer to ground level, Wolfman's SAT phone was able to make a connection with Moore at NSWC.

"Admiral, we need a favor," I said. "Can Big Bird get eyes on the house where Serna is staying? It's a heavily fortified hacienda in the foothills of Culiacan. It's the only one around, so will be easy for you to pick out. We are about to breach it. Can Big Bird pick up my location via satellite?"

"Let me check. Hold on."

Before Moore came back online, Stinger had found another escape hatch and carefully searched it for trip wires.

"We found you, Mac," Moore said, coming back online. "You're less than two hundred meters from the main house." He paused. "The house has three thermal outlines. Looks to me like the only shooters they have left. Just so you know, they're stationed in the kitchen."

"Can your people keep Big Bird on station for the next two hours? We're not keen about assaulting this place without a detailed map."

"From where you are, Mac, the only people you'll be facing are the three losers in the kitchen ... the three guys that were left behind. I'm thinking you could just tell them to drop their weapons and come out to you."

"Brilliant, Admiral," I said with a laugh. "We've already done that. We're going to take these losers back to base with us.

We'll interrogate them as best we can on the way and then report to you where to find where Serna is this very moment."

Fifteen minutes later, we started to head to our extraction point. We were within half a mile when we heard an airplane revving its engine. We all turned back toward the hacienda to see a single-engine Cessna take off from what had to be a runway behind the house.

"Dammit, Mac," Stinger said. "This guy had a landing strip back there. We were sooo close, but now he's getting away. Is there anything we can do?"

"In this case, discretion is certainly the better part of valor," I said. "We have to be at the LZ at 0500. Can't be late. Besides, we'll probably be back tomorrow night with our Mexican Naval Infantry cousins to finish this thing once and for all."

"I'm with you, Mac," Stinger said. "At the very least we've still got Big Bird tracking his playmates. By the time we get back to base, we'll know where he is. The good news is ... Serna can no longer hide."

Big Bird tracked the plane in its flight from the hacienda— but didn't have to track it far. Shortly after it took off, the Cessna blew apart in the night sky. We watched with a mixture of anger, joy, and unfinished business as fiery pieces of Serna's aircraft showered the terrain below. I closed my eyes and saw my father smiling.

# CHAPTER 61



After Serna's plane went down, we double-timed over to meet Delgado and Martinez at the LZ. The helo picked us up at 0500, depositing us in Moore's office two hours later.

"As soon as we wrap up the AA Report," Moore said, "let's get you guys some sleep. You gotta be dog-tired."

"Most of us got some sleep on the inbound, Sir," I said. "We're ready to go wherever you want us."

Moore took out some papers from the top drawer of his desk and spread them out on the table. "We received this report about an hour ago. It says SEMAR, a Special Forces unit of the Mexican Naval Infantry, raided the 'house on the hill' as they're now calling it."

"Son-of-a-B, Admiral, those guys must have been there only minutes after Serna's plane exploded. No warning. Glad we didn't crash into them."

"Yeah! Extraordinarily dangerous on their part. I'll call my counterpart and give him an earful. No question Serna closed up his operation at the house, and no doubt he sanitized the place before leaving."

"That accounts for all the activity we saw in the house when we came out of the tunnels," Stinger said.

"The report says they found two bodies in one of the bedrooms. Both shot through the head execution style," said Moore.

"With all due respect, Sir," I said, "Not sure any of us care about those particular details. What about the plane? We still have to get a handle on whether Serna was on board that plane or not."

"Gonna be hard to tell one way or the other," Moore said. "Though, if I were him, I would have wanted to get out in a hurry."

"But his body hasn't yet been found," I said.

"True," said the Admiral. "But it was a small plane he was in, so the explosion would have scattered whatever and whoever was on that plane over a large patch of real estate. It'll take weeks to comb the area, and my guess is the Mexican government won't put much effort into finding Serna's body parts. In fact, I'll bet they can't wait to close the book on our friend Victor Serna once and for all."

"And if he does turn up later?" I asked.

"Then I'll bet his own government would simply close the book on him."

"We can only hope," I said. "If truth be told, I'm too tired to even care." I went back to the barracks and promptly fell into a deep sleep haunted by dreams of planes exploding in midair. Delgado woke me six hours later with the news that Moore wanted us back in his office ... pronto.

# CHAPTER 62



"Good news, gentlemen," Moore said as we gathered in his office. "When I told you the only thing the Mexican government cared about was closing their book on Victor Serna, I wasn't kidding." Moore smiled, then said, "But guess what? While they were closing their book on Serna ... we weren't.

"Remember I told you about my friend Eric Rogers, the DD at SIGINT? He was the one who tracked Serna's phone call to Rinaldo Ruiz and got the confirmation he was in Culiacan. Well, guess what? That idiot Serna called Ruiz again less than an hour ago ... and, if you can believe it, on an unsecured line. Ruiz had the smarts to cut him off, but not before our guys tracked the signal back to the source."

Moore paused, then said with a smile, "Sorry ... we just

found your boy Victor Serna alive and well in a place named Yecora."

"The airplane, then, was used as a diversion?" I asked.

"That particular one was," Moore said. "A genius of a contingency plan though, if you ask me. Would have worked, too, if Serna could've kept his mouth shut."

"A win for the good guys," I said, pounding the table. "Let's take this jerk and his pals out once and for all. And oh, by the way, where on god's green earth is Yecora?"

"We have it on a map," Moore replied, "but we can't afford to ask anyone about it because as soon as the authorities start nosing around, Serna will be out of there in a heartbeat ... no doubt moving to a place that's even more remote and even harder to find."

"And they'd know we're on their tail," said Wolfman.

"In a heartbeat," I said. "So, let's just find 'em in this Yecora place, and be done with all of them. Can you tell us exactly where it is?"

"As the crow flies," Moore responded, "it's about two hundred and sixty klicks northeast of Culiacan. In the Sierra Madre Occidental range. A tough place to get to, and nobody seems to know much of anything about the region. Probably some business venture of Serna's back in the day."

"Anybody live out there now?" I asked.

"We pulled all the land records," Moore said. "The property is, in fact, registered in Serna's name. Not much more than sagebrush and a few dirt roads out there. The land was once used for ostrich farming but has remained unoccupied and unused for the past ten to fifteen years. At least that's what the records tell us."

"Is the Bird on him?" Delgado asked.

"As of the past two hours," Moore said.

"How much of a posse does he have?"

"On our first pass, the Bird counted some thirty men, give or take," Moore said. "The Bird's next pass, however, counted fifty-two … all armed." Moore paused, then added, "on the last pass, the Bird counted one shy of a hundred guys. From the looks of their weaponry and the four distinct camps they're sectioned into, they don't look to be a formidable foe."

"They've also got themselves a big problem, Sir," Delgado added. "The encampment is spread out over at least twenty acres, each camp sectioning itself into its own little fortress. Hard to get leadership in that spread-out pile of manure."

"They'll have their problems, that's for sure. But we'll also have problems," I said. "The mountains around there are not particularly suitable for helicopter insertion. Landing a helo or two, or even ten, on top of them is a sure way to get us all killed. Got any better ideas?"

"Well, right off the top of my head," Delgado said, "I'd say the five of us could HAHO in. It would be a tricky jump, but give us time to get comfortable free falling from an airplane over terrain like this, and I'm sure we'd be good to go."

All heads nodded in unison. "Then let's get to it," I said.

# CHAPTER 63

HAHO PARACHUTE JUMP

"A High Altitude, High Opening parachute jump, huh?" Delgado said, trying to look reassuring. "It's got to be a damn tricky maneuver in those mountain passes. If we don't get it right, bad things will happen to us. Like, for example, dying."

"I'm with you, Vinnie," I grinned. "So, what do we want as a takeaway?"

"Well, for one thing, Mac, just telling Serna he has no better choice than to come with us. We can promise him a couple years behind bars in a lush prison in Mexico, near where he now lives, and then, presto, he'll become a free man. Why wouldn't he go for something like that?"

"He'd be an idiot not to," Moore said. "But, before we all get entangled with Serna, we've got a lot of things to work on. For example, you're going to be jumping at an altitude of thirty thousand feet … forty miles from the target." Moore hesitated, then said, "in the middle of Mexico. And, as a FYI for you people, I'm going to have trouble getting permission from the Mexican government to even insert you."

"With all due respect, Admiral," Stinger said, "why not just do it without their permission? You know … the 'easier to seek forgiveness than permission' attitude."

"Sorry! That's not the way things work in international circles," Moore said, "especially when you have an unidentified aircraft flying over your country."

"We'll be going early in the morning," FT said. "The map shows this place to be about seven hundred klicks from the Arizona border, right?"

"Six hundred and seventy-two, to be exact," said Moore.

"Even better, Admiral. For the plane flying us in, it would be an hour in and an hour out. If there was an issue, couldn't we claim pilot error?"

Moore cocked his head to the right and smiled. "No way that would work, FT. But something you *did* say ignited a spark. How 'bout flying the plane in under the radar? Then, when we're forty miles from the drop zone, we'd pull you up to thirty thousand, drop you off, then immediately slide back down under their radar again. We could very well get away with something so audacious. Let me confer with my Air Force buddies to see if they could pull it off."

"Hey, forty miles from thirty-thousand feet?" I shrugged my shoulders and, with palms out, said, "Should be a piece of cake, right?"

"Absolutely, Mac. How many times in our careers have we done this same jump?" FT asked. "Maybe a hundred?"

"Somewhere around there," I said. "Only downside is we may not get a chance to practice in real-time."

"You guys think you could pull this off?" Moore asked. "If it's not feasible, I won't put you at risk."

"I think FT's right, Sir. We're not amateurs. This shouldn't present a huge problem for us."

"If that's your consensus, then I'm one hundred percent behind you," Moore said. "Now, all I have to do is get our people to furnish you with a pilot and plane that would deposit you in hostile territory."

"Piece of cake, Admiral," Stinger said with a smile. "Let's not forget, we were in Pakistan undetected for over forty minutes when we killed bin Laden. I'm positive we could do the same thing here."

"Okay. Let me give you a quick briefing on what's been going on in DC," Moore said. "The drug raids a day or so ago caused some flak from a few of our more liberal friends in the press. Now some of our elected representatives are getting twitchy about pushing the drug issue any further. They're saying we've essentially crippled the cartels, so let's just pick up our gear and go home. I'm about to push through a request for Air Force assets to go after Serna but, given the times, I can't be one hundred percent certain it will be approved."

"What about the President?" Delgado asked. "How does he stand on this?"

"He wants everything to go away as quickly as possible."

"What if we presented him with the best of both worlds?" I asked. "Ever since I supposedly saw Serna's plane explode, I've been thinking ... we Americans love to win, right?" Moore sat in silence, like he was waiting for the other shoe to drop. He didn't have to wait long.

"What if the President went on television," I said, "claiming America has won, or at the least is winning, the war on drugs? He could use the Sinaloa Cartel, just recently raided, and hopefully just shut it down, as an example. The President would be a hero ... his second term assured."

"That's what every President since Reagan has claimed ... *victory* in the War on Drugs," said Moore. "Problem is we're still in the drug business and still sinking. Tell me how we're going to pull ourselves up and change the narrative?"

"I'm going to capture and jail Serna, Sir. The President would then be able to signal to the world that America is serious about its battle on drugs, and is, once and for all, putting a dagger in the Mexican cartels' drug business."

"Did I miss something?" Moore asked. "Did you forget to tell me how you're going to capture Serna?"

"Well, Admiral, after my crew and I clandestinely HAHO into the hill country above Serna's camp, I'm going to walk down into his camp and convince him to come back with me. I'll promise to pull the US military off him. He'd no longer be a target. Of course, Mexico would want him to go to jail for at least a year or two in order to salve their sense of justice. However, from what I've seen of Serna's wealth and reputation, he'd own whatever jail they put him in within the first two weeks of his lockup. He'd have his own suite, for goodness' sake. Parties every night. Girls, drugs, you name it. He'd be living large ... and be out within two years, max. Wouldn't you go for something like that?"

"The question on the table is, would not the Ángel de la Muerta want to live up to his reputation and just shoot you?"

"Well, if he goes there, I guess it would mean I wasn't successful. But I will be successful because I'm going to make Serna an offer only a fool would reject."

"And, if I may ask, what would that be?"

"Well, that's where the second half of our offer comes into play. I'll tell him he's on the clock. We have Big Bird stationed off the coast right over where his yacht used to be. I'll even show him the pictures of his former yacht, just to stick the knife in further. I'll tell him straight out that if my team doesn't hear from me within thirty minutes, then Big Bird will rain down Hellfire missiles on his entire camp, obliterating him and everyone in it."

"I'm surprised you're letting Serna off so easily, Mac," Moore said. "Given he killed your father, I thought the revenge factor would dictate the Hellfires would come first."

"Turned out seeing the plane explode last night when I was sure Serna was on it, gave me no joy nor satisfaction. All I want, and I'm sure all my father would have wanted, is to see this drug war finally come to an end. It's killing the country. It's murdering our young people. And, if truth be told, once Serna is in jail, no matter how secure, some rival gang will put out a contract to kill him. My hope is the rival gang, or gangs, are sick and tired of Serna, and would have their own Kite system ready for getting him."

"Well, if we can get an okay from Washington for the air support to pull this off," said Moore, "and you don't get your fool-self killed, I'll personally pin those medals on you and your entire squad on the front lawn of the White House."

"No medals necessary, Sir. Just get us all home in one piece. My dad, for one, will thank you and finally be able to rest in peace."

"You can count on it for sure," Moore said. "So, let's meet again tomorrow. As long as the Special Forces loan us one of their air assets, you all will be going in."

"Let's hope" I said.

# CHAPTER 64

YECORA, MEXICO, FRIDAY 3:30 A.M.

Our air assets arrived a day early which allowed us to practice most of our day HAHO jumping off San Clemente Island. It took three jumps and glides of between thirty and forty miles before we felt comfortable with the operation. By 6 p.m., we were back on Mother Earth. By ten o'clock, we were asleep.

By the time the aircraft door opened the next morning at 4 a.m. at its predetermined stand-off distance, we had already completed the required thirty minutes of breathing one hundred percent oxygen from the tanks the Air Force provided. With oxygen bottles attached to our vests and breathing tubes sitting securely in our mouths, we were good to go.

Less than an hour later, we were stowing our gear and checking our weapons on the backside of a peak three hundred feet above Serna's camp. We then belly crawled up the peak until we crested the hill. The eastern sky was just turning a golden orange.

"He's got an army down there," FT whispered, looking through his binoculars. "Serna's guys are forward ... all sleeping in six-man tents."

"Has anybody counted how many tents are spread out over that entire valley?" I whispered back.

"I counted forty-four, Mac," Delgado replied. "Means we'll be facing somewhere north of 250 bad guys."

"A good size army, for sure," I replied, "but I'll bet most of them have never pulled a trigger in anger before."

"We can only hope," Stinger said with a smile. "By the way, have you noticed that tent right below us? It sits on its own promenade ... fifty yards or so in front of the first compound." I focused my binoculars where Stinger was pointing. "That's the only four-man tent in the entire compound," he continued. "Guess we all know who's living large in that tent, huh?"

"Our good friend Victor Serna, of course," said Wolfman. "Living large on his own acre of land."

"How many *tent cities* are we seeing down there?"

"I count four separate cities, Mac," Wolfman whispered, "not counting the one we think must be Serna's. Aside from his, though, each camp has eight or nine 10-man tents. The four camps spread out together fill about two-thirds of the valley down there. Shouldn't cause us any trouble."

"God bless amateurs," I said.

"We caught a break the way they split their camp," Delgado said, lying in the brush on the mountain top. "We're going to be able to focus solely on Serna and whoever shares his tent with him."

FT pointed to some of the men walking into the brush line on the far side of the clearing. "A long walk to take a crap, huh?" he nodded knowingly.

"Yeah. I'm glad I won't have to wade through the latrine on the way back to you guys," I said.

At that moment, the generator in the back of the first commissary tent kicked in, a signal, no doubt, to the other three camps that breakfast was about to be served.

"I don't see any sentries, Mac," Delgado whispered, who was now lying next to me. "Do you?"

"No. The whole camp must think they're invisible. Nice to be looking at amateurs in front of us though, huh, Vinnie?"

"Hope so, Mac," Delgado whispered. "Though Serna and some of the crew with him don't look amateur to me."

"If he doesn't take our offer, he'll die there," I replied. "I'm sure he knows that. And I, for one, couldn't care less one way or the other."

"But we'd prefer we take him with us, right?"

I hesitated, then said, "Yes ... we'd prefer we take him with us. But if Serna becomes belligerent and doesn't believe we mean business, Stinger will radio the Bird and tell the operator to obliterate the camp in the 4th quadrant. That will get his attention."

FT nodded. "Amen to that," he whispered.

"Guaranteed," I replied. "We all know Serna is first and foremost about survival ... and we can offer him that. I am gonna tell him he'll probably spend *some time* in a Mexican prison ... but no more than two or three years, max. He'll no doubt go for that, thinking he'll simply buy people off and be a kingpin within three or four weeks."

"And, of course, that won't happen," Vinnie said.

"Absolutely not. I've made up my mind to take him directly to the States. He'll end up like his pal El Chapo Guzman. Seven life sentences. Once he's locked up, the world, including you and me, will thankfully never hear another word from, or about, Victor Serna."

"Okay," Vinnie replied with a smile as he unfastened his pack and laid out a series of grainy photos of the backside of the mountain upon which they sat. "Let's go over again how we're going to get down to their camp."

I pointed to one of the photos. "That's the trail I'll be walking down. The way it looks to me is I'll come out of that tree line by the camp's food tent and the running water. I'll even get myself a drink ... let them discover me there."

"And once you convince Serna to go with us, how do you expect to get back up here?" Delgado asked.

"Quickly, Vinnie. Quickly," I replied with a laugh. "I'm hoping no one sees us, but if we are compromised, and the guards start firing, you guys have to suppress their fire until Serna and I are in the brush. Be sure to keep those dudes pinned down until we're back up there with only you and the Hellfires' arrival. Shouldn't be more than six minutes, max."

I got everyone settled in. "We all know what to do tomorrow morning, right?" There were nods around. "Okay everyone ... let's get a good sleep, and then kick ass."

# CHAPTER 65



It took a few moments before anyone noticed me standing by the sink, helping myself to a cup of water. However, once people started shouting, it was just a matter of seconds before I was surrounded by ten to twelve guys, screaming and pointing their weapons at me. Someone clubbed me in the back of the head with the butt of his rifle. I went down on all fours, blood seeping into my eyes, blurring my vision. I sensed, rather than saw that the men who had surrounded me had now started to back away. When I tilted my head back up, I was staring into the face of Victor Serna.

At his command, they searched me. Finding nothing but my handkerchief, they dragged me up the hill to Serna's tent and threw me on the dirt floor. "Fortune has shined on me once again, Señor McArthur," Serna said, flashing a wide smile. "We missed each other at Borrego, but you wanted to meet me so badly you came all the way to my camp in the mountains." He laughed contemptuously.

"I was sorry to have missed you in Borrego," I said, through a mouth now puffy from the hits I'd taken. "You ran away before I had the chance to introduce myself." I sat back on my heels.

"You come to my camp unarmed, huh?" said Serna, his voice now threatening as he walked in a circle around me. "And you dishonor me that way? You must have a death wish!" Without waiting for me to say anything, he walked over, raised the tent flaps, and dismissed all his guards. "You stay here with me, Diego." After the guards left, Serna approached me and sat on his haunches.

"You know," he said, "I used to dream that a giant was after me. I'm thinking now that you just might be that giant."

"I can assure you that I'm not the giant of your dream. The truth is, I've wanted to meet you ever since you murdered my father."

"Ah, yes, I forgot ... McArthur senior. That was a mistake, my friend. I never even knew your father, but he told many people, even friends of mine, that he wanted nothing more than to put me out of business. Ironically, it was *me killing him* that has sentenced *me* to this hole when I could be living a life of luxury in any of a dozen Mexican towns." He bent down and growled, "I wish I'd never heard of your father. And now, because of him, you are here to put me out of business." He stepped back, looked over at Diego, nodded his head and proclaimed, "I tell you, my friend, isn't it always families that cause the worst problems?"

He left me on my knees in the middle of the tent and

walked back to get himself a bottle of water. "Did you know, Señor, I tried to kill you ... *twice*?"

I nodded.

"I must say, you have proven tougher than most."

"You have me at your mercy now, Mr. Serna. You can kill me this very minute, but if you do, my friends will come and get you. You will have ten of me after you, not just one. And when they find you, they will rip you apart limb by limb. There's no way you can beat us." I paused, then said, "But enough of this talk about killing one another. I'm here to offer both of us a way to return to our normal lives. Luxury living. Rich friends. Beautiful women."

"Ahh ... a salesman," Serna crowed, waving his hand to Diego. "Come over here, Diego. We have a salesman in our midst. Shall we hear what he has to offer?"

"No, my friend. Do not waste your time on him. Kill him now and throw his carcass to the dogs."

"That's not very hospitable, Diego. Señor McArthur is our guest. You should be ashamed of yourself." He laughed, then turned back to me and said, "And what do I have to do to receive those gifts from you?"

"Surrender to me."

Serna looked at me as if I were a crazy man, then laughed long and hard. Diego followed his lead. "You must have eaten the locoweed from the top of the mountain from where you came, Señor," he said, bringing himself under control. Gesturing towards Diego, he continued. "In case you haven't noticed, Señor, the two of us have the only guns in this tent, and they are both pointed directly at you. I also have more than fifty soldiers within forty yards of where I am currently standing. You, my friend, have no one. You will soon die."

"I came here to die with you," I said. "Or save you. It's your choice. In case you didn't know, I'm not alone. I have an entire platoon of US Navy SEALs in the hills surrounding your camp. I also have a drone three hundred miles from here carrying six Hellfire missiles. At the first sound of a weapon discharging in your tent, my people in these hills will tell the operator to launch those missiles. Thirty-some minutes after that call is made, this valley and everything in it will be nothing but dirt, smoke, and blood. Your blood, Señor Serna." I paused, looked around the tent, then asked, "Can I sit in a chair and have a glass of water? I'm thirsty."

Serna snapped his fingers. "Diego, water and a chair for our guest." When Diego brought me a chair and water to drink, Serna said, "I know you're lying to me. You don't have anyone out there."

"Oh, really?" I asked, reaching under my shirt. I stopped when I saw Serna narrow his eyes, leveling his pistol at my head. "Wait a minute! Wait a minute," I said. "I'm simply trying to show you the earbud taped to my chest. For just such moments as these."

Serna pursed his lips, thinking through his alternatives. Finally, he nodded and lowered his gun.

"Vinnie?" I said into the earbud's mic. "You read me?" Vinnie clicked once in reply. "Good. Tell Mr. Serna what you see." I handed Serna the earbud. He tentatively put it to his ear. I beckoned him to come closer as I wanted to join the conversation.

"Mr. Serna? My name is Vinnie Delgado. I'm one of the

SEALs on the ridgeline right above your camp. I can see your tent. Just so you can believe me, a few minutes ago there were twelve men standing guard in front of the tent. Now there are none. I can also see another twenty or so still eating breakfast. Just wanted you to know they're all in our sights. If anything happens to my friend, every person in the four camps you have in this valley will die. You, Mr. Serna, won't be alive to see the massive destruction that's going to take place here."

Serna waited a moment, then handed the earbud back to me. "You must think I'm an idiota, Señor, to believe such a fantastic el cuento."

"Not at all, Victor." I paused for a moment, then, with a small chuckle, said, "You don't mind me calling you Victor, do you?"

Serna flicked his hand dismissively, as if swatting at an annoying fly. Smiling inwardly, I put the bud back in my ear. "Vinnie, you read?"

"Loud and clear, Mac."

"It seems Mr. Serna doesn't know what the US military is capable of doing. Can we show him? Maybe start the process a little early?"

"No problem, Mac. Only thing I'm worried about getting you out in one piece."

"I'm hoping that won't be a problem, either. How long before the Hellfires go live?"

"Got one going live as we speak," Vinnie answered. He went silent for a few moments, then said, "Okay, Mac, missile number one was just fired. In exactly eight minutes, it will blow up quadrant four."

At that very moment, the drone's operator was sitting in

Wyoming maneuvering it into position. Five miles above the Pacific Ocean and four miles west of Manzanillo, Mexico, the drone's electronics making it invisible, the cameras in the Big Bird saw the city of Culiacan in the distance. It saw its hotels and taxicabs, its bars and nightclubs. It even saw Serna's *Casa* high on the hill. But the cameras bypassed all those. They were looking for red laser beams. They found four of them in a mountainous region some three hundred miles to the north and east of where Big Bird was hovering. The operator in Wyoming armed all four of the AGM 114M Hellfire missiles simultaneously. He then programmed the sequence. The first missile would fire in thirty seconds. When the operator saw the cameras identify the laser beams, he pressed a button starting the first firing sequence. The first of the four missiles dropped from one of Big Bird's outboard pylons. Four seconds after release, its engine ignited. Quickly going supersonic, it traveled faster than the roar made by its engine. In precisely eight minutes thirteen seconds, that missile would fulfill its purpose. The operator would wait until he made sure that first missile had fulfilled its mission before he was told to launch all his missiles and call it a day.

"PERFECT, Vinnie. We're counting on you." Taking the bud from my ear, I turned to Serna. "Give or take a second or two, the first Hellfire has been launched from a drone hovering over where your yacht used to be moored in Manzanillo. In exactly ten minutes from right now, the camp furthest away from where you are currently sitting will cease to exist. After that, at our discretion, your other camps in this valley will also cease to exist. You don't have to take my word for it. You'll hear and see with your own eyes what these missiles are capable of." I let that sit there, then said, "Victor, the three of us here are tied to the same leash. Either we all leave this tent in the next ten minutes to rendezvous with my team, or the three of us will die together when the camps behind are obliterated from the face of the earth by a Hellfire missile."

For the next five minutes, I laid out what would happen if the two of them surrendered. It took Serna all of two minutes to agree to our conditions. Turning to Diego, he said, "You are coming with me, correct Diego?"

"Don't trust him, Victor. He's the wolf in sheep's clothing."

"Nonsense, Diego. You just don't want to lose your job." Serna laughed, then said, "We've been together a long, long time. You have nothing to worry about. I promise I'll take care of you the same as I do now. And when we are out of jail in a year or so, things will return to normal. Actually, better than normal. This Americano," he pointed to me, "will have gone back to his own country, finally letting us live our own lives." He turned to me and gave me his gun. "I accept."

"A wise choice, Victor," I said. "How about you, Diego? Are you coming?"

"Never," Diego yelled. "I will never go. And you must stay with us, Victor. The gringo is lying to you." He picked up his pistol and tried to pull Serna back.

Turning the gun on Diego, I said, "First of all, drop the weapon." He didn't, letting it hang by his side. "Let me tell you what's going to happen here, my good friend. Two minutes ago, a drone, sitting right about where your boss's yacht used to be in Manzanillo, released a Hellfire missile. In a little more than ten minutes, it will have traveled over three hundred miles, slamming into the back quadrant of your camp. Obliterating it." I paused for effect. "Safe to say, everyone in that quadrant will die."

Another pause, then, "There will be casualties in areas adjacent to where that missile exploded, of course, but nothing like what will occur just a few minutes later when the second missile pulverizes quadrant two."

"Madre de Dios," Serna muttered.

"Missile three will slam into the third quadrant approximately ten minutes later, and missile four will obliterate whatever is left of the camp ten minutes after that."

I let that sit for a few beats, then said, "Bottom line is we have exactly twenty-seven minutes to get our asses as far away as we can. The question I have for you, Diego, is ... are you coming with us or not?"

"Never," he spit.

"Sorry, wrong answer," I said. Raising the pistol, I shot him through the forehead. Turning toward Serna, I asked, "I'm hoping you still want to come."

"Yes, of course I do," he murmured, looking over at Diego lying in his own blood on the floor. "But we are going to have to hurry, Señor. My people would have heard the shot. They will come running."

"Then let's get the hell out of here."

WHEN I OPENED the tent's flap, I saw six men running in our direction and shouting. I shoved Serna out of the tent and steered him hard right. "We gotta make it to the brush line, understand? Run as fast as you can. I'll be right behind you."

I saw the puffs of dirt kicking up in front of me before the sound of the gunfire registered in my brain. A part of me was relieved by Serna's guys being such poor shots, though the more rational side told me those puffs of dirt were getting closer.

Serna and I had traversed more than a third of the distance to the brush line when two major events coincided. First, Stinger's MP7 joined the battle from the hill to our left, leveling the playing field considerably; and second, Victor Serna got hit by a bullet and went face down in front of me.

I ran to him, hoping Stinger could neutralize the shooters while I tended to Serna. Stinger did better than neutralize the shooters, he silenced them. But me? I couldn't help Serna. The top left side of his head was missing.

I looked at his body, raised my eyes heavenward, and mouthed, *For you, Dad. I wish we could have jailed him for the rest of his life in the worst prison in the United States. But having him lying there with part his head blown off is a good second place. Rest in peace, Dad.*

# CHAPTER 66



It was late afternoon when we turned off Highway 1 and onto the paved road that led to our destination. A quarter of a mile in, we came to an electronic gate and pushed the red button as instructed. A moment later, the gate retracted silently on steel runners. Before us, across a vast highland meadow, the sun dipped below a series of dark clouds that speckled the horizon. The ocean had turned a blue-black, topped with tiny whitecaps as far as the eye could see. We were thankful for the mild weather, unusual for this part of the Mendocino coastline in the dead of winter.

The road bent slightly right, and we could see a modern, medium-sized house with an attached garage sitting on a rocky outcrop high above the Pacific's churning surf. Motion sensor lights came on as we stopped in front of the stone pathway leading to the front door.

"Hope he's not waiting inside the door with a gun," Vinnie said. "The long road in, coupled with motion sensors, is designed to keep him from being surprised by guests."

"Vinnie's right, Mac," Navarro said as he put the car in park at Gilardi's front door. "You sure you don't want us to come with you?"

"No, but thanks. I've got to take care of this myself. I've waited long enough already." I disengaged my hand from Shira's and put on a pair of latex gloves. Finishing, I gave her a light kiss on the lips, exited the car, and walked to the front door. Before I could ring the bell, the door opened.

"Ken McArthur," exclaimed Bill Gilardi with no surprise in his voice. He looked out at the three people in the car parked in his driveway. He shrugged. "I've been expecting you. Come on in," he said.

Gilardi had noticeably aged since I'd last seen him. His salt-and-pepper hair was now totally white, and the stomach spilling over his belt attested to the fact he'd given up both the gym and Weight Watchers.

His retirement from the DEA six months prior was national news. At the ceremony, the President himself awarded Gilardi the prestigious Homeland Security Medal.

He led me through the living room to a large, freshly painted kitchen with walls lined with leaded glass cabinets and filled with dishes and pottery of every kind. An antique four-legged green stove stood proudly in the far corner. Gilardi guided me to a small breakfast nook off to his right and offered me a seat at an old-fashioned yellow Formica-topped table.

"Coffee?" he asked.

I nodded. "Black."

He disappeared around the corner and came back holding two mugs. He set them on the table, then sat down opposite me, his back to the kitchen's outer wall. "I like the gloves," Gilardi said with a nod of his head as he sat down. "Nice touch." He took a deliberate sip of coffee, swallowed, then said, "I've been following your adventures for the past few months. Through the obituaries, mostly. Through them, I knew you'd show up on my doorstep one of these days."

"You're the last," I said.

"How did you find out about my involvement?" he asked, then quickly switched gears, and said, "surface-to-air missiles ordered up by Mexican Naval Infantry supposedly got Serna. At least that was the official word. I knew that wasn't the case. I knew it was you and your people. Did you get to talk to Serna?"

"I did," I said. "I sat in his tent the day his own people killed him. He told me everything. Nothing you didn't already know, so I won't bore you with the retelling." I sat in silence for a few minutes as I sipped my coffee, then asked, "Did you ever get a chance to meet Diego? He was Serna's friend." Gilardi's face remained impassive. "Just wondering is all. He was an okay person but overly suspicious."

"Stop being such a condescending jerk, okay? Just cut to the chase and tell me how you found out."

"Hey, you asked, so I'm telling you. Be patient." I smiled, enjoying the discomfort he exhibited. I paused, looked skyward, then said, "Oh, yeah. Now I remember. Well, surprisingly, Serna gave me his gun. So, I asked him if he minded answering a few questions for me. That there were some things I didn't quite understand. He surprisingly answered that he didn't mind at all. So, I asked how he knew my dad's flight number. With no hesitation, Serna told me he got it from you." Gilardi stiffened ever so slightly. *Gotcha, you slimy SOB.*

"Serna told me Rinaldo received a phone call from you, Bill. Out of the blue. He told me neither he nor Ruiz even knew who you were. Said they were skeptical. So, Ruiz called a few people in Northern California to check you out. Serna told me you, Bill, were the one who told Rinaldo about *Snowplow,* and even gave him my dad's flight information. When I got back from Mexico, I checked. The DEA's office in San Francisco made the flight arrangements for my father's flight to El Paso, so all your people knew the airline, the flight number, and the scheduled flight my dad was taking. Including you, Bill. And you told Ruiz and the Tormentas."

"It was Mike Gray who talked to Ruiz. He and Brian. I never spoke to the man personally."

"But you ordered him."

Gilardi sat up straight, looking directly into my eyes. "When I heard you were back and the mission was successful," he said, "I had a hunch you may have extracted some information from Serna. I knew for sure when I started to read the obituaries. If I remember correctly, the first of the 'unexplained deaths' were the baggage handlers. Correct? The ones who actually planted the bomb?"

I stared at him but kept silent.

"Being in the business I'm in ... or was in, I had access to hundreds of reports. It was through those reports that I followed your path to my door. I'm not for sure that you're the one who killed the baggage handlers personally, but it wouldn't surprise me. Their deaths are still listed, at least as of three months ago, as robberies gone awry. No clues. No suspects."

"There are still no clues nor suspects," I said.

Gilardi nodded his head in acknowledgment. "Then the female, Lupe Mendoza, from San Jose. Everyone knew she had ties to the cartels. The truth was, she played it both ways. We were using her, too. She happened to be the one who sent the gangbanger to San Francisco to kill you. The press reported that she drowned."

"In her bathtub ... under suspicious circumstances ... was the official report," I said. "And let's not forget Agent Torres."

"Ah, yes. Poor Pete. He was the rational one. The other two were so volatile. They really got worked up over *Snowplow*. Remember when Gray went after you in my office the first day, and Torres came to your defense?" Gilardi smiled sadly and shook his head. "But, like the others, he wanted it to succeed so badly he'd do virtually anything to assure it."

"Including killing my father," I said.

"Including killing your father. He was against it at first, but finally succumbed to the pressure from the other two."

"Did you send Jackson and Gray to kidnap Shira Lipkin and hold her until I came for her?"

"The way things operated in our Task Force was by consent. For the most part, I didn't order anyone to do anything. They would come and tell me what they had in mind, and my response was either yes or no."

"But mostly *yes*, correct?"

"Mostly, but again, for the most part I had nothing to do

with the planning. The kidnapping was Gray's doing. He was the one who thought you were a fly in the ointment. Even counseled us to eliminate you." He paused. "We should have listened."

I remained silent.

"And then just two months ago ... Rinaldo Ruiz."

I nodded, reached into the small of my back, pulled out a Glock 19, and laid it on the table in front of him. The Glock was given to me by Navarro. Untraceable. I took great pleasure in seeing the panic in Gilardi's eyes ... a small payback in and of itself.

"And yes, there was Mr. Ruiz," I said, tracing the outline of the Glock with my gloved index finger. "He was as bad as the *Angel of Death* himself. Serna told me a lot about Rinaldo Ruiz. Did you know they were childhood friends?"

Gilardi sat silently for a few moments, then said, "Did you kill Ruiz, or was it the guy sitting in your car outside? In any case, it was bloody. It's the reason I remember it so vividly. They found Ruiz outside a warehouse on our side of the border. His right hand had been sliced off, and his throat slit. The official report was gang warfare. But we both know that gangs don't slit throats. Cartels maybe, but not gangs. Gangs use guns. Much faster and quicker. So, it wasn't hard for me to see Rinaldo Ruiz was your kill."

I nodded but remained silent.

"And now you have come for me, correct?"

"Why did you have my father killed?"

Gilardi hesitated a moment, then said, "I know this part is hard on you. It was hard on me, also. I liked your father. He and I worked together for many years, and worked together very closely on *Snowplow*. While not my best friend, he was, in an odd sort of way, a friend. More like a distant brother than a friend. You have to understand, none of what happened to your father was personal. Walt was brilliant. *Snowplow* was brilliant. But Walt began to have reservations about the ethics of the operation, even though that operation was entirely his baby at the beginning. He got everyone excited about it, then he decided it was unethical."

"You had him killed because he was having second thoughts?"

"No. Your dad died because the President wasn't going to sign the order to send Special Operations personnel into Mexico. He was backing out on his commitment to your father. To all of us. He needed his backbone stiffened, and the only way, in our estimation, to give him the courage he needed was to have the cartels murder Walt. If you had asked Walt, I guarantee you he would have thought it was a good trade-off. A means to an end."

"Did you ask him?"

"No. And I know whatever I say cannot take away your pain, but I hope you can see from all the good that has come from *Snowplow*, your father's death was not in vain."

"Did my dad know about the use of fentanyl?"

"Of course, he did! Don't forget, fentanyl *was* Walt's plan. It's what I meant by his death not being in vain. He knew we were in a war, and in war, civilian casualties are inevitable. When he conceived the plan, he was willing to sacrifice thousands of people to win the war, but as it got closer to becoming operational, he did start to have some second thoughts."

"I have a few questions about the fentanyl part."

"Ask away."

"At the beginning, you presented it as an attack by Al Qaeda, right? That's how you wanted it seen?"

"Of course. It wouldn't have made any sense otherwise. It's what most Americans would have expected. And *Snowplow* was going to give it to them. A terrorist attack using fentanyl? It got everyone's attention, that's for sure. The public demanded action."

"And how were you able to switch it from Al Qaeda to the cartels?"

"Well, that part was tricky, for sure. It was a testimony to your dad's genius. Obviously, Task Force 64 couldn't come out one day and say, 'Oops. Sorry, we made a mistake. It's not Al Qaeda that's causing the trouble, it's the cartels.' That would never have flown. So, your dad came up with a way to let the discovery of fentanyl be seeded in the drug supply and evolve naturally. He knew once the data came in, people would see the inconsistency and finally discover the drug angle. We had to doctor the data a little at the beginning to highlight the ambiguities, but it wasn't hard."

"How did you get fentanyl powder?"

"Over a year ago, now, your dad took Task Force 64 to New Orleans. I stayed here to run the shop. We contracted with some street gangbangers to steal fentanyl from a local university lab. The gangbangers never had a clue as to what they were stealing."

"And seeding it? How'd you get all the drugs you needed?"

"Come on, Ken. Don't play naïve with me. You're aware that law enforcement warehouses hold enough drugs to rival the cartels. All we did was mix it and get it out on the street. Once out, it had a life of its own. Though how so much made it to the East Coast, I'll never know."

In a perverse way, I was proud of my father. The complexity of *Snowplow,* in all its moving parts, was truly remarkable.

"Your dad did this country a big favor," Gilardi said. "Through his sacrifice, we accomplished what American society and American politicians have been trying to do for decades ... to get Americans off narcotics. *Just Say No*, right? In case you hadn't noticed, drugs are a cancer to this society. Most of the violence in this country is a direct result of drug use and is manifested most visibly in our inner cities."

I remained silent.

"Have you seen the stats lately?" When again I offered no response, he just simply said, "Inner-city crime is down thirty-eight percent in the last six months, and that's because the demand for drugs in those neighborhoods have dropped drastically.

"Have you've seen the latest polls? Since we put *Snowplow* into play, drug use in this country has dropped roughly fifty-six percent. Roll *that* number off your tongue. *Fifty-six percent.* And since the demand is still dropping, what's happening in Mexico? I'll tell you what's happening. The cartels are not as rich as they once were and are therefore losing some of the lifeblood they had. A few of the cartels are even branching out. Diversifying. Taking up extortion and human trafficking. More like old-time Mafioso stuff, and that's good because it's easier for us to monitor and control."

I stayed silent.

"Did you know that the violent death rate in Mexico has dropped by fifty percent since *Snowplow* went operational? Your dad would have willingly given his life for those numbers. He did a great thing for this country, Mac. You have to agree ... right?"

I pursed my lips and said, "No, I don't have to agree." Looking into Gilardi's eyes, I said, "Way too many people died because of what *you* did." I picked up the Glock. "I'm not smart enough to be the moral arbiter about what my father and Task Force 64 did or didn't do. I'll let history sort that out. But I can be the moral arbiter for you, Agent Gilardi, for murdering my father. And I'm bringing you to justice for that crime."

"Is this where you shoot me?" he asked.

"No," I replied. "I'm going to give you the same chance I gave Victor Serna. Well, maybe not the *same* chance, but close enough. I'm going to give you three options. Option One: I'll leave here and go directly to the press. I'll lay out exactly what you did. Exactly how you organized *Snowplow*. How you had a direct hand in killing fifteen to twenty thousand Americans, most being under the age of twenty-five. And their only offense? They did drugs."

"They died because of choices *they* made," Gilardi said defiantly.

"I think most people in this country would say the responsibility for their deaths lays directly on your shoulders."

"I'll take my chances," Gilardi replied. "To most people, I'm a hero."

"In any case, Agent Gilardi, here's Option Two: My testimony will convict you for the murder of my father and the other two hundred and eight people that died aboard that airplane you blew up."

"You're forgetting you have no proof."

"How can you be so sure?" I asked.

Gilardi looked down at his hands without responding.

"People around the country will look at you as the monster that brought down that airplane, killing over two hundred and some innocent men, women, and children. You'll be put away for life. And think, as a former law enforcement officer, your living conditions in prison would be ... well, let's just say ... difficult."

Gilardi continued to look at his hands, the muscles in his cheeks starting to reflect his anxiety.

"And lastly, Option Three. I'm going to give you a chance, Agent Gilardi, to retain your dignity. I'm going to leave a gun here on the table. It has one bullet in it. The gun has no history so it will be impossible to trace. You can do the honorable thing. The manly thing. It's a chance you didn't give my father. I'll give you time to write a note of explanation."

"And if I don't choose any of them?" Gilardi asked.

"Then I'll shoot you myself."

AN HOUR LATER, as the three of us stood on a bluff a quarter mile from the house watching the sun settle into the sea, we heard the shot.

Returning to the house, we found Gilardi sitting in the glass-enclosed porch facing the Pacific Ocean. A typed and signed letter, more of an *apologia* than a confession, was found on his desk in the study. He'd used his own weapon to kill himself. Navarro retrieved and pocketed his Glock. We made one last pass through the house, locked the front door, and exited through the garage. At a pay phone in a small fishing marina three miles down the main highway, I called the local police and reported hearing a gunshot at Gilardi's house. I gave the location and hung up.

THEY LAID Special Agent in Charge Gilardi to rest with full law enforcement honors. The Deputy Director of the DEA, John Dunnigan, was flown in from Washington DC to provide the eulogy. He began by saying no one can ever comprehend what personal demons prompt people to take their own life. He praised Gilardi as the brilliant leader of *Snowplow*, the operation that single-handedly won America's War on Drugs, the longest active war in the nation's history. Never mentioned, however, was the thousands of young Americans who died of fentanyl poisoning.

Walter McArthur was posthumously awarded the DEA Medal of Valor for his part in designing *Operation Snowplow*, now used as the blueprint for dealing with drugs and drug trafficking.

Alex Navarro, Vinnie Delgado, Shira Lipkin and her dog Buck were present at both ceremonies. Many of the players in the drama known as *Snowplow* paid the ultimate price for their participation. We were all satisfied with the outcome. It was now time to move on.

In January of the following year, I presided over the

opening of the Red Squadron Security Agency's new headquarters in San Francisco. At the event, Shira Lipkin was introduced as the firm's general manager. After purchasing San Francisco Giants season tickets next to the Navarro's, Shira and I went to Arizona to watch the Giants in spring training.

A week before the season opened, I proposed to her.

Business is booming. The Giants look to be contenders again this year, and, if so, Shira and I will be at every game. Buck is living his best life. Most importantly, though, I'm home ... and soon to be a married man.

Life is good.

# Acknowledgments

I want to thank my awesome wife Sarah who was as important in getting my novel finished as I was.

But the publication of a book requires many hands, including my publisher, editor, cover designer, and technical advisors. I also thank my loyal fans who have supported my writing for over a decade.

# About the Author

Dennis Koller was raised in San Francisco. After spending a good deal of his adult life in Higher Education, he gave it up in order to concentrate on writing novels.

He has published several mystery-thriller-suspense novels. "The Oath" and "The Custer Conspiracy" were both awarded Silver Medals from the Military Writers Society of America. *The Custer Conspiracy* was labeled *Intriguing* by Publishers Weekly, while *The Oath* was acclaimed the winner of the Independent Press Award for Fiction. His third thriller, *The Rhythm of Evil,* was honored as a finalist in the 2024 American Legacy Book Awards.

Dennis is proud to be a member of the Writers' League of Texas. He and his wife Sarah live in the Dallas metroplex.

For more about the author, visit his website here denniskoller.com or scan the QR Code below.

# THANK YOU FOR READING

If you enjoyed *One Death Too Far*, we invite you to leave a review and share your thoughts and reactions online and with friends and family.

Publish Authority